KISS
OF THE
FUR QUEEN

Tomson Highway

Doubleday Canada Limited

Canadian Cataloguing in Publication Data

Highway, Tomson, 1951–
    Kiss of the fur queen

ISBN 0-385-25652-3

I. Title

PS8565.I433K57 1998   C813'.54   C98-931194-5
PR9199.3H53K57 1998

Jacket design by Pylon Design
Jacket photograph of dancer by Frank Richards/
    photograph of snow scene by Martin Rogers/Tony Stone Images
Text design by Heidy Lawrance Associates
Printed and bound in Canada

Published in Canada by
Doubleday Canada Limited
105 Bond Street
Toronto, Ontario
M5B 1Y3

FRI 10 9 8 7 6 5 4 3 2 I

Igwani igoosi, n'seemis

A NOTE ON THE TRICKSTER

The dream world of North American Indian mythology is inhabited by the most fantastic creatures, beings and events. Foremost among these beings is the "Trickster," as pivotal and important a figure in our world as Christ is in the realm of Christian mythology. "Weesageechak" in Cree, "Nanabush" in Ojibway, "Raven" in others, "Coyote" in still others, this Trickster goes by many names and many guises. In fact, he can assume any guise he chooses. Essentially a comic, clownish sort of character, his role is to teach us about the nature and the meaning of existence on the planet Earth; he straddles the consciousness of man and that of God, the Great Spirit.

The most explicit distinguishing feature between the North American Indian languages and the European languages is that in Indian (e.g. Cree, Ojibway), there is no gender. In Cree, Ojibway, etc., unlike English, French, German, etc., the male-female-neuter hierarchy is entirely absent. So that by this system of thought, the central hero figure from our mythology – theology, if you will – is theoretically neither exclusively male nor exclusively female, or is both simultaneously.

Some say that Weesaceechak left this continent when the white man came. We believe she/he is still here among us – albeit a little the worse for wear and tear – having assumed other guises. Without the continued presence of this extraordinary figure, the core of Indian culture would be gone forever.

ACKNOWLEDGEMENTS

There are many people to whom gratitude has to be expressed for the support, inspiration, faith, and love that they gave me during the writing of this book. In alphabetical order, they are: William Aide, Keith Anderson, Merrick Emlyn Anderson, Lilly Barnes, Micah Barnes, Elizabeth Bateman, Linda Beath, Jack Blum, Denise Bolduc, Elaine Bomberry, Peter Bomberry, Rita Bomberry, my agent Denise Bukowski, Jim Burt, Catherine Cahill, Tantoo Cardinal, Teresa Castonguay, Kennetch Charlette, Celia Chassels, Marsha Coffey, Cathie Cooper, Sharon Corder, Dale Crosby, James Cullingham, Jennifer Dean, my agent Suzanne DePoe, David Doze (Vox Management), David Earle, Bernice Eisenstein, Gloria Eshkibok, Barker Fairley, Jonathon Forbes, Carol Hay, William (Bill) Henderson, Daniel Highway, Pelagie Highway, Kathleen Jamieson, Edwin Jebb, Alexie Lalonde-Steedman, Florence Lalonde, my partner Raymond Lalonde, Thérèse Lalonde, Jani Lauzon, Larry Lewis, Doris Linklater, Edna Manitowabi, Tina Mason, Pamela Matthews, Maya Mavjee, Elva McCoy, Ann-Marie MacDonald, Linda Merasty, Louise Merasty, William (Billy) Merasty, Mary Jane McCallum, Gloria Montero, Jim Morris, Rena Morrison, Daniel David Moses, John Neale, Maxine Noel, Margarita Orszag, Ken Pitawanakwat, James Reaney, Anne Robbins, Svend Robinson, Carol Rowntree, Buffy Sainte-Marie, Jaydeen Sanderson, Jenna Sanderson, Jennifer Sanderson, Jonathon (Little Joe)

Sanderson, Don Sedgwick, Richard Silver, Mary Stockdale, Iris Turcott, Isabel Vincent, my editor Charis Wahl, Don Winkler, and everyone at Doubleday. As well, the following institutions are to be recognized for their generosity: the Canada Council, Concordia University, Simon Fraser University, University of British Columbia, and University College (University of Toronto). Thank you all from the bottom of my heart.

Lastly, a heartfelt thanks has to be extended to the storytellers of my people, the myth-makers, the weavers of dreams. For it is on their shoulders that we, the current and upcoming generation of Native writers, stand. Without them, we would have no way of telling our stories and, ultimately, no stories to tell.

This book, of course, is a novel — all the characters and what happens to them are fictitious. Moreover, some liberty has been taken with the chronology of certain historical events — the Fur Queen beauty pageant, for instance. As a certain philosopher of ancient Greece once put it, the difference between the historian and poet/storyteller is that where the historian relates what happened, the storyteller tells us how it might have come about.

Kiss
OF THE
Fur Queen

*"Use your utmost endeavours to dissuade the Indians from excessive
indulgence in the practice of dancing."*
—From a letter by Duncan Campbell Scott,
Deputy Superintendant General of the
Department of Indian Affairs, Ottawa, Canada
sent out as a circular on December 15, 1921.

*"At night, when the streets of your cities and villages are silent, they will
throng with the returning hosts that once filled them, and still love this
beautiful land. The whiteman will never be alone. Let him be just and
deal kindly with my people. For the dead are not powerless."*
—Chief Seattle of the Squamish, 1853,
translated by Dr. Henry Smith.

PART ONE
Allegro ma non troppo

ONE

"*Mush!*" the hunter cried into the wind. Through the rising vapour of a northern Manitoba February, so crisp, so dry, the snow creaked underfoot, the caribou hunter Abraham Okimasis drove his sled and team of eight grey huskies through the orange-rose-tinted dusk. His left hand gripping handlebar of sled, his right snapping moose-hide whip above his head, Abraham Okimasis was urging his huskies forward.

"*Mush!*" he cried, "*mush.*" The desperation in his voice, like a man about to sob, surprised him.

Abraham Okimasis could see, or thought he could, the finish line a mile away. He could also see other mushers, three, maybe four. Which meant forty more behind him. But what did these forty matter? What mattered was that, so close to the end, he was not leading. What mattered was that he was not going to win the race.

And he was so tired, his dogs beyond tired, so tired they would have collapsed if he was to relent.

"*Mush!*" the sole word left that could feed them, dogs and master both, with the will to travel on.

Three days. One hundred and fifty miles of low-treed tundra, ice-covered lakes, all blanketed with at least two feet of snow — fifty miles per day — a hundred and fifty miles of freezing temperatures and freezing winds. And the finish line mere yards ahead.

The shafts of vapour rising from the dogs' panting mouths, the curls of mist emerging from their undulating backs, made them look like insubstantial wisps of air.

"*Mush!*" the hunter cried to his lead dog. "Tiger-Tiger, *mush.*"

He had sworn to his dear wife, Mariesis Okimasis, on pain of separation and divorce, unthinkable for a Roman Catholic in the year of our Lord 1951, that he would win the world championship just for her: the silver cup, that holy chalice was to be his twenty-first-anniversary gift to her. With these thoughts racing through his fevered mind, Abraham Okimasis edged past musher number 54 — Jean-Baptiste Ducharme of Cranberry Portage. Still not good enough.

Half a mile to the finish line — he could see the banner now, a silvery white with bold black lettering, though he couldn't make out the words.

Mushers numbers 32 and 17, so close, so far: Douglas Ballantyne of Moosoogoot, Saskatchewan, at least twenty yards ahead, and Jackson Butler of Flin Flon, Manitoba, another ten ahead of that.

"*Mush!*" the sound a bark into the wind.

"Please, please, God in heaven, let me win this race," a voice inside the caribou hunter's body whispered, "and I will thank you with every deed, every touch, every breath for the rest of my long life, for hallowed be thy name . . ." The prayer strung itself, word by word, like a rosary, pulling him along, bead by bead by bead, "Thy kingdom come, thy will be done on Earth . . ."

Less than half a prayer and already God the Father was answering. Wasn't that his voice Abraham Okimasis could hear in the northwest wind? Less than a quarter of a mile to go, he was sure of it, and already he had passed musher number 32, Douglas Ballantyne of Moosoogoot. And now, not forty yards away, the banner hovered over the finish line like the flaming sword of the angel guarding paradise – "The World Championship Dog Derby, Trappers' Festival, Oopaskooyak, Manitoba, February 23–25, 1951!" And now musher number 21, Abraham Okimasis of Eemanapiteepitat, Manitoba, was only ten feet behind musher number 17, Jackson Butler of Flin Flon, the finish line not thirty yards away. Twenty-five. Twenty. Fifteen. Ten . . .

The screams of children, of women, of men, the barking of dogs, the blare of loudspeakers crashed over the hunter, submerging him, drowning him. A sudden darkness knocked the breath clean of his lungs, the vision from his eyes. And in his blindness, all he could sense was a small white flame, as if perceived through a long, dark tunnel, fluttering and waving like a child's hand, beckoning him. All he knew was that he wanted to lie down and sleep forever, and only the waving flame was preventing him.

When Abraham Okimasis surfaced, he found hands reaching for him, other hands clutching at his arms, his shoulders, his back, manoeuvring him through a mass of human flesh. Cameras, microphones were aimed at him. Men with notepads and pencils, women with pens and large red moving mouths, prying, babbling in this language of the Englishman, hard, filled with sharp, jagged angles.

Then the caribou hunter felt himself levitating towards a platform. Wings must have been attached to his shoulders by guardian angels posing as minions of the festival, Abraham would reason some days later. And on the platform a man like a white balloon, so large, so pale, his voice thunderous and huge.

"Boom," the voice went, "boom, boom." Something about "Abraham Okimasis, forty-three years old, caribou hunter, fur trapper, fisherman, boom, boom." Something about "Abraham Okimasis, musher, from the Eemanapiteepitat Indian reserve, northwestern Manitoba, boom." Something having to do with "Abraham Okimasis, winner of the 1951 Millington Cup World Championship Dog Derby, boom, boom." Something about "Mr. Okimasis, first Indian to win this gruelling race in its twenty-eight-year history . . ." The syllables became one vast, roiling rumble.

Whereupon another darkness came over the Cree hunter. And in his blindness, all he could sense was the long, black tunnel, the small white flame so far, far away, flickering and fluttering, waving and swaying — a child's hand? a spirit? — beckoning, summoning.

A mile away, on a makeshift stage at one end of the high-ceilinged temple of ice hockey, seven fresh-faced, fair-haired women stood blinking under glaring lights. The youngest was eighteen, the eldest no more than twenty-three. Across the stage, a banner read: "The Fur Queen Beauty Pageant, Trappers' Festival, 1951, Oopaskooyak, Manitoba."

A panel of judges had sized up these seven finalists from every angle conceivable: height, width, weight, posture, deportment, quality of face, length of neck, circumference of leg, sway of hip, length of finger, quality of tooth, lip, nose, ear, eye, and eyebrow, down to the last dimple, mole, visible hair. The women had been prodded, poked, photographed, interviewed, felt, watched, paraded around the town for the entire three days of the Trappers' Festival, for the delectation of audiences from as far afield as Whitehorse, Yellowknife, Labrador, and even Germany, it had been reported in the *Oopaskooyak Times*. These seven beauties had cut ribbons, sliced cakes, unveiled snow sculptures, made pronouncements, announcements, proclamations. They had given out prizes at the muskrat-skinning contest, the trap-setting contest, the beard-growing contest, the dreaded Weetigo look-alike contest, the bannock-baking and tea-boiling contests. They had coddled babies, kissed schoolchildren, shaken hands with the mayor and his wife, danced with lonely strangers whose sole desire it was to pass one fleeting minute of their lives in the arms of a Fur Queen finalist. And now, the judges were about to reveal the most graceful, the most intelligent, the most desirable, the most beautiful. The Fur Queen.

All puffed out in timber-wolf-lined top hat and tuxedo, the mayor, who had graciously volunteered as chairman of the judges' panel, stepped up to the microphone at centre stage, cleared his throat, thumped his chest, opened his mouth, and trumpeted the entrance into the arena of the brave and daring men who had risked life and limb to take part in the Millington Cup World Championship Dog Derby. The crowd roared.

The chairman again cleared his throat, thumped his chest, opened his mouth, and boomed into the microphone.

"Results of the 1951 Fur Queen Beauty Pageant, for which the decision of the judges is final. Third runner-up, Miss Linda Hawkins, Silver Lake, Manitoba." A young woman burst into a tearful smile and stepped up to the chairman to receive her cash award and a bouquet of yellow roses, had her upper body draped by the two other judges with a yellow satin sash, and was photographed a hundred times until all she could see was showers of stars. The crowd roared.

"Second runner-up, Miss Olivia Demchuk, Eematat, Manitoba," boomed the chairman's voice. And a second young woman burst into a tearful smile, stepped up to the chairman to receive her cash award and a bouquet of pink roses, had her upper body draped with a pink satin sash, and was photographed a hundred times until all she could see was showers of stars. The crowd roared louder.

"First runner-up, Miss Catherine Shaw, Smallwood Lake, Manitoba," boomed the chairman's voice. And a third young woman burst into a tearful smile, stepped up to the chairman to receive her cash award and a bouquet of crimson roses, had her upper body draped with a crimson satin sash, and was photographed a hundred times until she was blinded by the light. The crowd roared. And roared again.

Then the chairman of the judges' panel cleared his throat, thumped his chest, opened his mouth, and boomed into the microphone: "And the Fur Queen for the year 1951 is . . ." One could hear the ticking of watches, the buzzing of incandescent lights, the hum of loudspeakers. "Miss Julie Pembrook, Wolverine River, Manitoba. Miss Julie Pembrook!" The young woman burst into a blissful smile, stepped up to the chairman to receive her cash award and a bouquet of white roses. The radiant Miss Pembrook was draped not only with a white satin sash but with a floor-length cape fashioned from the fur of arctic fox, white as day. She had her head crowned with a fox-fur tiara ornamented with a filigree of gold and silver beads, and was photographed a thousand times until all she could see was stars and showers of stars. And the crowd roared until the very ceiling of the building threatened to rise up and float off towards the planet Venus.

In the thick of this raucous, festive throng, Abraham Okimasis stood, Cree gentleman from Eemanapiteepitat, Manitoba, caribou hunter without equal, grand champion of the world, unable to move, barely remembering to breathe.

Because of the stars exploding in his own eyes, all he could see was bits and pieces of the scene before him interspersed with the vision of his lead dog Tiger-Tiger, panting out his puffs and clouds of vapour, striving for the finish line. And before the hunter could collect himself, a third darkness came upon him, the roaring in his ears gigantic. And at the far end of this new darkness appeared again the small white flame, flickering on the platform. Floating, whispering sibilance and hush, blooming into a presence, the white flame began to hum, a note so pure human ears could never have been meant to hear it. Then the presence began to take on shape – the caribou hunter could just discern a flowing cape seemingly made from fold after fold of white, luxuriant fur, swelling like the surface of a lake. The caribou hunter thought he saw a crown, made of the same white fur, hovering above this cape. And the crown sparkled and flashed with what could have been a constellation. Then Abraham Okimasis saw the sash, white, satin, draped across the upper body of a young woman so fair her skin looked chiselled out of arctic frost, her teeth pearls of ice, lips streaks of blood, eyes white flames in a pitch-black night, eyes that appeared to see nothing but the caribou hunter alone. And then the caribou hunter and the woman in white fur began floating towards each other, as if powerless to stay apart. And as the two moved closer, Abraham Okimasis could decipher the message printed across her sash, syllable by syllable, letter by letter: "The Fur Queen, 1951."

Then he became aware – he must have been dreaming,

surely — that this creature of unearthly beauty, the Fur Queen, was wafting towards him with something in her arms, something round and made of silver, carrying the object at waist level, like a sacred vessel, a heart perhaps, a lung, a womb? The goddess stopped in front of him, her face not half a foot away, her eyes burning into his, her person sending off ripples of warm air redolent of pine needles and fertile muskeg and wild fireweed. He couldn't look away, not even when he felt something falling gently, almost imperceptibly, into his hands.

When the queen turned for one fleeting second to smile at the screaming throngs below, Abraham looked down at his hands. There lay the large silver bowl, the Millington Cup, the coveted first prize of the World Championship Dog Derby, and, in the bowl, a cheque in the amount of one thousand dollars.

He had won. He was the king of all the legions of dog-mushers, the champion of the world! All realization, all sense, all time suddenly became entangled in some invisible glue. Abraham pulled his stunned gaze from the silver bowl to the Fur Queen's brilliant smile, where it became imprisoned once again.

And then the Fur Queen's lips began descending. Down they came, fluttering, like a leaf from an autumn birch, until they came to rest on Abraham's left cheek. There.

After what seemed like years to Abraham Okimasis, she removed her lips from his cheek, expelling a jet of ice-cold vapour that mushroomed into a cloud. Her lips, her eyes, the gold and silver beads of her tiara sparkled one last time and then were swallowed by the billowing mist.

The next thing Abraham knew, or so he would relate to his two youngest sons years later, the goddess floated up to a sky fast fading from pink-and-purple dusk to the great blackness of night, then became one with the northern sky, became a shifting, nebulous pulsation, the seven stars of the Great Bear ornamenting her crown. And when she extended one hand down towards the hunter on Earth, a silver wand appeared in it, as simple as magic. Now a fairy-tale godmother glimmering in the vastness of the universe, the Fur Queen waved the wand. Her white fur cape spread in a huge shimmering arc, becoming the aurora borealis. As its galaxies of stars and suns and moons and planets hummed their way across the sky and back, the Fur Queen smiled enigmatically, and from the seven stars on her tiara burst a human foetus, fully formed, opalescent, ghostly.

The Fur Queen disappeared, leaving her cape and crown, and the ghost child drifting in the womb of space, the wisps of winter cloud its amniotic fluid, turning and turning, with a speed as imperceptible yet certain as the rhythm of the spheres. And slowly, ever so slowly, the ghost baby tumbled, head over heels over head, down, down to Earth.

TWO

The pinewood sled and eight grey huskies glided, free of gravity, among the northern Manitoba stars, or so Abraham Okimasis would relate to his two youngest sons years later. Occasionally, a stray beam from the frosty midwinter moon became entangled in the ornate surface of the World Championship Dog Derby trophy, and needles of silver light shot out.

For by the time he had rested a day and a night in an Oopaskooyak hotel and then set off on his journey north – and home – the northwest wind had been replaced by a kinder, gentler wind from the south. Still, the caribou hunter knew only too well how suddenly these winter storms could pounce upon the northern traveller. The evenings were so unseasonably balmy that he drove on well past dusk, for he couldn't wait to see his wife and children.

The six nights he spent bedded down by his campfire,

under a lean-to of spruce boughs, became one long night. The six days he spent crossing ice-covered lake after ice-covered lake, island upon island — the snow, soft and pure, covering their stands of spruce and pine and tamarack — these six days melded into one. In the grip of the moment when he crossed the finish line, the moment of the Fur Queen's kiss, he wasn't even aware that he had entered the southern end of Mistik Lake until he was well on his way across the first great bay. The snow was so white, the sun so warm, the spruce so aromatic, the north so silent; and the moon, drifting from passing cloud to passing cloud, seemed to howl, backed up by a chorus of distant wolves.

And all the while, among the stars and wisps of cloud, the silvery foetal child tumbled down, miles, light years above the caribou hunter's dream-filled head.

At dusk on the sixth day, the hunter caught sight of the Chipoocheech Point headland and his heart swelled, as it always did when he knew Eemanapiteepitat would be coming into view within the next half hour. Chipoocheech Point was a mere five miles south of where his wife awaited him patiently. When he rounded the point and the toy-like buildings began to glimmer in the distance, his heart jumped and his mouth flew open to yodel in a falsetto clear and rich as the love cry of a loon — "*Weeks'chiloowew!*" — a yodel that always spurred his faithful team of huskies on to even more astonishing feats.

Before he could count to one hundred, Abraham Okimasis

was racing past the lopsided log cabin of Black-eyed Susan Magipom and her terrible husband, Happy Doll. Black-eyed Susan Magipom boldly thrust her spindly thorax out the door, gazing ardently at Abraham as though Happy Doll Magipom didn't exist.

"*Mush!*" the hunter yelled out to Tiger-Tiger, "*mush, mush!*"

Before he could count to a hundred and ten, Abraham Okimasis was racing past the red-tiled roof of Choggylut McDermott and his wife, Two-Room; the lonely shack of Bad Robber Gazandlaree and his dog, Chuksees; the house of the widow Jackfish Head Lady, who once had a near-death encounter with the cannibal spirit Weetigo just off Tugigoom Island; the silver crucifix crowning the steeple of the church that had killed Father Cheepootat when its brick wall collapsed on him during confession; the dark-green rectory where Father Cheepootat's successor, Father Eustache Bouchard, received the faithful, for everything from marriage counselling to haemorrhoid examinations, and passed out raisins to small children on Easter Sunday mornings. And then Abraham Okimasis, for the very first time in three weeks, saw the little pine-log cabin he had built for his wife, the lovely Mariesis Adelaide Okimasis, and their five surviving children.

He was only vaguely aware that people were gathering: stragglers trundling home from the store at the north end of Eemanapiteepitat hill, young men sawing firewood in front of old log cabins, laughing children romping in the snow with barking dogs, even Crazy Salamoo Oopeewaya arguing with

God from a rooftop; all had abandoned their current pursuit and rushed after Abraham's sled as it raced up the hill towards the Okimasis cabin. Their gesticulating arms, their babbling voices were indecipherable to the tired though elated hunter. His only two scraps of thought were that this ragtag bunch was ready for a party such as it had never had, and that it was clearly Jane Kaka McCrae's enormous new radio that had spread the news of his triumph throughout the reserve; for there was Jane Kaka, the most slovenly woman in Eemanapiteepitat, braying like a donkey to a gaggle of women with mouths and eyes as wide as bingo cards.

Before he could alight from his sled, Annie Moostoos, his wife's addled fifty-five-year-old cousin, renowned throughout the north for the one tooth left in her head, was dancing among the woodchips in the front yard, round and round the sawhorse, wearing Abraham's silver trophy on her head, like a German soldier's helmet. How the skinny four-foot widow got the trophy Abraham never did find out, for when he turned to ask, who should be standing there holding out Abraham's battered old accordion, his face as pink as bubblegum, but his own crusty, half-crazed fifty-five-year-old cousin, Kookoos Cook, renowned throughout the north for having chopped a juvenile caribou in the left hindquarter with a miniature axe and having been whisked off to the horizon by the terrified animal because Kookoos Cook had refused to let go of his only axe. Before Abraham could say "*Weeks'chiloowew*," Kookoos Cook had shoved the ratty old instrument into the musher's hands.

"Play my dead wife's favourite jig, play '*Kimoosoom Chimasoo*' or I'll never talk to you again."

So the caribou hunter pumped and pulled his screechy old accordion, playing "*Kimoosoom Chimasoo*" like it had never been played, which is how Mariesis Okimasis first saw her husband after three whole weeks: through her kitchen window, her apron bloodied by the shank of caribou she was wrestling with, Mariesis Okimasis, forty years of age, black-haired, brown-eyed, lovely as a willow tree in spring. Her bloodied butcher knife missing Jane Kaka's left breast by half an inch, she zoomed through the door and flew into her husband's arms.

A mere two hundred yards south of the Okimasis cabin, one could have seen the priest in his study, a nail in one hand, a hammer in the other, poised to nail a brand-new crucifix into a wall. No good Catholic danced on Sundays, Father Eustache Bouchard had told his flock repeatedly. He considered marching over to tell the revellers to go home to supper and do their dancing some other day. His hammer came down, very hard, on his left thumb.

One trillion miles above the aboriginal jamboree, the ghostly foetus continued its airy descent towards Earth. And only medicine women, shamans, artists, and visionaries were aware that a star-born child would soon be joining their dance.

Mariesis Okimasis had once won a contest for which the prize had been to have her picture taken by an itinerant British anthropologist who had claimed that never in all his travels had he seen cheekbones such as hers.

"That guy never did send us a copy of the picture," moaned Mariesis into her husband's tingling ear as she slipped under him, he over her, their mountainous, goose-down-filled sleeping robe shifting like an earthquake in slow motion. Mariesis could see the left side of her husband's face, and for this she was glad, for nothing in life gave her more pleasure than the sight of his thick, sensuous lips.

The moonlight drifting in the little window over their bed made them look like large ripe fruit.

"That's all right," the large ripe fruit breathed into her ear as she struggled with her white flannel slip. "I don't need a picture when I have the real thing." He slid out of his underwear.

The moonlight led Mariesis's eyes to the floor beside the bed where her sleeping children lay, those four still at home; she listened to their delicate snores wheeze their way in and out of her husband's heavy breathing, a sweet kitten's purr floating up to her. Then the light took them to the dresser top, where sat the trophy her champion of the world had brought for her from the distant south. Beside it stood a photograph: Abraham cradling in his arms the silver bowl, his cheek being kissed by the young woman radiant in her white fur cape and her silver-beaded fur tiara: "The Fur Queen," he had explained, "the most beautiful woman in the world. Except for Mariesis Okimasis," of course.

Suddenly, the light was coming from the Fur Queen's eyes. Mariesis half-closed hers and let this moment take her, out the little window above the bed, out past the branch of the young spruce tree bending under its weight of snow, out to millions of stars, to the northern lights: the ancestors of her people, ten thousand generations, to the beginning of time. Dancing.

And somewhere within the folds of this dance, Mariesis saw, through tears of an intense joy — or did ecstasy inflict hallucinations on its victims? — a sleeping child, not yet born but fully formed, naked, curled up inside the womb of night, tumbling down towards her and her husband.

The ancestors — the women — moaned and whispered. Mariesis could hear among them her mother, who had left this Earth mere months after Mariesis had become a bride, one among many to have succumbed to tuberculosis. And though barely audible where she lay in her pool of perspiration, the women's voices said to her: "And *K'si mantou*, the Great Spirit, held the baby boy by his big toe and dropped him from the stars . . ."

And that was all she remembered.

Poof! he went on his bum, smack into the most exquisite mound of snow in the entire forest, making crystals of silver spray shoot up to join the stars. He disappeared into the mound and would have stayed down there indefinitely if it hadn't been for his bouncy baby flesh and his supple newborn bones.

"If you throw them on the floor," one-toothed Annie Moostoos would brag about her nine brown babies to all who cared to listen, "they'll bounce right back into your arms — it's true. Why would I lie to you?"

And the baby boy came shooting out of the mound of snow in two seconds flat and landed on his feet, right beside a small spruce tree that happened to be sleeping there. The little spruce tree opened one drowsy eye to see who could have made the whispering bump in the night and just managed to catch the tail-end of a spirit baby sprinting off into the darkness. There being nothing left to see but the little whirlwind in the baby's wake, the spruce tree went back to sleep.

The spirit baby ran through the forest, and ran and ran and ran. Hunch led him on, guided him, something having to do with warmth, he knew, something to do with hunger, with appeasing that hunger, something to do with love hunger, with appeasing that hunger, something to do with the length of string that led from the middle of his belly, a string almost invisible, so refined it could have been a strand of spider's web. This string and hunch. That was all.

Bang! The baby tripped, falling flat on his face, with a shriek more of surprise than of pain, in front of a cave. Growling like an ill-tempered bitch, a large, hairy animal lumbered out of the cave, admonished the prostrate child for having roused him from his winter sleep, and gave him a swift kick in the bum. The baby yelped, jumped up, and dashed away from the cave and its cantankerous occupant through the forest towards a tent standing on the shore of a lake.

Then the child bumped into a rabbit, who took pity on him, for, by this time, the naked child was shivering. The rabbit slipped off his coat and wrapped it around the child's shivering, plump midsection. The as-yet-unborn infant made his gratitude clear to the rabbit, who turned out to be a writer of lyric rabbit poetry, and the travelling baby and the now naked, shivering animal would be friends for life.

Finally emerging from the forest, glinting with crystals of snow and frost, the child ran around the tent by the lake, across the pile of woodchips strewn at the entrance, just missing getting sliced in half by a man flailing away with an axe, and burst through the tent flap like a comet.

The tent interior glowed golden warm from the kerosene lamp. Moaning and whimpering and crying softly, Mariesis Okimasis lay on a bed of spruce boughs, a minuscule and very ancient woman hovering over her like the branch of an old pine tree: Misty Marie Gazandlaree, Chipewyan, ninety-three years of age and one of the most respected midwives in the north at that time. The silver baby scooted under the old woman's left arm, took a little hop, two small skips, one dive and half a pirouette, and landed square on top of Mariesis Okimasis's firm round belly: 5:00 A.M., Saturday, December 1, 1951.

He lay puffing and panting, when the man with the flailing weapon entered the tent, his arms piled high with firewood, his eyes aglow at the sight of the child. And the last thing the child remembered, until he was to read about it years later, was shutting his eyes and seeing up in the dome of his miniature skull a sky filled with a million stars, the northern lights pulsating, and somewhere in the web of galaxies, a queen waving a magic wand.

The baby boy was floating in the air, his skin no longer silver blue but pinkish brown. As he floated, he turned and turned and laughed and laughed. Until, lighter than a tuft of goose-down, he fell to Earth, his plump posterior landing neatly in a bowl of silver.

"*Ho-ho!* My victory boy!" the fun-loving caribou hunter trumpeted to whatever audience he could get, which, at the moment, was his wife. "*Ho-ho!* My champion boy!"

"Down! Put him down, or his little bum will freeze!" cried Mariesis Okimasis, though she couldn't help but laugh and, with her laughing, love this man for all his unpredictable bouts of clownishness. Jumping up and down, the short Mariesis was trying to get the tall Abraham to put his World Championship Dog Derby trophy down so she could put their baby back into the warmth and safety of his cradle-board. This was, after all, a tent, not a palace, not even a house, and this was, after all, mid-December and not July, in a region so remote that the North Pole was rumoured to be just over that next hill. In fact, if it hadn't been for the curl of smoke from its tin chimney, the little canvas shelter would have been invisible, that's how much snow there was when Champion Okimasis was born.

THREE

$\mathcal{A}$top a low, moss-covered rock that overlooked Nameegoos Lake, Champion Okimasis stood singing a concert to his father and the caribou. The three-year-old stretched and pumped the miniature accordion strapped to his chest with such abandon that its squawk was frightful. Somewhere out on that lake, Abraham Okimasis and his team of eight grey huskies were giving chase, and if Champion performed with sufficient conviction, the Okimasis family would be feasting on fresh hindquarter of young caribou before the sun touched the prong of that first pine tree.

"*Ateek, ateek, astum, astum, yoah, ho-ho!*" Champion's robin-like soprano rang out, his lungs small balloons. By the time he got to the tenth repetition of the phrase, a herd of caribou would come bursting out the other side of that first island, his father not twenty yards behind them.

"Caribou, caribou, come to me, come to me, *yoah, ho-ho!*"

Down the rise of land, Champion's mother was squatting on bare ground, clearing used dishes from a lunch table of spruce boughs three feet from the smouldering remains of their campfire. The early afternoon sun, amiable enough for early January, wasn't making much headway on the top layer of snow, but its golden light made Champion Okimasis and his family feel warm and at ease with life.

Covered in earth-toned cotton dress and winter parka, midriff ripe as a full moon, Mariesis Okimasis looked, to the singing Champion, like a boulder, a part of the earth. She was nine months into her twelfth pregnancy and the fateful event could pounce upon her any minute now, so Champion had been informed by his older sister, the pouty and bossy Chugweesees Okimasis.

"*Ateek, ateek, astum . . .*"

So proud was he of his first original composition that Champion wanted it to be appreciated, not just by his father and the caribou, not just by the two other hunting families on the other side of the island, but by the world. Her face glowing with an inner light, Mariesis smiled at the impassioned, swaying, rocking musical wonder and said, "Champion. My boy. You will soon have a brother who can dance to that little caribou song of yours."

Champion would have had ten older siblings but for TB, pneumonia, and childhood ailments, Mariesis had explained to an uncomprehending Champion; but here at least were Josephine, five, and Chugweesees, seven, playing with sticks and stones, and Chichilia, eleven, repacking the grub box for her mother. William William, nineteen, was up in Kasimir Lake, just south of the Northwest Territories border, helping one-eyed Uncle Wilpaletch trap mink and otter and arctic fox; and Marie-Adele, twenty-one, was married with children of her own and moved to her husband's home community of Ootasneema, Saskatchewan, so far away that Marie-Adele Weechawagas-née-Okimasis barely existed for Champion.

Sure enough, before he could launch into his forty-third verse, a herd of caribou came charging out from behind that first small island on a lake so white that it was difficult to look at for any length of time. Umpteen-umpteen caribou, Champion estimated their number as he squinted and banged his accordion with even greater vigour, the song kicking into a tempo he would later come to know as allegro con brio. When he saw his father zoom out behind the stampeding animals, hunting rifle in the air, his huskies racing as though demons were nipping at their tails, he yelped his father's famous "Weeks'chiloowew!" Two other rifle-waving hunters came dashing out behind Abraham.

At this distance, Champion, his mother, and his three sisters couldn't see the details, much less hear the sounds; but the thunder of caribou hooves was so familiar they would hear the rumble in their dreams of any ordinary night. They also knew that Abraham was expressing his joy by yodelling the only word in his yodelling repertoire, the word Champion loved with all his heart.

Josephine and Chugweesees and their puppies Cha-La-La and Ginger went tumbling, screaming, yelling, and barking down to the lake and would have run clean across the ice to join their father if the wise-beyond-her-years Chichilia Okimasis hadn't grabbed them and dragged them back to shore. "You wanna be stomped to death by wild caribou?" she screamed. "You wanna leave this Earth looking like two ugly little meat patties?"

Champion knew that the most effective way to help his father was to keep singing, and this he did, the song now more a furious jig than the anthem of hope it had been. Champion was so surprised by the new effect that he slipped into the key of D, although C was the only key he knew.

"Champion! Champion, call your father!" Alarmed by the sudden sharpness in Mariesis's voice, Champion saw that her face was contorted, her arms wrapped around her belly, her body rocking back and forth. The little musician stopped in mid-vibrato. Accordion still strapped to his little torso, he scampered down to the shore.

"Chichilia! Chichilia!" cried Champion, the accordion bouncing up and down on his little belly, squeaking and sputtering out random clusters of semitones. "There's something wrong with Mama! There's something —"

Splat. He had tripped on the root of a dying tree and lay on his accordion with the breath knocked out of both of them.

When he looked up, his face covered with dirt and dirty snow, all he could see was Chichilia's feet striding up to his face. Her dog, the remarkably intelligent Suitcase Okimasis, sniffed around his neck for a trace of broken vertebrae.

"Mama's belly is hurting! Mama's belly . . ."

Chichilia wasted not a word; the young woman strode across the ice towards her father and the stampeding herd.

Though he couldn't hear it from such a distance — at least a mile was his estimation — Abraham knew that his son was singing for him. For wasn't it his greatest pride to have finally sired a child with a gift for the making of music, one to whom he could pass on his father's, his grandfather's, and his great-grandfather's legacy? The assurance that this ancient treasure of the Okimasis clan could rest intact for at least another generation inspired him to glide across the ice with even greater skill, greater precision, greater speed.

"*Mush*, Tiger-Tiger, *mush!*"

The caribou now loomed a mere fifty yards in front of him; his soul began to sing.

Then a yearling veered to the left. The hunter's heart jumped three half beats. Separated from the herd, this yearling would give Abraham the perfect opportunity to display to the other hunters trailing him what was admired throughout northern Manitoba as caribou-hunting prowess without equal.

"*U*, Tiger-Tiger, *u!*" Abraham yelled to his lead dog, and Tiger-Tiger swerved, his seven team-mates following; the sled made an elegant turn to the left.

"Such a prince, my Tiger-Tiger, such a prince," Abraham whispered, for he and his part-wolf, part-husky had learned, over the seven years of Tiger-Tiger's eventful life, to communicate both with and without words. This was fortunate because Tiger-Tiger's Cree vocabulary was limited, though he had learned how to ask for "black coffee" on blizzardy Tuesday mornings. Keeping his left hand firmly hooked around the handlebar of the sled, Abraham took aim at the frightened caribou with his right. The sled's sudden encounter with patches of unevenly packed snow, however — and the fact that the fleeing animal, knowing death was imminent, was running erratically — was making his aim unsteady. His finger was about to press the trigger when a human figure beyond and to the right of his quarry drew his focus. He shot and missed.

"Damn," he cursed the ill-timed appearance of this human, who was waving frantically. He would have taken a second shot but recognized his intrepid daughter, Chichilia. She may not be able to sing a note, much less play one, try as Abraham might to teach her, but she could shoot a slingshot with such accuracy that, at eight years old, she killed an entire warren of rabbits, whose ears she made into a stunningly succulent stew. For a girl who astonished audiences with highly polished displays of level-headedness and self-possession, Chichilia's current agitation was downright alarming.

"*Cha*, Tiger-tiger, *cha!*" the hunter yelled into the wind. The leader of the team swerved to the right so suddenly that the left side of the sled came off the ground. Abraham was now heading straight for Chichilia.

"Whoa, Tiger-Tiger, whoa!" he shouted, and the dogs began to slow down, though not fast enough for Abraham's comfort.

"Whoa!" he screamed, dropping his rifle into the sled as Chichilia's legs took great strides through snow that, in places, hadn't hardened quite enough to bear her weight. But all the hunter had to hear was "*nimama!*" to understand her message.

He pulled his sled to a halt beside the girl, sending fountains of powder snow everywhere. With well-practised motion, Chichilia leapt into the canvas-sided conveyance with the intention of sitting at the bottom. But Abraham had already slashed the air with one grand sweep of his moose-hide whip, shouted "*mush!*" and the dogs were off like bullets, making a beeline for the campsite. Chichilia went flying and slammed headfirst into the handlebar.

The caribou hunter was in such a rush that he forgot his normally fine-tuned manners. It was a few days before he remembered to apologize to his daughter for causing the rather spectacular bump on her head that would remain with her for the rest of her long and passionate life — a bump that would become the subject of many hours' quality conversation.

It couldn't have taken more than four minutes for father and daughter to reach the spot where they had stopped for lunch on their way to Eemanapiteepitat one hundred miles south for the birth.

Mariesis was not, however, bent over in pain or crying for help. She was unpacking their tent with the intention of erecting it, help or no help from her three small children. Josephine and Chugweesees were gathering sticks for tent pegs, and handling the hatchet with a less than admirable skill. Champion sat perched on the grub box, singing and playing his only song, "to make her feel better," he would explain to his father later, "so she wouldn't hurt so much."

Not waiting for his sled to come to a full stop, the caribou hunter leapt out and ordered his wife to lie down on a blanket.

"Won't stop jumping up and down" were all the words she could muster.

"*Ho-ho!*" the caribou hunter exclaimed. "Gonna be a dancer, this one." And in no time, the tent was standing.

That night, Mariesis lay half-covered by her enormous goose-down sleeping robe, the light of a kerosene lamp dancing on her perspiring face. To Abraham, hanging a white flannel bed-sheet across the middle of the small room to give his wife a measure of privacy, she looked beatific, the darkness of her deep-set eyes bottomless wells of love. From a carpet of newly cut spruce boughs, a fresh, moist, minty aroma filled the room to overflowing.

He tested the twine that held the sheet, then bent to put more wood into the stove he had fashioned out of a once-red oil drum, black from years of use. Abraham had to keep the hardy little appliance going, for if it stopped, they froze to death, it was as simple as that. Having refilled the stove, the hunter went outside to chop more wood.

Champion lay on the other side of the hanging sheet, his head next to the accordion he loved so much that he refused to be parted from it, day or night. Josephine and Chugweesees wiggled like worms beside him. Covered by a puffy down-filled sleeping robe, they whispered furiously.

"The Great Spirit must be holding our little sister up by her big toe by now," said the bossy Chugweesees. "Getting ready to drop her, right from the centre of the sky." She left no room for anyone to argue that the new arrival might be a boy; Chugweesees Okimasis simply assumed she could predict the future.

Across the lake, a lone wolf raised its howl, the string of notes arcing in a seamless, infinitely slow, infinitely sad glissando, then fading into silence, leaving the hearts of its listeners motionless with awe. Then two wolves joined the first in song. One of Abraham's dogs, tethered to trees behind the tent, answered, then a second dog, and a third, until a chorus of weeping souls, as if in mourning for one irretrievably lost, filled the night air, numbing the pain of the woman now deep in her labour in this snow-covered tent on this remote island.

Stifling a yawn, Champion looked up at the hanging bedsheet and made up his mind that he was not going to miss a second of whatever shadows played on it. He made the mistake of blinking, however, just once, which was enough to send him slipping across a river to the world of dreams, where he had long ago learned how to fly, where he might fly up to meet the falling baby halfway and tell him to go back. For was not this brazen new arrival about to depose the unique Champion Okimasis from his status as not only baby but star of this illustrious caribou-hunting family?

On the other side of the island, Chichilia Okimasis was dragging a one-hundred-year-old woman through knee-deep snow.

The crone's spine was as crooked as the gnarled pine walking stick with which she propped herself up; she was not much more than four feet tall and so fearfully thin that eleven-year-old Chichilia looked as large as a moose. Abraham had heard from another hunter that the campsite two miles away might harbour just such a woman and so had dispatched his strapping daughter to fetch her. Peroxide Lavoix by baptism, the midwife of births so numerous that she had long ago lost count much preferred her Indian name, which was Little Seagull Ovary.

"Not so fast, my girl," Little Seagull Ovary wheezed, like an accordion. "These spindly old legs of mine aren't what they used to be." The black silk kerchief she wore tied tight over her snow-white head — the trademark of all good mid-wives everywhere, she explained to her extremely impatient young escort — lent her the air of a fearsome one-eyed pirate.

To shorten their passage, the elder of the pair entertained the younger with a tale that her listener had heard at least one hundred times yet would never tire of hearing. This was the tale of newborn babies falling from beyond the stars, rousing cantankerous, hibernating bears, magnanimous lyric-poet rabbits, and such. Chichilia giggled as the midwife embell-ished the ancient yarn as only her very advanced age earned her the right to do. Little Seagull Ovary, for instance, insisted that the hibernating bear, being an actor bear, celebrated throughout the bear community, had missed a vital entrance cue on stage as a result of the newborn baby's interruption; his audience had complained to the management and he was in danger of fading into obscurity.

A star shot across the heavens, arced, and landed with a little explosion of light so close that Chichilia could almost catch it in the palm of her hand. The earth rumbled faintly; a shiver leapt up their spines.

"The child has landed. The child is running through the forest now," said Little Seagull Ovary.

In the land of dreams, the child-about-to-be-born was fluttering through a forest lit in hues of mauve and pink and turquoise, the wings that had sprouted on his back whirring soundlessly. He alighted on the occasional spruce, the occasional pine, the occasional birch as the fancy tickled him, like a subarctic hummingbird. A distance off, he spied another flying creature, compressing and pulling at a funny corrugated box strapped to his scrawny chest; in response, the box produced an irritating, squeaky whine. The infant-not-yet-born and the itinerant musician were about to fly to each other for a better look when they were interrupted by a cry, half wail of lamentation and half shout of triumph. Suspecting the cry as his entrance cue, the infant-not-yet-born dove into the nearest mound of snow, images of the sour-tempered actor bear and the sweet-faced lyric-poet rabbit he had met minutes earlier flashing across his memory. He dove with such enthusiasm, however, that he was way below the permafrost before he remembered to turn around.

Back beside his snoring sisters, Champion stirred and looked up at the hanging bedsheet. He rubbed his eyes. Eventually, with an effort that caused him to become wide awake, he was able to grasp that a shadow splashed across the sheet might be a very large fish hook.

"*Athweepi*," an ancient voice intoned, gentle as morning dew. The fish hook was, in fact, an old woman, and she was addressing a largish mound that moaned and shifted in front of her.

Champion could discern in the old woman's hands scissors, a length of cloth, and perhaps a bowl. And he heard, amidst the moans and the whispered, calming words, the sloshing of liquid on metal. Then the old woman reached so deep into the mound that she almost disappeared.

The journey back up to the surface was not as easy as the journey down, the spirit baby in the loincloth of rabbit fur discovered. For he had to squirm and wriggle and flail and punch his way through soil and rock and minerals so thickly layered they were all but impassable, through permanently frozen clay, tangled roots of trees and dormant fireweed, and shards of animal and human bone. He pushed and pushed until a tunnel eased his passage, replete with a viscous wetness. The earth around him rumbled and gurgled as if it would split open. The rumble became a roar. The roar became a scream. And the flash of light was the second-last thing he would remember about his first journey on Earth.

When the scream was gone, only moans and whispers remained, subdued currents of wind, a chorus of ancient women whispering, "*Awasis, magawa, tugoosin.*"

The hook-backed old woman resurfaced and from her hands, to Champion's great astonishment, dangled neither scissors nor cloth nor bowl. It looked like legs, arms, and a head, although so spindly they were hardly worth mentioning.

"The baby!" The realization slapped Champion square across the face. He stopped his breathing so his ears could open wide: not a peep, not a sigh, not even half a burp. Maybe it was dead, Champion dared to hope, then blushed. He would have crossed himself in repentance had he already learned the labyrinth of Roman Catholic guilt.

The midwife jerked one hand away from the baby, then jerked it back, the resulting slap on its bum resonating like a small gunshot. Only then did the child admit that it was a living, breathing being. It wailed.

"*Napeesis awa*," the midwife said tenderly, "*napeesis*." Mariesis sighed like the cooing of a ptarmigan.

Champion yawned and drifted across the magic river. Sitting side by side on the shore of dreams, he and his newly arrived little brother watched as, high above their heads, the seven stars of the Great Bear sparkled from a queen's tiara. Glimmering faintly through the Milky Way, the monarch waved her wand. A spray of stars exploded across the universe, turned back, regrouped, and made a perfect, inverted dipper above the Okimasis tent. The midwife's voice intoned: "*Ooneemeetoo. Kiweethiwin. Ooneemeetoo.*" And so the child was named: Dancer.

Father Eustace Bouchard, thirty-five, handsome, strong of body, strong of mind, French-Canadian, Roman Catholic, priest and missionary *extraordinaire,* stood between the altar and the communion rail, exuding holiness and mouthing words without sound. Cascades of starched, lace-bordered white garment gave off ripples of pungent sweetness. In one hand, he held a weighty black book from whose pink-lined pages he was reading. The other hand was thrust in front of him as if to slap the face of anyone who dared to interrupt. High above him, a naked, bleeding man hung from a wooden beam. Years later, Champion Okimasis would insist that the man was dead, Ooneemeetoo that he was still alive, that morning anyway.

The burning incense almost choked the breath out of one-toothed Annie Moostoos, who stood across the baptismal font from the muttering priest, the two-week-old Ooneemeetoo clutched to her trembling breasts. For Annie Moostoos had never stood this long before the holy altar of God in all her fifty-nine years. Only the sign of the cross that Father Bouchard wove at one point saved her from collapsing to the floor, she would later swear, thus saving the life of her twelve-pound godson.

From the pew behind his aunt, Champion Okimasis scrutinized the curious ritual. His parents, who were standing on either side of the untrustworthy Annie Moostoos, were listening to the man in the long white dress with marked deference. The priest dipped his free hand into a hollow place at the top of the pedestal of shining wood. His hand emerged with a handful of water, which he held over the baby's forehead, apparently intending to give it a good scrub.

Then his full lips parted, his white teeth glinted, and his tongue formed the words, *"Abrenuntias satanae?"* The words, meaningless to Cree ears, pierced the infant's fragile bones and stayed there.

"But he already has a name," squawked Annie Moostoos. The strapping priest turned with airy contempt to the tiny widow, confident that one arched eyebrow would render the source of this rash remark immobile.

Like a bullmoose ramming its antlers into those of some fearsome, lust-filled rival, Annie Moostoos charged ahead. "His name," she stated, "is Ooneemeetoo. Ooneemeetoo Okimasis. Not Satanae Okimasis."

"Annie Moostoos," the voice sliced through the smoky air as through a bleeding thigh of caribou, "women are not to speak their minds inside the church." The blast was so potent that the tooth, yellowed by age and the smoke of two million cigarettes, yet so celebrated for its stubborn solitariness, hung in its airless void like an abandoned oracle.

"Neee, tapwee sa awa aymeegimow," the disempowered god-mother whined to her cousin. Returning to the business at hand, the priest poured the holy water over the baby's fuzzy cabbage of a head. The water was cold. The child cried.

"Gabriel Okimasis," the oblate stated, as if to nail "Gabriel" permanently between quotation marks, *"Ego te baptizo in nomine Patris, et Filii, et Spiritus Sancti,"* to which the bundle in Annie Moostoos's aching arms responded with a sudden hush.

"Amen," said the parents.

To his dying day, Kookoos Cook claimed to remember floating glumly about in his mother's womb, mere days before his birth. Jane Kaka McCrae claimed to remember, clear as crystal, the filthy white ceiling high above her cradleboard well before she reached the age of one. Little Seagull Ovary recalled her father lifting her into the air, the tent awash in golden light.

Gabriel Okimasis, for as long as he was to live, would insist that he remembered his entire baptismal ceremony. Champion Okimasis would accuse him of lying; it was he, he would point out, who had told Gabriel the story. In truth, it was Kookoos Cook, sitting on the pew with Champion on his lap, who would never tire of telling his nephews the yarn, which, as the years progressed, became ever more outrageous, exaggerated, as is the Cree way of telling stories, of making myth.

FOUR

On their annual spring migration from the caribou-hunting grounds of the lower barren lands south to Eemanapiteepitat on Mistik Lake — there to await the arrival of the summer fishing season — Abraham Okimasis and his family had stopped for a midday break. There, on a largish island in the middle of a lake that, some say, had once been fished by someone named Weesageechak, the hunter and his wife lounged by their waning cooking fire, sipping steaming cups of muskeg tea after a lunch of fresh-broiled whitefish. The remains of their feast — here a fish's head, there a morsel of bannock — were strewn across the small round banquet table of freshly cut spruce boughs.

"Come December," said Mariesis with an undercurrent of sadness, "Champion will be seven years old." Like all lovers of long standing, they could read each other's thoughts.

"Seven years," replied Abraham, casting a sweeping glance

over the thawing lake before them. "That's a good time. Myself, when I was seven, I bagged my first moose." Abraham loved teasing his wife; he had been fourteen when the legendary event had taken place, and she well knew it. A breeze from the south ruffled a strand of her long, black hair. Her heart was too heavy; the hunter's joke had missed its mark.

"He will be leaving us soon. Champion. Does he have to go to that school in the south?"

The question fell upon the hunter's chest like a cold hand. His weather-worn brown face furrowed and his left hand raked absent-mindedly through a clump of pale green caribou moss, patches of which had begun to peek their way through the melting snow.

"What Father Bouchard wants, I guess," he finally admitted, wishing dearly that he had some say in the matter.

"But couldn't he wait two years? Until Gabriel can go with him? That school is so far away."

"*Sooni-eye-gimow*'s orders, Father Bouchard says. It is the law."

Then the wind changed direction ever so slightly so it carried the laughing voices of their two children, like the tinkle of small bells.

"Okay. I sing. You dance. Like a caribou," one little voice chirped.

"Like an old caribou? Or a young caribou?" echoed the other little voice with a silvery, chiming laugh.

"A young one, of course!" replied the first voice, sounding bossy.

Behind Abraham and Mariesis, up the slight rise of land that led from the lake to the forest, Champion was teaching his little brother to move like a young caribou. Gabriel's salt-and-pepper terrier, Kiputz, sat and watched the two boys, bemused. A large grey rock jutted mightily from immediately behind the happy trio.

Champion had his little accordion strapped to his chest, as if he had emerged from his mother's womb with the instrument attached. It had grown a little the worse for wear, however, and could do with a visit to the accordion hospital, Champion had explained craftily to his father earlier that day, meaning to say that he had, perhaps, outgrown it. Abraham had merely smiled, as there was no money for a new instrument.

"Okay," Champion said to Gabriel, "I sing" – and he sang – "'*Ateek, ateek, astum, astum!*' and you go . . ." and he demonstrated how to move like a young caribou, his arms high over his head for antlers, his moccasined feet taking elongated, loping strides.

Three years of age and graceful as a birch sapling, Gabriel tried to imitate his brother. He stuck his little arms up above his head and lifted his left leg so high for the first step that he staggered dangerously. But the leg made it back to the ground safely and he had just begun to raise his right.

"Your arms aren't high enough!" Champion yelled. His concentration broken, Gabriel toppled over with a little yelp. "Higher. Higher. And you should bend your wrists. Like this. Antlers are crooked," said Champion as he marched around the prostrate beginner.

Tired of being ordered around, Gabriel struggled back up to his feet. "But I shouldn't even have my arms up."

"Why not?"

"Because a young caribou doesn't have antlers, ha-ha!" laughed Gabriel and hopped three silly little circles around Champion so that he would be irritated.

"Well, this one does!" Champion placed his left hand hard upon the button side of the accordion to play the first chord of his most recent composition, "*Ateek, Ateek* II," written in G major, Champion's favourite key because it made him think of oranges.

The moment Gabriel heard the music, his body began to glide across the bed of moss as though he were floating on a bouncy summer cloud.

"*Ateek, ateek! Astum, astum!*" went Champion's song in its simple circle of three chords, limpid with honey-coloured sound. "*Yoah, ho-ho!*"

Back at the fire, now mere embers from which weak curls of smoke rose, Abraham and Mariesis found, for one disturbing moment, that they did not know whether to look down at the ground, at each other, or up at the sky. Their eyes stung, as though whipped by an icy blast of wind. Finally, the hunter peered into Mariesis's pupils, which looked like two long, dark tunnels at the far end of which appeared two tiny, waving flames. He could see that she was frightened, that she wanted to cry. He placed one hand over hers, to reassure her that he, at least, would never leave her.

"*Ateek, ateek!*" Champion's bell-like voice wafted to Mariesis's ears, nudging her, tickling her, coaxing her face back into a wide, if reluctant, smile. Now the couple could hear Kiputz's silly bark, which never failed to make them laugh, for it was a cross between a yodel, a woman's shriek, and a gander's honk.

A low rumble welled up beneath the children's voices, almost imperceptible, but enough to provide Champion's song with a muted ostinato.

"Thunder? In May?" Mariesis asked herself, incredulous. She looked up at the sky. Not a cloud. Clear blue far as the eye could see.

Abraham craned his neck to look to the rear of the island. Could the earth be opening up? Could the dreaded Weetigo have snuck up on them? It couldn't be the thunderbirds, for they swooped down on northern Manitoba only in July and August.

Without warning, two dozen head of caribou burst out of the forest at the northern end of the meadow, so fast that Abraham and Mariesis didn't even have time to blink. Only later would they explain to themselves, with some embarrassment, that the thought of losing Champion to boarding school had so befuddled them. And that southeast wind, Mariesis tried to convince Annie Moostoos, with extreme discomfort, had done so much to hide any sound coming from the north.

"Even if it had been an explosion of the most powerful of German dynamite," she had said, "we wouldn't have heard it."

How else could northerners possibly have missed a sound that they should have heard from five miles away?

The mouths of Abraham and Mariesis hung open, their lower lips trembled, and their throats swallowed once but made no sound. Their eyes were frozen on the rock in front of which, seconds before, Champion and Gabriel had been dancing and cavorting.

The thunder of hooves now made it seem as though whole mountains of rock were cracking and then crumbling. One hundred, two hundred caribou — it could have been ten thousand, their sound was so massive — had filled the open stretch of land in no time flat, their legs a moving forest, their antlers the surface of a stormy lake. Years could have passed before the hunter and his wife managed to look with horror deep into each other's eyes.

"The children!" The only sound Mariesis's mouth could emit should have come out as a piercing shriek; instead, against such a monolithic rumble, it was small and distant. Everything now moved as though swimming through a sea of honey. Mariesis floated up from her sitting position, intent on plunging headlong into the herd, but her husband clamped both arms around her waist. Hissing like a cornered wolverine, she stabbed her elbows viciously into his belly, which only made him cling with greater tenacity. She flailed and kicked, over and over, screaming.

"No! No! No! No!" he shouted, over and over and over. But his words had no sound.

Mariesis couldn't see. The tears were nothing; it was rage

that was blinding her, rage at this man who dared to call himself the father of her children, rage for giving up, so soon, so easily. How could he, this champion of the world? And rage at herself for being caught unprepared.

In the meadow, by the large grey rock, Champion and Gabriel, too, had been caught by surprise, surrounded by hooves pounding the earth, making pulp of what had been elegant puffs of pale green reindeer moss, sending it flying at their bodies, in their faces, in their eyes. Champion could just make out Gabriel sitting, legs spread on the ground not ten feet in front of him, his tear-stained face bewildered, his mouth open like a little beak expecting food, his arms spread like small wings. He may have been crying, but thunder was the only noise in the world.

No one has ever been able to explain what entered Champion Okimasis. The earth may have been caving in beneath his feet, the stone exploding, the northern forest gone mad and marching off to war. The sun may as well have fallen from the sky, the early afternoon was suddenly so dark.

But Champion Okimasis walked. He calmly raised his right foot and then calmly raised his left, eight paces forward in one unbroken line, a thousand caribou swirling around him like rapids around rocks.

Champion bent down, took Gabriel's hand in his, and the pair glided off towards the shimmering grey rock, as in a gavotte, Champion would shamelessly ornament the story years later.

On top of the large rock, Champion sat, legs splayed, Gabriel on his lap, Champion's arms clamped hard around his waist, Gabriel's hands gripping Champion's forearms, Champion's right cheek pressed to the grey felt back of Gabriel's parka. Both had shut their eyes tightly as if to blot the noise out with pressure on their eyelids. And there they clung, stiff as wood yet pliant as willow saplings buffeted by autumn winds.

Champion may have had Gabriel's back to hide behind, but Gabriel had nothing but wind, warm and moist and rank with animal breath and fur and sweat and sinuous muscle, blasting his face. When he opened his eyes, slowly, fearfully, all he could see was antlers, antlers far as the eye could go, jostling, careering, twisting, mangling air. Eventually, the blur without end took on form, but what? Dancers? Spirits? Whirlpools of light and air and shadow? The shapes became one pulsing wave of movement, throbbing, summoning him, beckoning him on. "Come with us, Gabriel, Gabriel, Gabriel Okimasis-masis-masis, come with us. Come with us, Gabriel, Gabriel, Gabriel Okimasis-masis-masis, come with us."

Champion began to sing, his soprano soaring above the pounding basses and timpani of hooves like the keening of a widow.

"*Ateek, ateek! Astum, astum!*" sang Champion, "*Yoah, ho-ho!*"

Slowly releasing his hold, Gabriel opened his arms to embrace this immense field of energy. And he began to weep.

By the campfire, of which only smoulders remained, Mariesis had her face crushed hard against her husband's chest.

When the last of the herd was but a low hum, the whisper of the southeast wind was almost jarring.

First came the sound of Mariesis sobbing, weakly, as if collapsing from the exertion. Then came Kiputz's excited bark. And last, Abraham's mellifluous baritone.

"*Ho-ho!*" he laughed, "My Champion boy, *ho-ho!*"

Mariesis raised her face, shocked, insulted by such uncalled-for exuberance. Abraham's weather-hewn brown face was lit up like a sun, suffused with an ecstasy she had never seen.

And then Mariesis saw her sons, perched atop the large grey rock, glowing with triumph, Champion and Gabriel Okimasis, laughing.

They had never been on an airplane. They had seen them, drifting in the wind like dragonflies. They had seen them berth at Father Bouchard's old dock, swallowing — or, better, spewing out — Josephine, Chugweesees, Chichilia, and other Eemanapiteepitat children. They envied them their wings, their ability to become airborne; it was said that they could climb above the clouds. So Champion was excited, Gabriel jealous, when the red seaplane arrived late that September morning.

Abraham wondered out loud, to other long-faced parents on the priest's old dock, what on earth their son was going to get "down there." Champion proudly replied that he was only going for a ride, that he would come back the next day to tell them all about "the south."

"At least Josephine and Chugweesees will be with him," Mariesis sighed wearily.

Inside, it smelled like gasoline and rubber. The glass in the window felt like plastic: yellowy, scratched, difficult to see through. Still, as the plane floated off and its propellers whirred to life, Champion spied Gabriel on the sandy shore, like a toy soldier, saluting him. For certain, he would be able to tell his little brother when he got back if *K'si mantou* really lounged lazily among the clouds as if they were giant fluffed-up pillows.

But there were no clouds that day, merely an eternal blue. And far below, endless lakes that looked like his mother's doughnut cut-outs, except of rabbits' heads, caterpillars, and human faces with great big eyes.

At noon, Gabriel sat across the table from his parents and Chichilia, refusing to cry. Instead, with a temerity that surprised his elders, he ordered his mother to put out some trout *arababoo* for Champion anyway. The plane would crash and Champion would swim back and be home by sunset, Gabriel insisted. He would be very hungry.

PART TWO
Andante cantabile

FIVE

*C*hampion Okimasis stood at the head of a line of seven small Indian boys watching the tall, pasty man in black cutting the hair of another small boy. At first, Champion thought the holy brother might take pity and leave some hair, but as the seconds ticked on, this appeared unlikely. The silver clippers made one last ruthless sweep, leaving a pate as shiny as a little moon. With a flourish of his great right arm, the brother gave the boy a gentle shove, swept the pale blue sheet off his shoulders — causing a rainshower of jet-black hair — and said "Next" in a tone as business-like as if he were counting money. Humiliated, the boy slid off the chair, which was much too high for him, and ran off, sniffling.

Champion had never seen such an enormous room, bigger than Eemanapiteepitat church; arctic terns could fly around in here with ease. "Gymnasium," he had heard the room called by the barber brother, the only word that Champion had found musical in this queer new language that sounded like the *putt-putt-putt* of Happy Doll Magipom's pathetic three-horsepower outboard motor.

Champion would dearly have loved to hide in some dark corner, perhaps even run all the way back to Eemanapiteepitat, except that his father had told him three hundred miles was too far for a boy of six to walk. Biting his lip, he waded through the river of discarded hair and scrambled clumsily into the chair in front of Brother Stumbo, who stood there waiting with his smile, the hair-sprinkled pale blue sheet, and sharp-toothed stainless-steel clippers. As Champion's weight sank in, the leather upholstery sighed. A split second before Brother Stumbo enveloped him in the sheet, Champion reached up and touched, with wistful affection, the strand of wavy hair around his right earlobe.

Brother Stumbo had to pause. "Down. Put your arm down." And though Champion didn't know what the man was saying, his body language clearly ordered Champion to lower his arm and sit as still as a rock.

Poised for the slaughter, Champion straightened his back and called forth every ounce of courage so he wouldn't burst into tears. The bristles of discarded hair made his neck itch. He wanted desperately to scratch but his arms were immobilized. If he started to cry, he wouldn't be able to wipe away the tears and he would be seen by all these strange boys from other places with a baby's crying face. He wished that he could look at his hair one last time. He wished he was on Nameegoos Lake with his family. And the caribou. He wished his accordion was strapped to his chest so he could play a melancholy song, he thought mournfully, flailing about for anything that could hold the tears at bay.

Clip, clip, clip. Champion could feel his hair falling, like snowflakes, but flakes of human skin. He was being skinned alive, in public; the centre of his nakedness shrivelled to the size and texture of a raisin, the whole world staring, pointing, laughing.

"And what's your name?" Brother Stumbo's voice hit the boy's neck with a moist, warm billow of air that smelled of days-old coffee and Copenhagen snuff. Champion assumed that he was ruminating on some sacred subject known only to men of his high station and remained silent.

"Name? What's your name?" the snuffy whiff came at him again. Champion's nerves began to jiggle, for he was beginning to suspect that he was being asked for something.

"John? George? Peter? Joseph?" The clipper-happy barber cut four incisions into what remained of Champion's mop of hair.

"Cham-pee-yun!" He countered the assault by ramming the three syllables in the spots where the ouches would have been. Not only did he now know that he was being asked a question, he knew exactly what the question was. "Champion Okimasis!" he reiterated, in challenge.

"Okimasis," a fleshy voice floated up behind Champion's ears. "So this is the one named Jeremiah Okimasis." A face surfaced, one he had not yet seen in this new place, one with eyebrows so black and bushy they could have been fishing lures. The face consulted a sheet of paper.

Champion's heart gave a little shudder. But he refused to admit defeat, especially now that there were two of them to one of him. He summoned forth the only English word he knew and, with it, shielded his name.

"No. Champion. Champion Okimasis."

"According to Father Bouchard's baptismal registry, you are named Jeremiah Okimasis," chortled the portly, elderly face, now attached to a great black cassock, starched white collar, and silver crucifix that dangled from a chain around his neck. As with Father Bouchard, Abraham Okimasis would have decreed that this man's word bore the weight of biblical authority and therefore was to be listened to; feeling his father's eyes looking over his shoulder, Champion would have knelt before the priest and crossed himself but for the pale blue sheet that held him prisoner.

"Ah, Jeremiah," said Brother Stumbo as he snipped merrily. "Jeremiah Okimasis. That's a good name." Champion felt the tear that, against his best intentions, had escaped from his right eye. "There now, Jeremiah. It's only Father Lafleur. You mustn't cry in front of the principal." His hair now gone completely, Champion had no strength left; he began to bawl.

Father Lafleur placed a hand on Champion's thigh and, like some large, furry animal, purred at him. "There, there. You'll be happy here with us." The scent of sacramental wine oozed off his tongue, and incense appeared to rise like a fog off the surface of his cassock. Cold air, like a large, gnarled hand, clamped itself on Champion's naked head.

With what looked like a hundred bald-headed Indian boys, Champion found himself climbing up several banks of stairs made of some grey, black-speckled stone. Stairs made him quiver with excitement — wait until he told Gabriel about them. You could slide up and down their pale green iron banisters all day long, he would report, stairs are such a clever, whimsical whiteman sort of thing.

Uniformly garbed in sky-blue denim shirts and navy denim coveralls, the boys marched out into a long, white passageway that smelled of metal and Javex — everything here smelled of metal and Javex — where lines of Indian girl strangers were marching in the opposite direction. But there was his sister Josephine, hair now cropped at the ears like all the girls, as though someone had glued a soup bowl to her head. He waved surreptitiously at her but, just then, one of the innumerable doors that lined this tunnel swallowed her. Ghost-pale, tight-faced women sheathed completely in black and white stood guarding each door, holding long wooden stakes that, Champion later learned, were for measuring the length of objects.

The echo of four hundred feet on a stone-hard floor became music: *peeyuk, neesoo, peeyuk, neesoo.* Until Champion became aware that music of another kind entirely was seeping into his ears. From some radio in one of these rooms? From some *kitoochigan* hidden in the ceiling? All he knew was that this music was coming closer and closer.

Pretty as the song of chickadees in spring, it tickled his eardrums. Like a ripe cloudberry in high July, his heart opened out. He forgot the odour of metal and bleach, and he forgot the funny shape of his exposed head that had caused such jeering from the boys of other reserves. He looked with hope to see which doorway might reveal the source of such arresting sweetness. His forced march, however, left him with no option but to put words, secretly, to a melody such as he had never heard, "*Kimoosoom, chimasoo, koogoom tapasao,* diddle-ee, diddle-ee, diddle-ee, diddle-ee . . ."

Finally, the music splashed him like warm, sweet water, in a cloud of black-and-yellow swallowtail butterflies. He wasn't even aware that he had stepped out of the queue and was now standing at the entrance to the room.

On a bench sat a woman in black, the stiff white crown stretched across her forehead, her hawk's nose and owl's eyes aimed at a sheet of white paper propped in front of her. Her fingers caressed the keyboard of the biggest accordion Champion had ever seen.

Except that it didn't sound like an accordion; the notes glided, intelligent and orderly, not giddy and frothy and of a nervous, clownish character.

He wanted to listen until the world came to an end. His heart soared, his skin tingled, and his head filled with airy bubbles. He even felt a bulbous popping at the pit of his stomach, rising up through the narrow opening of his throat, making him want to choke. His lungs were two small fishing boats sailing through a rose-and-turquoise paisley-patterned sky, up towards a summer sun lined with fluffy white rabbits' tails. His veins untwined, stretched, and swelled, until the pink, filmy ropes were filled to bursting with petals from a hundred northern acres of bee-sucked, honey-scented, fuchsia-shaded fireweed.

Something soft and fleshy brushing up against his left shoulder made him flutter back down to Earth, unwillingly. He turned to look. What met his gaze, to his great surprise, was the upper body of Jesus, nailed to a silver cross, wedged into a wide black sash.

"Jeremiah," said Jesus, "class will be starting soon." Champion blinked at the thrice-punctured man, to be assured that he had indeed spoken, and could he please say more? But the victim's mouth remained unopened, leaving Champion to look elsewhere for the source of these words.

Champion turned his face upward until the little bones of his neck began to smart. There, way up, hovered the giant, beaming face of Father Lafleur.

SIX

*C*hampion-Jeremiah — he was willing to concede that much of a name change, for now — sat with his black-covered scribbler, his stubby yellow pencil, and the mud-caked fingernails he was anxious that nobody see. Twenty-nine other Cree boys and girls his age sat in rows around him, thirty little wooden desks dappled with late-September sunlight filtering through the yellow, brown, and orange leaves of birch and poplar trees. This golden light culminated at the front of the room, the usual domain of the fearsome grade-one teacher, Sister Saint-Antoine. In her place now stood the even more fearsome principal of the school. As he spoke, the oblate scraped a metal-edged wooden ruler across a large paper chart on which was drawn — in complex detail and swirling, extravagant colours — a cloudy place that he referred to as heaven. Champion-Jeremiah suspected that this might be the same locale Father Bouchard called *keechigeesigook.*

Heaven had a substantial population of beautiful blond men with feathery wings and flowing white dresses, fluttering about and playing musical instruments that Champion-Jeremiah had never seen before: some resembled small guitars with oval contours and humped backs, others oversize slingshots with laundry lines strung across them. The caribou hunter's son noted, with stinging disappointment, that accordions were nowhere to be seen. The men with wings played and sang all day long, so Father Lafleur appeared to be explaining, and escorted people from their graves beneath the earth to one side of an ornate golden chair on which sat an old, bearded man.

Among the people rising from these graves to heaven, Champion-Jeremiah tried to spot one Indian person but could not.

Taking a chunk of white chalk in hand, Father Lafleur printed "GOD" on the black slate beside the chart, evidently intending that the meaningless word be copied down.

"But to see God after you die," he lectured on, pointing to the old man in the chair, "you must do as you are told." The words swept over the students like a wind. Champion-Jeremiah peered at the image of God and thought he looked rather like Kookoos Cook dressed up as Santa Claus except that his skin was white and that, for some reason, he was aiming a huge thunderbolt down at Earth and glaring venomously.

Slowly, laboriously, Champion-Jeremiah scrawled the word "GOD" on the left page of his scribbler and finished off his handiwork with a great black period. The word loomed large and threatening; he felt an urge to rub it out.

"Hell," the priest yanked Champion-Jeremiah out of his doleful rumination with his stabbing emphasis, "is where you will go if you are bad."

Hell looked more engaging. It was filled with tunnels, and Champion-Jeremiah had a great affection for tunnels. A main tunnel snaked from just below the surface of the earth to its very bottom and others ran off to each side in twists and knots and turns, not unlike the Wuchusk Oochisk River and its unruly tributaries. Champion-Jeremiah thought of the tunnels he and Gabriel made every winter in the deep snow of Eemanapiteepitat, then realized that Gabriel would have to make tunnels by himself this winter.

Skinny, slimy creatures with blackish-brownish scaly skin, long, pointy tails, and horns on their heads were pulling people from their coffins and throwing them into the depths with pitchforks, laughing gleefully. At the ends of the seven tributaries were dank-looking flame-lined caves where dark-skinned people sat.

Aha! This is where the Indians are, thought Champion-Jeremiah, relieved that they were accounted for on this great chart. These people revelled shamelessly in various fun-looking activities. One cave featured men sitting at a table feasting lustily on gigantic piles of food: meats and cakes and breads and cheeses. In another, women smoked cigarettes and sashayed about in fancy clothing, and in a third, men and women lay in bed together in various states of undress. In another, people lay around completely idle, sleeping, doing absolutely nothing. There appeared to be no end to the imagination with which these brown people took their pleasure; and this, Father Lafleur explained earnestly to his captive audience, was permanent punishment. Champion-Jeremiah was hoping to find an accordion player in at least one cave but, to his great disappointment, there was no place for musicians of his ilk in hell or heaven.

"And this," Father Lafleur crowed, "is the devil. D-E-V-I-L. Devil." He scratched the word on the blackboard at least a foot below "GOD" and finished with such force that the chalk broke and fell to the floor. Excellent student that he intended to be, Champion-Jeremiah copied the word, slowly, painstakingly, on the right-hand page of his scribbler: "DEVIL." The L took such effort that he completely forgot to add a period.

In the largest, most fiery, most fascinating cave of all, on a huge black chair of writhing, slime-covered snakes with flicking tongues, sat the being with the biggest horns of all, the longest tail, the most lethal-looking pitchfork, his head crowned by a wreath of golden leaves. Champion-Jeremiah wished that he could understand what the priest was saying, for this king was absolutely riveting. He narrowed his eyes to slits so that he could peer into the eyes of this shameless, strutting personage to whom, apparently, modesty was unknown. He took careful note of the fact that the king — "Lucy," the priest called him — was not glaring venomously. King Lucy was grinning, King Lucy was having a good time.

"And the sins that will get you there," said Father Lafleur in a tone that Champion-Jeremiah was sure had a tinge of something not unlike enjoyment, "are called the seven deadly sins."

Champion-Jeremiah looked down at the word on the right-hand page of his little scribbler and found the *D* of "DEVIL" not quite perfect. He reached for his eraser. "And these seven deadly sins are called . . ." Champion-Jeremiah applied the eraser to the *D*, "pride, envy, gluttony . . ." – erasing was such a waste of time – "sloth, covetousness, anger, and . . ." Champion-Jeremiah hated making mistakes, "lust." The word burst forth like a succulent, canned plum. The priest wiped his brow with a rumpled white handkerchief. Champion-Jeremiah seized the moment to look down at his scribbler: "EVIL" was right there at his fingertips.

He thought it rather pretty, especially the way the *V* came to such an elegant point at the bottom, like a tiny, fleeting kiss.

A cold wind came sweeping down over the vast field of gravel that was the boys' playground, a six-foot, steel-mesh fence holding at bay the surrounding forest of pine and spruce, birch and poplar and willow. If you stood on the monkey bars or flew high enough on the swings, you could see Birch Lake in the distance, down the hill behind the school building, transparent emerald, unlike the opaque blue of Mistik Lake.

"The winds of late October . . . ," said Champion-Jeremiah to himself, then stopped. His Cree must not be heard or he would fail to win the prize: the boy who acquired the greatest number of tokens from other boys by catching them speaking Cree was awarded a toy at month's end. Last month, the prize had been an Indian war bonnet; this month it was to be a pair of cowboy guns. Sitting in the gravel with his back against the orange brick wall of the school, Champion-Jeremiah suddenly didn't care whether he lost or won the guns. "The waves on Birch Lake must be climbing higher and higher and there will soon be ice. Later than on Mistik Lake." On the gravel between his knees, he placed eight pebbles in one neat row with a rectangle of wood at the end.

"*Mush!* Tiger-Tiger, *mush!*" whispered Champion-Jeremiah as he made the pebble at the head of the line jump up and down. In the make-believe windswept distance, the caribou were flying across his invisible ice-and-snow-covered northern lake.

A wisp of snow flew by, the first that Champion-Jeremiah had seen this fall. He half-heartedly tried to catch it, but it's hard to catch a wisp of snow, even with mittens.

Cree boys small and large — some almost young men — were scattered like leaves across the yard, near and not so near, even way to the other end of the fence, a good quarter of a mile away. Girls had their own yard on the other side of the giant building, out of sight, away from the view of lusty lads who might savour their company, so Champion-Jeremiah was to learn in the nine years he would spend here. Even his sisters

Josephine and Chugweesees were marched away to their own world the minute they got off the plane. He would find a way to visit them someday, as sure as the moon was round.

A whimsical shift in the direction of the wind brought to Champion-Jeremiah's attention something other than snow. Two floors up, a window was slightly open. There was that lilting melody again, the undulating bass, the rising and falling harmonies so shiny with light that he could wrap them around his fingers, lick his hand, and let the liquid music spill onto his lips, over his chin, down his neck.

He missed his accordion dearly.

His hair had now grown to a downy brushcut. The caribou hunter's son stood before an old oak desk so mountainous he could barely see over its top. Beside this desk stood a Christmas tree, and behind it sat Father Lafleur, peering over his reading glasses at the tiny lad who stood at stiff attention, like a drummer boy.

"Yes?"

"Yes." The second English word Champion-Jeremiah had learned. After "no" and then "yes," he had learned about twenty others. He paused to see if the priest's furry eyebrows would curve upward. They didn't. But he was not going to shy away from attempting, for the first time, in public, a complete sentence in English, curving eyebrows or no.

"Play piano?" The two words popped out of the nervous crusader's mouth like the chirping of a newly hatched bird. Champion-Jeremiah cursed himself for not sounding more impressive, more stentorian. But then the holy eyebrows formed two crescents, furry caterpillars arching for a meal over the edge of some green birch leaf.

"Ah, you can play the piano," said Father Lafleur to Champion-Jeremiah, doubtful but taking his time with the terrified child.

Aha! he was about to exclaim with a hearty slap to his desk. The organ! The organ at Father Bouchard's church, of course!

But Champion-Jeremiah's chirp beat him to the punch.

"No! Wan play piano!"

"Ah, you *want* to learn to play the piano." The principal treated every second word as if it were a stepping stone to a sacred shrine.

Thrilled that he had finally gotten through to the man, Champion-Jeremiah nodded, almost violently.

"Hmm-hmm," purred the priest, for he seemed to find the boy's vociferous nodding entertaining.

Champion-Jeremiah knew he was about to be tested. He knew the answer to his prayer wasn't going to fall from the sky. He knew he was going to have to work for it when he saw the principal's lips virtually disappear into one small, hair-thin slit.

"Do you make any other kind of music?" Leaning forward, Father Lafleur tapped his pen on the desk. Such gestures made Champion-Jeremiah nervous – besides, he didn't understand the question.

"Music," the man in black boomed, elongating the vowels as if they were some tragic dirge. "Do you make any other kind of music?" as if the seven-year-old would understand better if he shouted. "Do you sing, perhaps?"

"Sing!" Another word in Champion-Jeremiah's English vocabulary. He jumped on it like Kiputz on a tibia of freshly boiled caribou. That's it! The idea flashed across his mind like lightning. I'll sing for him. I'll *weeks'chiloowew* like Dad.

"Yes. Me sing it. Me sing it liddle song."

"Then sing for me," drawled Father Lafleur. Putting lighted match to a thick, brown cigar, he sank back into his giant leather chair, which hissed at Champion-Jeremiah.

Dismissing the hiss as an idle threat, Champion-Jeremiah cleared his throat, wiped his lips with the cuff of his shirt, dropped his hands to his sides, and puffed out his lungs.

"*Ateek, ateek! Astum, astum!*" The opalescent gems floated into the air in slow, swooping curves and circles. "*Yoah, ho-ho!*"

The priest watched the heart-shaped lips, pink as bubble gum, with wonder and astonishment. The notes of the song climbed up and up and up until they reached the silver angel at the top of the Christmas tree, making her wings shimmer and undulate. For all the priest knew, Jeremiah Okimasis himself had sprouted wings and was flitting about like a warbler or a finch, lending sparkling light to each golden ball, each silver bell, each piece of tinsel.

The priest's spine began to buzz, ever so vaguely, ever so faintly, but he was unaware that once — just once — his tongue darted out and licked his lower lip.

Champion-Jeremiah saw it. "*Ateek, ateek . . .*" And he knew then that he had the principal of the Birch Lake Indian Residential School squarely in the palm of his hand.

When Champion-Jeremiah arrived back in Eemanapiteepitat late that June, Gabriel found himself faced with a dilemma: if he could speak no English and his older brother no Cree, how were they to play together? Fortunately, before the week was out, Champion-Jeremiah experienced an epiphany. At their fish camp on Mamaskatch Island one stormy evening, inside the tent, he tripped over Kiputz, causing him to burst out in a torrent of Cree expletives that shocked his mother. From that moment, he chattered with such blinding speed that people could barely understand him. The family breathed a collective sigh of relief. And shortly thereafter, Gabriel learned English: "yes," "no," "yes-no," and "hello, merry."

SEVEN

*L*ike a seagull surfing the autumn wind, the red seaplane circled above the Birch Lake Indian Residential School. Jeremiah and Gabriel Okimasis could see the splashes of yellow in the deep green forest that surrounded the sprawling orange-brick edifice and the two enormous gravel-covered, fenced-in yards flanking it. Between them, the boys counted fourteen people in black and white — at this distance, who could tell if they were men or women? — walking single file down the gravel path towards the lake. They resembled a row of penguins the boys had once seen on a *National Geographic* cover at Father Bouchard's rectory. Descending foot by foot, the plane approached the lake, the water so clear the limestone bottom was visible.

At the dock, the chorus line of penguins — who turned out to be nuns, priests, and brothers — stood jammed together, the clipper-happy barber brother towering over them like his namesake, the famous comic book *Stumbo the Giant.* Father

Lafleur stood with feet apart, hands on hips, his eyes squinting against the brilliant midday sun.

When the pilot opened the passenger door, there stood Jeremiah Okimasis, eight years old, mop of jet-black hair, the riot of multicoloured beads on his caribou-hide jacket sparkling magically, a smile splashed across his chubby, brown face. It had been a summer of good fishing.

The pilot helped him down the little steel ladder and lifted him into the waiting arms of the principal.

"So, Jeremiah," said Father Lafleur, all sunny and jovial, "you've decided to come back for a third year."

Jeremiah dearly wished he could toss off an English sentence just as jazzy, but he couldn't. The priest grunted, "Aha! You've gained some weight," and deftly deposited him on the dock with two delicate pats on the lad's burgeoning posterior.

The next passenger to appear was Gabriel Okimasis, five years old, black hair even fuller and wavier than Jeremiah's, skin transluscent, eyes doll-like.

"Can that be Jeremiah's little brother?" asked a nun, her voice filled with doubt.

"Naw, it can't be."

"Impossible!" harrumphed a short dumpy nun. "Much too pretty." The pilot passed the object of adulation over to Father Lafleur, whose chunky ruby ring momentarily got entangled in the fringes of Gabriel's beaded home-tanned caribou-hide jacket. The priest just managed to save Gabriel from falling into the lake by clamping his hand onto the boy's thigh.

"So, Jeremiah," chortled the priest as he set Gabriel lightly down on the dock, "you've brought your little brother this time."

"Yes," piped Jeremiah in a tiny, humble voice. We didn't have much choice, he would have added, if the language had been his.

Jeremiah took Gabriel by the hand and started walking him, proudly, onto shore. Josephine and Chugweesees, now ten and twelve, were somewhere behind him, but he couldn't say goodbye. He didn't want to look at them. He didn't want to cry in front of these people.

Cooing like a wise old owl, a nun reached out to ruffle Gabriel's hair. Never having seen such a creature before, Gabriel recoiled in fear, his voice teetering on the edge of tears.

"*Awiniguk oo-oo?*"

"*Mootha nantow. Aymeeskweewuk anee-i,*" Jeremiah replied with as much reassurance as he could muster.

As if from thin air, a grinning Father Lafleur appeared behind the brothers and, with a gentle touch to Jeremiah's left shoulder, purred.

"Now, Jeremiah. You know you're not to speak Cree once you're off the plane." Jeremiah felt a choke breaking against his throat. Small brown suitcases in hand, the Okimasis brothers silently trudged up the grassy slope, past a dying clump of fireweed.

The Okimasis brothers took a last wistful look at their sisters and waved a shy farewell. Chugweesees, like Champion, had long been divested of her illustrious name and was now known simply as Jane, a regrettable change, for it reminded them of the unfortunate halitosis-stricken Jane Kaka McCrae, the most slovenly woman in Eemanapiteepitat.

"Hail Mary, full of grace, the Lord is with Thee; blessed art Thou amongst women and blessed is the fruit of thy womb, Jesus," recited Brother Stumbo in a sleep-inducing monotone as he paced down one aisle and up another, his large black rosary beads swinging from both hands. Identically attired in pale blue flannel pyjamas, thirty-seven newly bald Cree boys knelt beside their little beds in the junior boys' dormitory.

"Hello merry, mutter of cod, play for ussinees, now anat tee ower of ower beth, aw, men." Gabriel rattled off the non-sensical syllables as nimbly as he could, pretending he knew what they meant. But, his knees hurting from the cold, hard linoleum, he couldn't help but wonder why the prayer included the Cree word *"ussinees."* What need did this mutter of cod have of a pebble?

"Glory be to the Father and to the Son and to the Holy Ghost," intoned Brother Stumbo as he swept by Jeremiah's bed, fingering the small wooden crucifix at the end of his shiny black rosary.

"Azzit wazzin da peekining, izznow and fereverer shallbee," answered, in imperfect unison, thirty-seven little voices. And then boys and brother brought the session to its grand finale with a lusty and unanimous "Aw, men."

Under his blankets, Jeremiah craned his neck to catch a

glimpse of his little brother seven beds away. With a weak little smile, Gabriel waved and he waved back.

Brother Stumbo addressed the assembly one last time. "Goodnight, boys." To which the entire room dutifully replied, "Goodnight, Brother Stumbo," their voices resonating like one large "aw, men." Brother Stumbo flicked the light switch, and the room was plunged into darkness.

In no time, Jeremiah heard the muted wheeze of sleeping children, like summer breezes flitting about the room, now here, now there. "Maple Sugar," the jig his father had taught him just before the boys had left home on the plane that morning, bounced merrily across his mind like a naked rabbit. Above the yard, a large three-quarter moon slid out from behind a clump of clouds. Jeremiah yawned and drifted off.

Like an otter surfacing for air, a shadow rose out of the darkness. The moon slid back behind the clouds and the moving figure was enveloped once again, though not before it sent a quick glint of silver light into the gentle rhythm of children sighing in their sleep. Then an errant wind, perhaps the motion of the earth in its nightly orbit, moved the clouds so the white, vapoury moon glowed once again.

The figure was caught in a web of moonlight, fleetingly, just as it rose from one bed and moved towards another.

With a swish of cloth, the figure resurfaced, large and looming, beside Gabriel's bed, its silvery point of light throwing off one final glimmer.

A small black-and-white photograph rested on the pillow,

glass-covered, gilt-framed. Next to it lay two sleeping heads whose gleaming pates bore witness to Brother Stumbo and his magic silver clippers. Covered by a sheet, a blanket, and a bedspread, the Okimasis brothers lay wrapped around each other, their snores all but nonexistent.

The Fur Queen laid her lips upon the cheek of caribou hunter Abraham Okimasis, grand champion of the world, the kiss frozen in time.

Father Lafleur watched the two boys for a minute, to him, Caravaggio's cherubs, pink and plump-cheeked, their lips full, ripe cherries. Then, gently, he shook Jeremiah's arm. Once. No response. Twice. Still no response. Father Lafleur bent over and shook him yet again, almost violently, and hissed: "Jeremiah!"

Jeremiah and Gabriel were flying across blinding white snow in their father's pinewood sled. The vapour of the February morning was playing havoc with the sun's rays. What should have been rainbows instead were isolated balls of pastel colour, now appearing, now disappearing, pink, purple, blue, orange, purple, sunburst yellow, turquoise, purple, pink, dazzling their eyes. Somewhere above these shifting spots of ethereal light arced Abraham's loon-like yodel, "*Weeks'chiloowew!*"

But it wasn't the caribou hunter yodelling "the wind's a-changing!" It was Father Lafleur whispering Jeremiah's name at his face. It wasn't rainbow-coloured dots through winter vapour that Jeremiah was seeing but the glinting eyes of the principal, inches from his own. And it wasn't flecks of snow from the racing dogsled that was spraying his face but the holy man's saliva.

"Get back to your own bed."

Jeremiah barely remembered, earlier that night, shuffling drowsily over to his brother's bed, to see if the sniffling he had heard was Gabriel's, which it was. Jeremiah had only meant to hold him until he fell asleep.

Briefly, the two had whispered about the herds of caribou and the hunting season. Gabriel had even taken their father's Fur Queen photograph from under his pillow and they had kissed it. "The Fur Queen will watch over you," Mariesis had said to Gabriel as she had packed it into his little brown suitcase. "The white fox on her cape will protect you from evil men."

"Come on," whispered Father Lafleur. "Up." He tugged at Jeremiah's arm. Jeremiah slid out from beneath the sheet and his brother's warm embrace. His hair was gone; he had no power. Childish sleepiness masking his defeat, he shuffled down the aisle of slumbering bodies, back to his own bed.

The priest stood watching Jeremiah's receding figure. Then he turned back to Gabriel, who remained oblivious. Suddenly, his eye was caught by the photograph. In the semi-darkness, the moon, playing her usual tricks on glassy surfaces, made the Fur Queen wink. Nonplussed, the priest replaced the photo on the pillow and slinked down an aisle towards the door, as another cloud broke the moon's silvery spell and enfolded him once more in darkness.

EIGHT

On a stage festooned with white crêpe-paper bells, large red satin bows, and deep red velvet curtains, Gabriel Okimasis was dancing. His little feet were kicking dust, his cowboy hat was bouncing up and down and would surely have flown right off his head if it hadn't been for the string under his chin, the white satin tassels on his red cowboy shirt were swinging left and right and back again. A six-year-old square-dance caller standing on a low wooden box called "Do-si-do and swing your partner round and round, promenade!" to the rhythm of Jeremiah's festive, jiggly piano music. The eight miniature cowboys and cowgirls did exactly that.

"*À la main* left," the caller shouted, and Gabriel swivelled to the left, grabbed the right hand of his partner, who grabbed the next male dancer's left as Gabriel moved on to the next female dancer's left hand. And so it went until the circle was completed and Gabriel had returned to Carmelita Moose.

Gabriel was so happy he wanted to grab Carmelita Moose and twirl her over his shoulder until she saw stars, but the choreography did not call for such elaborate moves. Instead, the dancers formed circles, squares, spinning wheels, and daisy chains. Their rhythm was so infectious, their enthusiasm so irresistible, that the audience tapped their feet and clapped in time.

Gabriel beamed with pleasure and once, in the middle of a turn and tap-tippity-tap of the feet that required particular panache, winked down to the place where, on the bare floor of the boy's gymnasium, beside a Christmas tree as tall as a house, Jeremiah sat, playing the piano as if he had been born for that sole purpose. In a crisp white shirt, perky black bow tie, and sleek black dress pants, his back as straight as a paddle, Jeremiah was banging out "Maple Sugar" in a way that would have made Abraham Okimasis's chest puff out with pride, had he been there.

But he wasn't, and neither was Mariesis. Nor was any other parent of these dancing children among the two hundred in their audience. The front row of seats was occupied by twelve nuns, two brothers, and two priests. The hawk-nosed, owl-eyed Sister Saint-Felix beamed like a car light at the keyboard-pounding Jeremiah Okimasis, who, she crowed every chance she got, was her best student in a fifty-year career tortured by one crushing disappointment after another. As Gabriel Okimasis bounded past centre stage, the principal followed the dancing form until it disappeared into the wings. The curtains closed and applause resounded.

Father Lafleur sat still for a moment, then clapped three slow thoughtful claps.

The fingernail of a giant index finger, a crescent moon hung in the sky, pointing into uncurtained windows to reveal sleeping children, row on row on row: white bedspreads, white sheets, white pillowcases, the hair on small dark heads grown to fluffy black brushcuts.

A sliver of light flashed once from the dark recesses of the room. It could have been a firefly except that this was mid-December. Other than the soft rhythm of children purring in their slumber, there was only the sound of cloth brushing against cloth, stopping briefly and then swishing on. The firefly reappeared and disappeared again as it approached the row where the dreaming Gabriel Okimasis was furiously engaged in a do-si-do made particularly complicated because his partner, Carmelita Moose, kept floating up, balloon-like, so that, while his feet were negotiating quick little circles, his arms had to keep Carmelita Moose earthbound. The undisputed fact was that Gabriel Okimasis's little body was moving up and down, up and down, producing, in the crux of his being, a sensation so pleasurable that he wanted Carmelita Moose to float up and up forever so he could keep jumping up, reaching for her and pulling her back down, jumping up, reaching for her, pulling her back down.

When Gabriel opened his eyes, ever so slightly, the face of the principal loomed inches from his own. The man was wheezing, his breath emitting, at regular intervals, spouts of hot air that made Gabriel think of raw meat hung to age but forgotten. The priest's left arm held him gently by his right, his right arm buried under Gabriel's bedspread, under his blanket, under his sheet, under his pyjama bottoms. And the hand was jumping up, reaching for him, pulling him back down, jumping up, reaching for him, pulling him back down. He didn't dare open his eyes fully for fear the priest would get angry; he simply assumed, after a few seconds of confusion, that this was what happened at schools, merely another reason why he had been brought here, that this was the right of holy men.

From some tinny radio somewhere way off – Brother Stumbo's room next door? – he could hear Elvis Presley singing "Love Me Tender."

Through his slitted eyes, he could see that the motion of the priest's hand obviously gave him immense pleasure: his eyes were closed, the furrows on his forehead smoothed out, his lips curved into a smile, his face glowing in the moonlight with the intense whiteness of the saints in the catechism book.

Gradually, Father Lafleur bent, closer and closer, until the crucifix that dangled from his neck came to rest on Gabriel's face. The subtly throbbing motion of the priest's upper body made the naked Jesus Christ – this sliver of silver light, this fleshly Son of God so achingly beautiful – rub his body against the child's lips, over and over and over again. Gabriel had no strength left. The pleasure in his centre welled so deep that he was about to open his mouth and swallow whole the living flesh – in his half-dream state, this man nailed to the cross was a living, breathing man, tasting like Gabriel's most favourite food, warm honey — when he heard the shuffle of approaching feet.

He shut his eyes tight. He held his breath.

Jeremiah had awakened with a start from a dream of playing concerts to vast herds of caribou. Why, he didn't know, but he thought he might have heard a whimper from Gabriel. Once his eyes adjusted to the darkness, he decided to check up on him, perhaps give him just one kiss.

With great reluctance, he slid out of bed, flinched from the cold and slipped into the night. His pale blue pyjamas glimmering, the little ghost, all vapour and mist, floated through the eerie light, down one aisle and up another.

But Gabriel was not alone. A dark, hulking figure hovered over him, like a crow. Visible only in silhouette, for all Jeremiah knew it might have been a bear devouring a honeycomb, or the Weetigo feasting on human flesh.

As he stood half-asleep, he thought he could hear the smacking of lips, mastication. Thinking he might still be tucked in his bed dreaming, he blinked, opened his eyes as wide as they would go. He wanted — needed — to see more clearly.

The bedspread was pulsating, rippling from the centre. No, Jeremiah wailed to himself, *please*. Not him again. He took two soundless steps forward, craned his neck.

When the beast reared its head, it came face to face, not four feet away, with that of Jeremiah Okimasis. The whites of the beast's eyes grew large, blinked once. Jeremiah stared. It *was* him. Again.

Jeremiah opened his mouth and moved his tongue, but his throat went dry. No sound came except a ringing in his ears. Had this really happened before? Or had it not? But some chamber deep inside his mind slammed permanently shut. It had happened to nobody. He had not seen what he was seeing.

"Silent night, holy night," sang a heavenly choir of angels. The little baby Jesus lay sweetly, all naked, rosy and plump, upon a bed of golden straw. Surrounded by cows and donkeys, shepherds and angels, his parents watched over him with a care that was, indeed, tender and mild.

Resplendent in white starched linen surplice, crimson satin bow exploding like fire from his throat, blood-red cassock falling to the floor, Gabriel Okimasis swayed lightly as he walked, dignified and stately, across the sanctuary, one of God's own cherubim. Hands held together against his chest, the six-year-old knelt on a prayer stool and bent low his perfect head.

Deep in complicated prayer upon an altar glowing with gold and silver and silk and fine taffeta, Father Lafleur intoned the Latin text of the Christmas midnight service.

"*Dominus vobiscum.*"

"*Et cum spiritu tuo*," the congregation chanted in reply.

Later, the priest knelt on the altar's second step, smote his breast three times with his ruby-fingered hand, and intoned, for all assembled there to hear: "*Mea culpa, mea culpa, mea maxima culpa.*"

Well-trained soldiers of the church, all dutifully recited with him. "Through my fault, through my fault, through my most grievous fault."

The Okimasis brothers had never discussed this phrase but both had concluded that they were being asked to apologize for something beyond their control. Under these circumstances, however — yards enclosed by steel fences, sleeping quarters patrolled nightly by priests and brothers — they had also independently concluded that it was best to accept the blame; it *was* their most grievous fault.

At the electric organ, Jeremiah launched into "O Come, All Ye Faithful." There were four verses to this particular carol, he recalled, with his usual precision for facts musical, so by the time the congregation got to the part about the three wise men from the East arriving in Bethlehem with what Gabriel had insisted were boxes of Black Magic chocolates, Holy Communion was about to begin.

After the hymn, Jeremiah could see Father Lafleur bent low over his golden chalice wherein lay pieces of the Body of Jesus Christ, muttering the last bits of prayer to give him the strength to serve it to the faithful. He was surrounded by eight altar boys, all Cree, aged five to twelve. And none among the congregation — other than twelve nuns, two brothers, one other priest, cooks, janitor, and nightwatchman — was over the age of sixteen.

The nuns filed down the centre aisle to the communion rail, there to kneel in a neat row of supplication before the miracle the high priest was about to offer them. As two hundred

Indian children sang, "Away in a manger, no crib for a bed," Father Lafleur, holding the host aloft with his right hand, descended the altar steps and walked slowly to the first nun.

As the priest made the turn, his gaze locked with that of his organist, Jeremiah Okimasis. The little angel, Gabriel, holding the golden paten to catch fragments of Christ's body from under communicants' chins, caught this telling exchange between his brother and the priest. He felt something heavy, cold and wet, at the base of his spine, a sensation vaguely like a bog-like squelch.

"*Corpus Christi*," said the priest, and the first nun's tongue lolled out like a piece of overchewed gum. The nun missed one small morsel of the white host, causing it to come twirling down, snowflake-like, but mumbled "Amen" anyway, somewhat too apologetically for Gabriel's taste.

He looked at the priest's hairy white right hand, reached with his paten, and neatly caught the fragment of falling flesh within the sacred vessel's golden hollow.

Three hundred miles to the north, Father Eustache Bouchard, silver chalice in one hand, round white host in the other, approached the communion rail, where knelt a line of Cree Indian people, not one of whom was between the ages of six and sixteen.

"*Corpus Christi*," Father Bouchard said to Abraham Okimasis, and placed the paper-thin wafer on his tongue.

"Amen," replied the champion of the world.

NINE

"Kill him! Kill him! Nail the savage to the cross, hang him high, hang him dead! Kill him! Kill him! . . ." ten million people roared.

Down went Jesus, down into the gravel, the crucifix crushing him, swirling dust playing havoc with his vision, his lungs, the very air he breathed. Pant, groan, and weep as fiercely as he might, he received no pity. Instead, the Roman centurion raised his whip and lashed God's sole offspring, lashed and lashed; he would stand back up, he would take up his cross, he would march up Eemanapiteepitat hill. Blood from the victim's lacerated spine splashed the soldier's scarlet tunic, his gold breastplate, his leather leggings, and naked thighs.

Slowly, Christ wobbled to his feet. What choice did he have? The crowd jostled, they slavered at his pain: "Kill him! Kill him! Nail the savage to the cross, hang him high, hang him dead! Kill him! Kill him! . . ." And this was only his first fall; the script demanded he have two more. The Son of God wailed at fate but dragged the cross around the bend.

And who should he run into but his mother, swathed in della robbia blue and laughing giddily, her hair a blizzard of confetti. Jane Kaka McCrae's last born, Big Dick, had finally married the lovely Asscrack Magipom – Mariesis Okimasis was so drunk she could barely stand.

"Jane Kaka ran out of wine!" she ululated, then paused to suck dry a Javex jug; like excess milk, red wine streaked her breasts. "At the dance! Can you believe it?" She reeled, her knees buckled, and she collapsed in a heap.

"Not now, Mother, can't you see I'm busy?" said Jesus.

"And Jane Kaka was so upset she fainted –" Mariesis burped, "right there in the church-hall kitchen. Banged her head against the statue of you, and *poof!* the water in Father Bouchard's tank turned into Baby Duck, can you believe it?" She fell again. "One week later, and the party's still raging!"

Crack! the whip struck the Lord's round buttocks. Mother or no mother, he could tarry no longer.

One week earlier, Gabriel had felt that same sensation, the stinging pain that brought with it a most unsaintly thrill. But playing Jesus was admired, even praised, by lay and clerical staff alike. It kept the children out of mischief, "supplemented" their religious instruction, and gave the principal food for thought: a course in drama for all altar boys was a virtual fait accompli, so Brother Stumbo had been overheard to say. No, far from being penalized for playing God the Son,

Gabriel's crime had been to be caught singing "*Kimoosoom Chimasoo*" when he was hanging from the cross and already seven tokens in the red.

In an office whose four walls verily vibrated with cigar smoke the principal had unbuckled his thick black leather belt and slid it off.

With Gabriel's now six-year-old posterior exposed to the light, the priest had lashed and lashed until, by the third blow, it had turned as red as cherry Jell-O.

"Bleed!" a little voice inside Gabriel had cried. "Bleed! Bleed!" He wasn't going to cry. No sir! If anything, he was going to fall down on his knees before this man and tell him that he had come face to face with God, so pleasurable were the blows. In fact, he clung to the vision with such ferocity that there he was, God the Father, sitting large and naked in his black leather armchair, smoking a long, fat cigar, little Gabriel's buttocks splayed across his knees, the old man lashing them with his thunderbolt, lashing them and lashing them until both man and boy gleamed.

"*Kimoosoom chimasoo*," Gabriel's little Cree voice rang out from the pit of his groin, even as a little English voice beside it pleaded: "Yes, Father, please! Make me bleed! Please, please make me bleed!"

Up the road, Jesus of the bleeding buttocks met the saintly Simon, who helped him bear the cross for two delicious yards until a phalanx of foul-mouthed soldiers clattered up and whipped him off. Next came Veronica, who dabbed once at the Saviour's face with a filthy dishtowel before she too felt the wrath of Jeremiah, the centurion.

To save time, Jeremiah had cut Christ's second fall, his consolation of the women, and his third fall, all without informing Gabriel. The company skipped to the strip.

Off came Gabriel's clothes at the hands of Jeremiah and his ragamuffin band and onto the prostrate cross went the Cree Son of God, naked but for his underwear, and shivering.

At which point Brother Stumbo's whistle announced supper.

Jeremiah and his nine-year-old soldiers hurriedly "nailed" Gabriel to the cross, swung it up, and banged its base into a groundhog hole. Veronica, saintly Simon, and drunk Mariesis in tow, they rushed off, leaving their spruce-branch whips and Jesus hanging in the gathering gloom. Call out as he might – "Come pack! Tone leaf it me here!" in his still dysfunctional English – the Saviour's pleas went unheard.

Wired haphazardly to the steel-mesh fence behind him and crackling in the dry June breeze, a scrap of cardboard read: "The Okimasis Brothers present 'The Stations of the Cross,' with a scene from 'The Wedding at Cana' thrown in."

Squirm by squirm, wriggle by wriggle, Jesus made the base of his pillory chew the groundhog hole. Next, he yanked until the cross fell, pinning him beneath its weight. Then he worked his wrists free of their binding ropes. Finally, praying to the Father that his supper would be saved, he ran.

In the dining room, one hundred boys looked up from apple pie half-eaten. The laughter was explosive, the pointing fingers worse than nails — Gabriel had forgotten to take off his spruce-root crown of thorns — but his vow of vengeance on one Champion-Jeremiah Okimasis rendered both laughter and fingers meaningless.

TEN

"There it is!" yelled Gabriel over the roar of engines and propellers. He wanted to run in circles and shriek with joy, but instead jabbed Jeremiah's stomach hard with his elbow. "There it is! There's Eemanapiteepitat!"

On the last day of June, the Okimasis brothers were in the red seaplane again, this time approaching Mistik Lake. At last! Mistik Lake with its thousand deep-green islands, its thousand gold sand beaches, its endless water.

Jeremiah strained to see over his brother's shoulder and his smile grew radiant. He yearned to reach right through the window, scoop up the toy village in the cup of his hand, kiss it tenderly, and put it in the pocket next to his heart. He could already taste the Cree on his tongue.

Late that night, hunters, beasts, and queens glimmered twenty trillion miles below the Okimasis brothers and twenty trillion miles above them. Gabriel and Jeremiah were the very centre of a perfect sphere, a gigantic bubble of night air, and glass-smooth lake, and stars. Gabriel told Jeremiah that the Okimasis family must look like Winken, Blinken, and Nod floating off towards the moon in a wooden shoe.

The wooden shoe was bearing the brothers, their father, their mother, and their sisters Josephine and Jane across one of the few open stretches of Mistik Lake to Kamamagoos Island, twenty miles south of Eemanapiteepitat, where Abraham had decided they would spend the summer fishing for trout that were the fattest in the world.

The only intrusion upon the vastness of the silence was the sound of paddles dipping and surfacing, dipping and surfacing, ripples of water gurgling sweetly in reply. Abraham sat in the stern of the canoe, thirteen-year-old Jane in the bow. Eleven-year-old Josephine slept on the floor behind Jane while Gabriel and Jeremiah sat idly in the middle with their mother between them. Infinitely happy that he had returned at last, Kiputz lay curled half-asleep in Gabriel's lap.

Suddenly, Gabriel saw a flame flickering faintly in the far distance.

"Look, a fire!" he exclaimed softly.

"Where?" asked Jeremiah, turning drowsily to look at Gabriel.

"There," replied Gabriel, pointing to the leeward side at what looked like a candle flame.

It must be Cree fishermen, Jeremiah concluded silently,

camped for the night on one of the islands. The brothers looked with wonder at the distant glow.

From some lonely place beyond the fading flicker, the sweeping arc of a lone wolf's howl reached out through the miles and came to a perfect landing beside the brothers, touching off a vague shudder that brushed the surface of their hearts, in perfect unison, like the ice-cold hand of someone waking after five hundred years of sleep.

Mariesis had seen such fires before. She had known this lake like an intimate friend, a relation, an enemy, a lover for nearly fifty years — such occurrences were not new to her. She merely kept her gaze straight ahead, as if nothing had happened.

Abraham, too, was looking straight ahead, focused on the three miles to Nigoostachin Island, where they could set up camp for the night.

"That's the island where Father Thibodeau's men caught Chachagathoo." It was their mother's voice, though as if someone else was giving expression to the words. "Don't look at it."

"Why not?" Gabriel asked, not moving his gaze from the sight. No response. Gabriel decided to be patient.

Mariesis's answer finally broke the spell. "Because Chachagathoo was an evil woman. Because she had *machipoowamoowin*. Father Thibodeau, oh, he hated that woman."

Like all children of Eemanapiteepitat, they had been told since early childhood that they were never to mention the name of Chachagathoo inside the house. And they didn't. All that they had heard of Chachagathoo was whispers that trickled through the village, from time to time, like some unpleasant, unwanted news.

When Father Thibodeau passed away, at the ripe old age of eighty-seven, he took his reason for hating Chachagathoo to his grave. His had been the first corpse Mariesis Okimasis had seen, when she was six years old, she had told her sons many times over the years: the waxen white mask with its eyes closed, its lips sealed tight, tiny Mariesis Eemoomineet standing in the summer breeze beside the open casket, wanting desperately to pinch the old man's nose to see if it would honk.

The boys had also heard the word "*machipoowamoowin*," but not often. All they knew was that it meant something like "bad blood" or "bad dream power." Jeremiah and Gabriel had once asked their uncle Kookoos about this ominous, disturbing word, but all they got was, "It means that when you dream you dream about things that go *chikaboom chikaboom* in the darkest corner of your mind, and that generally happens when you don't have no money to make the good home-brew." Gabriel thought to ask his mother about it, but a better idea poked him in the ribs.

His eye still on the receding flame, he decided to show off the English he had learned in his year at Birch Lake School.

"Do '*machipoowamoowin*' mean what Father Lafleur do to the boys at school?" Although he wanted to tickle his brother with this light-hearted joke, Gabriel's question ended with an eerie, spectral chuckle that could have popped out of a bubble in his blood.

Jeremiah's words, in English, were as cold as drops from a melting block of ice.

"Even if we told them, they would side with Father Lafleur."

Selecting one of the three Native languages that she knew — English would remain, for life, beyond her reach and that of her husband's — Mariesis turned to Jeremiah. "What are you saying, my sons?"

If moments can be counted as minutes can, or hours or days or years, one thousand of them trickled by before Jeremiah was absolutely sure Gabriel's silence would remain until the day they died. And then he said, his voice flat, *"Maw keegway."* Nothing.

ELEVEN

"Dominoes, dominoes, do the Cree Indians of northern Manitoba know how to play dominoes?" The little-boy voice of Gabriel Okimasis drifted through the radiant August afternoon on one extended note. Gabriel was draped in one of his mother's famous quilts, tied in a bulky knot at his neck and dragging on the ground a good two feet behind him.

Facing a clump of young spruce trees, a spray of fireweed flaming pinkish mauve at his feet, Father Gabriel raised a host the size of a frying pan — in fact, one of Mariesis's golden bannocks — above Abraham Okimasis's World Championship Dog Derby trophy.

"No dominoes, no dominoes, the Cree Indians of northern Manitoba were never taught how to play dominoes, oh dear," responded Jeremiah Okimasis from where he sat on a pale green carpet of reindeer moss at the opposite end of the clearing. Although Gregorian chant was the order of the day, the nine-year-old musician was softly playing "O Come, All Ye Faithful" on the worn, browned keys of his father's two-sizes-too-big blue accordion.

Father Gabriel's congregation consisted of sticks broken off at various lengths and arranged in three neat rows across the meadow. Kiputz, the most devout among the faithful, sat in respectful silence at the end of one row.

The accordion soloist modulated from the key of G to its relative minor, as one of the more sombre sections of the service was about to unfold.

Gabriel lowered his chalice and host and genuflected gently, his head bent in humble, wordless prayer on the moss. He raised his right hand to his heart, a butterfly hovering over fireweed. "Me a cowboy, me a cowboy, me a Mexican cowboy," he chanted, and he smote his chest, one smite for each "cowboy."

Suddenly, behind him, a squirrel dashed across the open space. Kiputz let loose with his first bark in a whole hour, leapt up and gave chase. "*Miximoo, miximoo, miximoo!*" being as Cree a dog as ever there was.

The priest whipped halfway around to glare at the perpetrator. "Kiputz," he stated coldly, "Kiputz. Shut up!"

The squirrel had scampered up a nearby spruce tree, the dog running round and round its base, jumping, barking, "*Miximoo, miximoo.*"

Father Gabriel whirled from the makeshift altar and took off after his errant parishioner, knocking host and chalice into the dirt with his robe.

"Kiputz! Kiputz, you're supposed to be in church, god-damnit!"

The red-furred rodent teased his pursuer. "Chiga-chiga-chiga-chiga-chiga-chiga-chiga!" ricocheted through the forest. "Come-and-get-me, come-and-get-me, come-and-get-me, you ugly little creep!" as Kiputz understood it.

Wars start when two parties haven't taken the time to learn each other's tongues.

"*Miximoo, miximoo, miximoo!*" Kiputz cursed like a drunken fisherman, which the squirrel translated as "You fucking god-damn son-of-a-bitch-rat-coward, come down off that tree!" The squirrel bared his teeth.

Leaving the memory of host and chalice, the trio of Mexican cowboys, and Cree Indians forever doomed to igno-rance of dominoes, Gabriel had but one thought: to put a stop to this ludicrous canine behaviour. Gabriel loved Kiputz dearly; he didn't want him getting damaged, much less dying right here before his eyes.

"Kiputz! Kiputz, stop it!" cried Gabriel, panting. The organist of the Church of the Sacred Meadow deftly segued from the solemn cadences of "O come, all ye faithful, joyful and triumphant" to a knee-slapping, finger-snapping, foot-stomping "Do your balls hang low, do they jiggle to and fro, can you tie 'em in a knot, can you tie 'em in a bow?" The froth of sixteenth notes cascaded down the smoke-stained accor-dion keys, joined hands at the bottom, and danced merrily in daisy-chain formation round and round the squirrel tree.

Suddenly, Gabriel felt a rough yank at his throat, for all he knew, the evil Chachagathoo reaching out to snatch him down into her grave. He fell back with a snap. His quilt-built chasuble had got caught, and ripped, on some wayward branch, it was later discovered by a miffed Mariesis. But for now, Gabriel Okimasis lay in the reindeer moss, the sense knocked out of him. All he saw was tiny bluebirds chirping merrily, tying pink silk ribbons in the Fur Queen's silver crown.

Jeremiah's sixteenth notes played on. For six years, they played without pause. Sprouting wings, they lifted off Kamamagoos Island that autumn, honked farewell to Eemanapiteepitat twenty miles to the north, then soared in semi-perfect V-formation over the billowing waves of Mistik Lake, past the village of Wuchusk Oochisk, over the craggy rocks where the Mistik River joins the Churchill River, past Patima Bay, Chigeema Narrows, Flin Flon, and – following the route Abraham Okimasis had raced back in February 1951 – through Cranberry Portage to Oopaskooyak, where they touched down to slake their thirst on the memory of the Fur Queen's kiss. After a detour of some years at the Birch Lake Indian Residential School twenty miles west of Oopaskooyak, the music curved south until it levelled onto the great Canadian plain and landed, just so, in the city of Winnipeg, Manitoba, eight hundred miles south of Eemanapiteepitat, in the pink salon of another woman in white fur.

PART THREE
Allegretto grazioso

TWELVE

Stately as an ocean liner, the woman in the portrait stood, a monument to pearls, pink cashmere, and white fox stoles, her white satin gloves blushing in the aura of the American Beauty rose grasped between their fingers. Beneath the painting, framed against unshuttered French windows, stood the subject herself, leaning against the crook of a Steinway grand piano. As her left hand pounded four-four time on the instrument's burnished top, her right wove patterns in the air as though conducting an orchestra: "And a-one and a-two and a-three . . ."

The resemblance of the portrait to the real thing was accurate enough, although the copy may have been twenty years younger than the original: Lola van Beethoven, piano teacher nonpareil, grande dame of the Winnipeg classical music scene, age sixty-five.

"And a-two and a-three and a-four," she half-sung in a

quavering dull contralto, her painted lips aquiver with passion while her rooster's crown of silvery bluish hair somehow remained completely undisturbed. "And stretch that phrase, and a-one and a-two . . ." The triplet sixteenth notes of Johann Sebastian Bach's D-major Toccata careered their robust, unfettered way from one pink wall of the room to another as the fading light of an early-September evening washed off the painting's giltwood frame.

At the keyboard laboured Lola van Beethoven's charge, grimacing when he judged his performance shoddy in one passage, beaming when he knew he had achieved the right effect in another. Jeremiah Okimasis, fifteen years of age, of rather bookish, intellectual demeanour, had just begun his first year of high school. Infinitely more important to him, however, was the instrument reverberating at his fingertips; for in this metropolis of half a million souls where he seemed to be the only Indian person, it was his one friend.

Toccata: the word is Italian for *touch*, the widow van Beethoven had embedded in her newest pupil's memory that day. *Toccata*: an exercise in touch — the touch of human fingers on keyboards — which, with persistent practice, can become a touch able to make pianos sing as if with a human voice.

The rhythmic underpinning of the piece brought to Jeremiah's mind Saturday nights in Eemanapiteepitat during those too-brief summer months when he and his siblings had been set free from residential school. As his left hand pounded out the rollicking, reel-like beat and his right flung out the reams of triplets, marionette images of Kookoos Cook, Annie Moostoos, Jane Kaka McCrae, his parents, and all the overanimated guests at those steamy wedding bacchanals bounced through his imagination, tugged at his heart — "Come home, Jeremiah, come home; you don't belong there, you don't belong there" — the rhythm of his native tongue came bleeding through the music.

As though tripping on the lump in his throat, he lost his concentration. Lola van Beethoven was about to pounce when, like a trout caught in a net, he resurfaced, flailing, grappling. Effortlessly, he slid into the coda — the largo, a hymn to the heavens — and thereby came back home to the tonic.

At the front door to the mansion half an hour later, Mrs. van Beethoven cupped her ingenu's hands admiringly in hers and, being a woman with no use for wasted verbiage, announced, "Five hours a day, six days a week, Jeremiah. Practise, practise, practise."

She raised one hand to brush a stray curl back against her patrician brow. "And within five years? Five years, Jeremiah. Boom. The trophy." A gentle gust of wind blew a whiff of some expensive fragrance up the Cree teenager's nostrils. "The Crookshank Memorial Trophy."

She pressed his hands one final time and, eyes wide with elation, shut the heavy glazed oak door. Jeremiah was so thrilled that he had been accepted into the indomitable doyenne's roster of exceptional students that he wanted to run back in and smother her with kisses.

Down leafy Red Deer Boulevard the young Cree concert-pianist-in-training strode, vinyl briefcase bulging with Bach and Chopin scores, his head a jangle of triplet runs, arpeggios, and trills. Revelling in the prairie breeze, he filled his lungs, astonished that the first week of September could be so hot. Up on Mistik Lake, after all, his relentless ululating father was already battling pre-winter gales and his gloved hands, as they hauled his nets in, would be laced with filaments of ice.

He found himself suspecting that he may mistakenly have gotten off the train at Mars. Or Venus. Here he was, back at school in the very distant south — it might as well have been Florida, or Rio de Janeiro — free, at last, of steel-mesh fences and curfews that chained you to your bed by 9:00 P.M., free of tasteless institutional food, free of nuns and brothers — and priests — watching every move, every thought, every bodily secretion, free to talk to girls.

Except that there were no girls to talk to. At his school, there may have been a thousand, but they were all white; not one spoke Cree. The exultation at his newfound freedom began to wilt just as he spied an orange-and-silver bus lumbering up the street. He sprinted towards it.

Sitting bolt upright, staring straight ahead, Jeremiah tried to appear as though he was on his way somewhere — dinner with rock-musician friends, a movie with a busty blonde, for God's sake, even bingo with his mother would do! — when in fact he had absolutely nowhere to go. All that awaited him was a basement room on the north side of the city, with a bed, a dresser, and a moth-eaten old piano. His landlady allowed him meals in her kitchen, and use of the washroom, but that was all. And what was there for him to do tonight? Play the piano. What was there for him to do tomorrow, Saturday night? Or all the nights of the week? Play the piano. His one consolation was that he would have no trouble meeting his daily practice quota, thereby becoming "the best goddamn piano player in Winnipeg," the Cree words whispering to him like a coded message from a secret agent. That's it! He would invent an imaginary friend, who spied on white people but conveyed the information to him in the language only they shared.

He thanked God that he had learned his father's lessons on solitude: how time alone could be spent without need for crying, that time alone was time for shaping thoughts that make the path your life should take, for cleaning your spirit of extraneous — even poisonous — matter.

Jeremiah's father would depart on any ordinary day to make the rounds of the more distant sections of his trapline, leaving his wife and children at camp with just the right amount of all they needed to survive until he returned. Abraham Okimasis would wade through banks of snow that grew to six feet high, through icy winds that blind and kill, through temperatures that freeze to brittle hardness human flesh exposed for fifty seconds to put food into his children's mouths. Days, sometimes weeks later, his dogteam would appear in the hazy distance of whichever northern lake the family happened to be living on that winter, his sled filled with furs for sale – mink, beaver, muskrat – the sole winter source of life-sustaining income for the northern Cree.

Jeremiah's father would tell his adoring children of arguments he had had with the fierce north wind, of how a young pine tree had corrected his direction on his homeward journey and thus saved all their lives, of how the northern lights had whispered truth into his dreams. And his soul was happy, his spirit full and buoyant, his smile a gift from heaven. Time alone, he said to them with just so many words: The most precious time one human being can have during his too few moments on Earth.

"Yes, but Father," he wanted to say from the back seat of a rapidly filling bus, "you never told us how to spend time alone in the midst of half a million people. Here, stars don't shine at night, trees don't speak."

The smells all mingled into one: of carbon monoxide, seventeen intensities of perfume, aftershave, cologne, breath of steak, chicken liver, onions, garlic, teeth gone bad, minty mouthwash, unkempt clumps of armpit hair overhead. Too much human living in one constricted space. The bus curved onto North Main Street.

Night had bled dusk dry; light from a thousand neon veins now stained the grey cement of street, of sidewalk, of rundown buildings. Traffic slowed to a laboured crawl. The sidewalk began to writhe. Strands of country music — tinny, tawdry, emaciated — oozed through the cracks under filthy doorways. The doors opened and closed, opened and closed. From their dark maws stumbled men and women, all dark of skin, of hair, of eye, like Jeremiah, all drunk senseless, unlike Jeremiah. Had the music student not looked upon this scene somewhere before? On a great chart with tunnels and caves and forbidden pleasures? He leaned forward to see if he could catch a glimpse, beyond the swinging doors, of horned creatures with three-pronged forks, laughing as they pitched Indian after Indian into the flames.

"You goddamn fucking son-of-a-bitch!" a woman of untold years screamed, as she landed with a crunch on the hood of a parked car and slid to the curb. "You can't do this to me," she shrieked. "This is my land, you know that? My land!" Precariously, she pulled herself up by clinging to a parking meter; her coat white, yellowed with age, polyester fur.

A tattooed, beer-bellied, bearded, greasy-haired white Cyclops stood at an open doorway and roared: "And this is my bar, you know that? My bar! Come back in here one more time and I'll rip the fuckin' eyeballs right outta that fuckin' ugly heada yours!"

The bus pulled up to a palace afloat on a nighttime sea, glimmering tantalizingly: the four-storey façade of glass and concrete, giant chandeliers, crimson carpet, swirling silver lettering over its entrance — the Jubilee Concert Hall. Like blackflies in June, ticket buyers clustered around the box-office wickets. Between them and Jeremiah's bus stood a

Plexiglas-covered display stand bearing the image of an exotic olive-complexioned man in a black tuxedo, a grand piano at his fingertips.

Tonight!
Vladimir Ashkenazy,
Russian pianist extraordinaire
with the Winnipeg Symphony Orchestra
Piano Concerto in E-minor by Frédéric Chopin

Into the curve of the propped-up piano top drifted, teetering dangerously on white high heels, a reflection of the Indian woman in soiled white polyester.

A car came by that would have looked at home framed by the Californian surf and sunset: open convertible, white, chrome gleaming. Four teenaged men with Brylcreamed hair lounged languidly inside, crotches thrust shamelessly, and laughed and puffed at cigarettes and sucked at bottles of nameless liquids.

"Hey, babe!" they hooted smoothly to the polyester Indian princess, "Wanna go for a nice long ride?"

A brief verbal sparring followed, from Jeremiah's perspective, in pantomime. Then the princess stepped into the roofless car and the bus pulled forward.

Gallantly, though not easily, Jeremiah left the episode behind him. Until, one week later, he thought he saw the woman's picture on a back page of the Winnipeg *Tribune*: the naked body of Evelyn Rose McCrae — long-lost daughter of

Mistik Lake — had been found in a ditch on the city's out-skirts, a shattered beer bottle lying gently, like a rose, deep inside her crimson-soaked sex. Jeremiah would report the image he had seen splashed across Mr. Ashkenazy's grand piano. But the Winnipeg police paid little heed to the obser-vations of fifteen-year-old Indian boys.

In Mrs. Slotkin's basement, all that year, Jeremiah Okimasis practised the piano until his fingers bled.

THIRTEEN

"Whachyou thinkin' about, *nigoosis?*" Abraham Okimasis stood at the bow of his blue canoe, hauling in a fishing net, yard by laborious yard, from the deep. As the dripping twine and blue-green nylon emerged, the fisherman fanned out its diamond-shaped webs, each holding captive an air-thin sheet of sparkling August sunlight. A trout surfaced, trapped in a convoluted tangle, and Abraham grasped its wriggling spine.

"Son?" he repeated. Gabriel's head came up over the stern in time to see the creature in his father's hand flailing, its glistening white belly punctured with a handhook, a spurt of blood. "You gonna miss Birch Lake?"

Gabriel looked into his father's laughing eyes — was he joking? Who could ever tell? — and wished desperately to ask, "Why would I miss that place?" Instead, his mouth said, quietly, "*Mawch.*" No.

"*Taneegi iga?*"

"Because . . ."

Abraham cast the dying fish into the wooden crate at his son's rubber-booted feet.

"That priest there," he went on, "the guy who runs the place, what's his name again?"

"Lafleur. Father Lafleur."

"Every time your mother and I ask Father Bouchard how you and Jeremiah are doing down there, he tells us that Father Lafleur is taking care of you just fine, that with him guiding you, your future is guaranteed."

Gabriel turned his gaze back to the depthless water. His fingers punctured the glassy surface and ripples shattered the reflection of his face. From his last encounter, two months earlier, he could still feel the old priest's meaty breath, could still taste sweet honey, the hard, naked, silver body of the Son of God. Of the four hundred boys who had passed through Birch Lake during his nine years there, who couldn't smell that smell, who couldn't taste that taste?

"You know, *nigoosis*." The fisherman's voice skimmed like the love cry of a loon across the silent lake. "The Catholic church saved our people. Without it, we wouldn't be here today. It is the one true way to talk to God, to thank him. You follow any other religion and you go straight to hell, that's for goddamn sure."

It was at that moment that Gabriel Okimasis understood that there was no place for him in Eemanapiteepitat or the north. Suddenly, he would join Jeremiah in the south. He could not wait!

"Ho-ho!" laughed Abraham as he spied another silver trout

glimmering just below the surface. Gabriel looked up. He would miss this dear old man. Across the wide expanse beyond the patriarch, Neechimoos Island – five miles into the province of Saskatchewan – was floating in midair, unrooted.

The Fur Queen kissed the caribou hunter gently on the cheek, waltzed him into the air, then made a perfect landing atop a pile of clothing folded in a dark brown vinyl suitcase. Mariesis Okimasis, squatting on the sun-splashed floor of her new two-bedroom house – pastel-painted plywood walls, white linoleum floor tiles, pine-log cabin receding in her memory – had discovered that her youngest child had almost left behind his copy of her husband's famous portrait. Wasn't that the drone of the airplane coming to take him away? Again?

Hearing footsteps, she turned. Framed in a wash of golden light, Gabriel stood, twirling in one hand – pink, mauve, purple – a bloom of fireweed. How handsome he was!

Flanked by his parents, Gabriel ambled down the yellow sand road that led to the new airstrip a mile behind the village. They passed three whitemen working on a new house beside the three already completed. Farther along, a gaggle of men and women and children and dogs and blackbirds was helping move Kookoos Cook's worldly wealth, such as it was, out of his beloved old log cabin to the first plywood house.

"Quit school, my son," Mariesis said, trying her best to sound matter-of-fact. "Stay home with us."

Kookoos Cook's ancient brown couch was banging its way out the one-room cabin's splintery doorway as Slim Jim

Magipom and Big Bag Maskimoot wheezed under its obstinate weight. For there was Kookoos Cook, plain as politics, perched on the top, his thighs crossed vise-like, trying to sip a steaming cup of tea.

Many had been the day over the last two years when Uncle Kookoos had complained venomously about the housing program *Sooni-eye-gimow* had foisted upon "this here reserve" – the new houses were mere cardboard boxes with plywood walls so thin a man could hear his neighbour fart and chip off the ice on February mornings. So when moving day arrived, Kookoos Cook had threatened to chain himself to his woodstove "like a common jailbird." Except that he had forgotten – "Jesus son-of-a-bitch goddamnit!" – that he had lost his rusty old chain at a poker game.

"I have to be with Jeremiah," replied Gabriel after a lengthy silence imposed by Kookoos Cook and his tempestuous sofa.

"You have been away since you were five. You'll be fifteen next January. For Jeremiah, it's too late. But you, you're our youngest."

The road opened out to the clearing where the landing strip began. Like every edifice in the new, emerging Eemanapiteepitat, the little terminal was fashioned out of plywood. The red Twin Otter Beechcraft that would be taking Gabriel to Smallwood Lake and the southbound train sat on the gravel runway Kookoos Cook had helped clear just the summer before. Village men alighted from the plane, some unloading cases of whisky, some falling in the dirt, others grunting accusations at empty air.

As Gabriel settled himself into a window seat, he caught a glimpse of Annie Moostoos deftly dodging a weaving man threatening to knock the single tooth out of her head with an empty whisky bottle. She scooted to safety inside the plywood outhouse that leaned precipitously to windward beside the terminal building. The man was about to rip the door from its hinges when Annie's gnarled brown hand reached out and pulled it shut.

"Tell Jeremiah to watch your wallet. I hear Winnipeg is full of crooks," his father laughed through the open door.

Mariesis's weather-worn oval face popped up beside her husband's. "He's full of shit," she said with a loving slap to her husband's shoulder. "Tell Jeremiah if he misses Holy Communion on Sundays, I'll never cook caribou *arababoo* for him again. Do you hear me?"

As the plane revved for take-off, Gabriel could see his parents leaning against a post beside the terminal, holding each other, waving sadly. Close behind them, hands on hips, stood Father Bouchard. And behind the priest, drink-filled revellers stumbled down the winding road back to the village.

With lynx-like stealth, Annie Moostoos's scrawny thorax emerged from the outhouse. The crone peered left, then right, like a hunter tracking ptarmigan. Assured her tooth was safe once more, she stepped out just as a gust of wind slammed the flimsy door against her head. And there she lay, lifeless as a day-old corpse.

FOURTEEN

"*Tansi*."

Jeremiah stopped breathing. In the two years he had spent in this city so lonely that he regularly considered swallowing his current landlady's entire stock of angina pills, he had given up his native tongue to the roar of traffic.

"Say that again?"

"*Tansi*," repeated Gabriel. "Means hi, or how you doing? Take your pick." He was smiling so hard that his face looked like it might burst. "Why? Cree a crime here, too?"

How strange Jeremiah looked. Clipped, his eyes like a page written in some foreign language. Even his clothes looked stilted, too new, too spick and span, as if lifted from a corpse in a coffin.

"It's . . . your voice. It's so . . . low." Jeremiah couldn't get over Gabriel's height, his breadth of shoulder, the six or seven black bristles sprouting from his chin. He didn't look fourteen going on fifteen, more like eighteen.

"Mom send me a jar of her legendary caribou *arababoo?*"
Jeremiah chirped as they waltzed, arms over shoulders, out
the station doors and into the white light of morning.
Gabriel's navy blue windbreaker, his red plaid flannel
shirt, his entire person sparked off microscopic waves of
campfire smoke, of green spruce boughs, of dew-laden
reindeer moss.

"Nah," said Gabriel. "She says city boys don't eat wild
meat."

"Yeah, right." Jeremiah rolled his eyes. "So. Tell me. How's
Eemanapiteepitat?"

"Annie Moostoos went and got killed by the airport outhouse door."

"Airport outhouse door? Yeah, right."

"*Tapwee!* We have an airport now. Uncle Kookoos helped
clear the land for it last summer. Before you know it, he pre-
dicts, jet planes will be landing in Eemanapiteepitat like flies
on dog shit."

"*Neee, nimantoom.*" Jeremiah laughed, light as a springtime
killdeer. For two brown Indian boys — not one, but two —
were dancing-skipping-floating down Broadway Avenue, tripping over each other's Cree, getting up and laughing, tripping
over each other's Cree, getting up and laughing.

"The mall," said Jeremiah early next morning as he reached for
the handle of the large glass door, "was invented in Winnipeg,"
his confidence in this stunning piece of information all the
greater by reason of its being utterly unsubstantiated. If he was

going to usher Gabriel into the rituals of urban life, then he was going to render the experience memorable, even if he had to stretch truth into myth.

Like a lukewarm summer wave, the silken strings of a hundred violins swept over them, the bulbs of twenty thousand fluorescent lights a blinding buzz. The chancel of a church for titans, the gleaming central promenade of the Polo Park Shopping Mall lay before them.

Gabriel gasped: at least three miles of stores if he was judging distance right. And the people! You could put fifty Eemanapiteepitats inside this chamber and still have room for a herd of caribou. And such an array of worldly wealth, a paradise on earth.

"Weeks," he whispered, his knees wobbly.

"Weeks what?" Jeremiah checked to see if the poor boy's eyeballs had jumped their sockets.

"Our shopping. It's gonna take us weeks."

"Not when a hundred bucks is all *Sooni-eye-gimow* gives you for a clothing allowance."

"*Anee-i ma-a?*" Gabriel pointed through the glass at a pair of tan knee-high leather boots, the toes so pointed that one kick and the victim would be punctured grievously.

"You wanna look like an Italian gigolo?" Jeremiah sneered.

Shoppers labouring under piles of merchandise passed by, their reflections wriggling in the floor-to-ceiling windows like fat suckers in a reedy cove.

"What's a gigolo?" Innocent as a five-year-old, Gabriel

scampered after Jeremiah, who had just walked up to the perfect store.

"A gigolo," the elder sibling proclaimed, as though from a pulpit, "is a man who sells a woman who wears shoes like these," pointing at multicoloured footwear with heels so sharp they could have roused the envy of a porcupine.

"You," Gabriel peered through the glass with grave suspicion, "can sell" — how could humans stand in such outlandish constructions — "a woman?"

"In cities," Jeremiah airily dismissed him, "it's done all the time, all the time. It's like selling meat. Come on, we gotta get you out of those rags. You look like you just crawled out of the bush."

"I didn't crawl," huffed Gabriel. "I took a plane. *And* a train." Grabbing Gabriel's sleeve, Jeremiah plunged deep into the entrails of the beast.

No-nonsense, flat-heeled oxfords winked at Gabriel, who rebuffed their gentlemanly advances as too no-nonsense, too business-like. If heels the height of coffee mugs came unrecommended — the price of cowboy boots, in any case, was prohibitive — then shoes of an athletic bent might be more to the point, with jazzy red or blue stripes down their sides. Jeremiah pooh-poohed the idea as too informal; white high school classrooms were not "gymnasia."

"What, then," asked Gabriel in mounting exasperation, "do city boys wear on their feet?"

Whereupon Jeremiah announced that white boys lived in dark penny loafers with socks so white they looked like snow.

As, like Odyssean sirens on treacherous shoals, the hundred violins slid shamelessly into "Ave Maria," socks began to wave at Gabriel, in colours, weaves, and textures that made his heart strings fibrillate. He had never heard of argyle socks, for instance, and was scandalized to hear that Argyle was a Scottish earl who drank his enemies' blood on the battlefield and then went home to eat their children. So brutal was the tale that Gabriel threw a curse at an entire rack of the lugubrious knitwear. He announced, instead, his preference for a six-pack of wool-polyester socks so white they looked like snow. The tricoloured bands around their tops would not be seen, of course, but knowing they were there would boost his confidence, Gabriel explained in understated Cree. He insisted, moreover, that he wear a pair home with his brand-new muskrat-coloured patent-leather penny loafers. Leaving his tarnished, near-soleless paratrooper boots and malodorous lumberjack socks with the bouncy bleached-blond clerk, the brothers went tittering out the door like Eemanapiteepitat housewives at a late-night bingo.

At Fischman's, they passed miles of sombre suits that made them think of priestly gatherings in Olympic-sized football stadiums. They mistook the *t* of "Eaton's" for a crucifix, missed their elevator stop, and ended up scrumming through racks of shift dresses waiting for nuns divorced from God. But for the mannequin in white fox fur who whispered "*ootee-si*" — "this way" — the brothers would have been suspected of transvestite tendencies.

By the time they entered Liberty's Fashions for the

Discerning Man, the lethargic mall air made Gabriel's head swim in circles, and the unkind lighting overhead became so oppressive that he swore the underwear at Liberty's had spirits of their own, that he could see their penumbra glowing like saintly haloes.

Jeremiah, however, was wrestling with visions of his own. "Remember Aunt Black-eyed Susan's story," he asked distractedly, his heart still palpitating from their brush with the Cree-whispering mannequin, "about the weasel's new fur coat?" A sudden swerve to Cree mythology might disarm such occult phenomena.

"You mean where Weesageechak comes down to Earth disguised as a weasel?" Gabriel alighted on a manly pair of spirit-white Stanfield's, and examined the Y-front with such rapacity that the bespectacled curmudgeon of a clerk, smelling sabotage, flared his nostrils. "And the weasel crawls up the Weetigo's bumhole?" Gabriel poked a finger through the opening.

"Yes . . ." Jeremiah, in spite of himself, exploded with jagged laughter. "In order to kill the horrible monster."

"And comes back out with his white fur coat covered with shit?" laughed Gabriel, dropping the Stanfield's on a pile of sky-blue boxers.

"You know," said Jeremiah, suddenly philosophical. "You could never get away with a story like that in English."

Gabriel's voice swooped down to a conspiratorial undertone, "'Bumhole' is a mortal sin in English. Father Lafleur told me in confession one time."

"He said the same thing about 'shit,'" said Jeremiah.

Gabriel dashed across the aisle to a selection of skin-hugging jockey-style shorts — with no hole for the penis. The nearby rack of neckties launched into "O Sole Mio" as Gabriel decided on three pairs of black jockeys designed by Alberto Bergazzi.

At Wrangler's, Gabriel wedged his lithe frame into a pair of blue jeans so tight that Jeremiah expressed concern. At Popeye's, the black patent-leather belt with a large silver buckle cost less than ten dollars. At Sanderson's, the red cotton shirt with pearl-white buttons became number one in Gabriel's heart. At Jack and Jill's, it was the red, white, and blue silk baseball jacket with striped knit wrists and collar, to Jeremiah's puzzlement.

At every store, Gabriel virtually danced into each article of clothing and stood before the mirror not so much preening as plotting "his Winnipeg years." Like moulted skin, his old wardrobe accumulated in multicoloured shopping bags. At Aldo's Barbershop, once the deed was done — to his specifications, not Brother Stumbo's — his appearance had changed so dramatically that if Jeremiah had not witnessed the metamorphosis, he would have taken his sibling for a rock star with a tan.

Which is when they came across the belly of the beast — one hundred restaurants in a monstrous, seething clump. Never before had Gabriel seen so much food. Or so many people shovelling food in and chewing and swallowing and burping and shovelling and chewing and swallowing and burping, as at some apocalyptic communion. The world was one great, gaping mouth, devouring ketchup-dripping hamburgers, french fries glistening with grease, hot dogs, chicken chop suey, spaghetti with meatballs, Cheezies, Coca-Cola, root beer, 7-Up, ice cream, roast beef, mashed potatoes, and more hamburgers, french fries . . . The roar of mastication drowned out all other sound, so potent that, before the clock struck two, the brothers were gnawing away with the mob.

"Why did Weesageechak kill the Weetigo?" asked Gabriel, as he washed down a gob of bleeding beef with a torrent of Orange Crush.

"All I remember is that the Weetigo had to be killed because he ate people," replied Jeremiah through a triangle of pizza. "Weesageechak chewed the Weetigo's entrails to smithereens from the inside out."

"Yuck!" feigned Gabriel, chomping into a wedge of Black Forest cake thick with cream.

They ate so much their bellies came near to bursting. They drank so much their bladders grew pendulous. Surely this place had a washroom hidden away somewhere. Gabriel went hunting.

There — glaring light, ice-white porcelain, the haunting sound of water dripping in distant corners — standing nearby was a man. Six feet, thin, large of bone, of joint, brown of hair, of eye, pale of skin. Standing there, transported by Gabriel Okimasis's cool beauty, holding in his hand a stalk of fireweed so pink, so mauve that Gabriel could not help but look and, seeing, desire. For Ulysses' sirens had begun to sing "Love Me Tender" and the Cree Adonis could taste, upon the buds that lined his tongue, warm honey.

The brothers Okimasis burst into the bronze light of late afternoon.

"'My coat!' moaned the weasel. 'My nice white coat is covered with shit!'" Gabriel continued the story of Weesageechak, the image of a certain man aflame with fireweed clinging to his senses with pleasurable insistence.

"Feeling sorry for the hapless trickster," said Jeremiah circumspectly, "God dipped him in the river to clean his coat. But he held him by the tail, so its tip stayed dirty."

"'And to this day,'" Gabriel took his brother's words away, "as Auntie would say, 'the weasel's coat is white but for the black tip of the tail.'" Exulting that they could still recall their wicked Aunt Black-eyed Susan's censored Cree legends, the brothers Okimasis danced onto the sidewalk.

Grey and soulless, the mall loomed behind them, the rear end of a beast that, having gorged itself, expels its detritus.

FIFTEEN

"*B*y ze tvilight of ze fifteens sentury and ze dawn of ze sixteens," Herr Schwarzkopf's German accent so grated on Jeremiah he wanted to hold the old man's mouth in place, "Spain's Keeng Ferdinand unt Kveen Isabella ver to set in motion ze vave vereby Roman Catolicism – unt Christianity in general – vas efentually to spread across ze Americas." At a wooden desk by the sheet-glass window, Jeremiah sat watching the grizzled geezer's jowls flap about. "All vas not vell, howefer," confided Herr Schwarzkopf like a gossip spreading slander, "vizin ze Roman Church itself at zis time. For efen as missionaries ver penetratink dipper unt dipper into ze New Vorld . . ."

"Penetration," wrote the seventeen-year-old Cree scholar in his notebook, "1492."

"In Europe itself, ze signs ver eferyfer zat ze church vas soon to break up into all manner of varring, hateful factions.

Martin Looser vould be only ze beginnink." Herr Schwarzkopf paused to extract a huge red handkerchief from a breast pocket, apply it to his generous Hanseatic nostrils, and honk so loud that Jeremiah envisioned a flotilla of boats in Danzig harbour.

Soundlessly, the door opened and a teenaged girl with straight black hair down to her slender waist slipped in, a clutch of textbooks in one hand, a beaded deer-hide purse with fringes hanging from one shoulder. In the overwhelming whiteness of complexions in the room, she was as dark as chocolate. Something inside Jeremiah cringed. With the subtlest of nods, Herr Schwarzkopf directed the girl to the one vacant seat, and lectured on.

"It is zerfore no coinsidense zat zis vas alzo ze era of ze burnink of vitches." Saliva spewed from his lips. "Any voman suspected of heretical zoughts against ze great patriarchy vas roasted alife at ze stake. Nine million vomen, szzzt! Like hot dogs." For Herr Schwarzkopf, it appeared, the more gruesome the account, the better; if the occasional man, too, had been burnt as a witch, he ignored the fact and, apparently, wished his students do so as well. "Ze Spanish Inkvisition, a powverful arm of ze Roman church . . ."

Hearing — and feeling — the new arrival sliding into the seat not far behind him, Jeremiah was put on his guard: was it because this young — and undeniably Indian — girl confronted him with his own Indianness, which his weekly bus sightings of the drunks on North Main Street had driven him to deny so utterly that he went for weeks believing his own skin to be as white as parchment? He had worked so hard at transforming himself into a perfect little "transplanted European" – anything to survive. He was suddenly enraged, unbalanced, diverting his terror by doodling, mindlessly, bloodlessly, into his notebook: "Nine million women roasted. Live. And they deserved it."

The corpse lay bloody and glistening on Gabriel's desk, its limbs splayed as if crucified, its innards exposed, disgusting. Was that the little pig's heart thumping lightly? Crinkling his nose, he poked at the organ with his pincers. The stainless-steel utensil came away with a drop of thickened blood clinging to its tip.

"The prostate," announced the wide-shouldered, white-shirted Mr. Armstrong in answer to a question from the room, "is the largest of the four accessory glands of the male reproductive system. Its main function is to produce prostatic fluid, one of several substances that compose semen." Thirty fifteen-year-olds, male and female, shifted audibly in their seats in tense anticipation. What next about this semen? What more about this all-important sperm? "Positioned immediately below the bladder and encircling, like a doughnut, the tube known as the urethra, the prostate gland may be small and puny looking – on this cadaver, in fact, it has not even yet formed properly – but it serves a complex and necessary function. Without it, a male would not be male."

Hands sheathed in latex gloves, Gabriel peered closer at the miniature hunk of flesh, veins, and bone, envisioning this gland with such a mystical allure. He poked around the bladder, the urethra, the genitals, amazed that such inconsequential size could hold such power.

"And we," Mr. Armstrong continued with grave circumspection, "the male of the species, that is, all have a prostate gland."

Gabriel stirred his way through the little swirl of blood.

And this is what they drink, he mused, the priests, as they celebrate their Holy Communion. Male blood. He removed his eye from the pan. This is what they eat, my mother and father, as they take the body of Christ into their mouths. The essence of maleness. He imagined himself shoving the dead pig foetus whole into his mouth and down his throat. The thought made him gag.

For refuge, he looked at the thirtyish, russet-haired, hazel-eyed Mr. Michael Armstrong, manoeuvring his chalk across the blackboard with practised skill. And he thought about the man's prostate gland, the essence of his maleness, which was considerable, especially in the way his buttocks bulged with such a daring yet delicate curve and then swooped under to join the well-muscled yet elegant thigh. It was a distraction that would affect his biology marks.

What was wrong with the essence of femaleness, as unabashedly illustrated by the dozen young women around him, that it should leave him cold as stone? He could hear Father Bouchard's words drifting through the sun-streaked Eemanapiteepitat church: the union of man and woman, the union of Christ and his church.

Like a jackbooted foot kicking at a padlocked door, a terrible guilt pummelled his heart. *Mea culpa, mea culpa, mea maxima culpa.* Suddenly, a terrible need came over him, to run into his mother's arms and hide, crawl back into her womb and start over. He heard his father calling him back home: "*Weeks'chiloowew!*"

The bell was shrieking, the room a bedlam of movement and gabbling voices.

Gabriel slid lethargically into his baseball jacket and shuffled down the corridor. What was there for a person like him – no friend, not one acquaintance, save Jeremiah, who did nothing but play the piano. Chattering teenagers with books brushed past him, locker doors slammed, and a bright orange sheet of paper with bold black lettering hung tacked to a door. A little hatted man stood in a boat, plunging a pole into what might have been water.

Gilbert and Sullivan's *The Gondoliers*
Auditions, November 12–13

"What's up?" Taken unawares, Gabriel had no ready answer. "Something on your mind?" With each passing month, the rising and falling of Jeremiah's Cree cadence was fading from his English.

Among the last of the stragglers was the dark new student with the buckskin handbag. She glanced at the brothers, the brothers glanced at her. Then she was gone.

"Jeremiah, I wanna go home."

"Okay, I'll walk with you."

"No. Home. Mistik Lake."

"Gabriel, it's taken me over two years to get used to it. You can't quit just like —"

"We don't belong here," retorted Gabriel. "Two thousand kids and —"

"Play football, basketball, take up bodybuilding, anything. Just do something with your time or you'll die of loneliness. Cities, they're like that."

Gabriel stood silent, wanting desperately to burst into tears.

"Come on, Gabriel. Buy you a Sweet Marie."

SIXTEEN

Tick-tock, tick . . . went the metronome atop Mrs. Bugachski's old brown piano, Jeremiah, straight-backed at its keyboard, mired in daily practice. Slumped in an armchair, Gabriel stared blankly at Jesus on the wall above his brother. Polish icons wallowed in grotesque extravagance, he mused, the gashes and crown of thorns particularly profuse with blood, the exposed heart glans-like in its voluptuous tumescence. The ticks and tocks, the heartbeat of Christ, the grandfather clock in Father Bouchard's Eemanapiteepitat parlour . . .

Gabriel remembered sitting beside his father on the varnished pinewood bench that April evening, as the priest thoughtfully informed the hunter that his younger sister, the wild and wilful Black-eyed Susan Magipom, had a place reserved in hell for leaving her husband, physically abusive though he may be, and for daring to move in with another man. With a great puff of smoke from his gnarled, black pipe, the priest advised the hunter that associating with the woman gave approval to her sin until she had returned to her rightful husband and repented. Gabriel had been all of five years old when this model father, husband, world champion, Abraham Okimasis, stopped speaking to his sister. In an isolated community of six hundred people, Mariesis and her children were forced to communicate with her by subterfuge: here a stolen smile and a whispered word, there a cup of tea behind closed doors. Except for the smoke-filled poker games that raged through the night whenever Abraham went off hunting with his eldest son, William William.

Gabriel could see the pendulous silver crucifix across the breast of the priest's black cassock. What was it about the naked man nailed to that beam of wood that caused his pulsing restlessness?

Tick-tock, tick . . .

The biology textbook sat open on Gabriel's lap, unread, the television blank, Jeremiah's endlessly repeated C-major scale unlistened to. Gabriel couldn't find a comfortable sitting position; his body ached for movement, freedom from this claustrophobic, kitsch-jammed living room, the only home Jeremiah could find where his banging on a keyboard five hours a day wouldn't drive the landlady to insanity, for Mrs. Bugachski was all but deaf. What sense was there in visiting — on a Friday night — when his brother paid no heed? *Tick-tock, tick . . .*

The orange-and-silver bus, empty but for five passengers, pulled up across the street from the Jubilee Concert Hall, leaving a solitary figure by the curb, the theatre glittering like a cosmic queen's tiara.

Gabriel surveyed North Main of a blustery mid-November evening, twenty-six bars — thirteen on each side of the boulevard — probing him with their oscillating lights, like the hundred eyes of some vapour-breathing beast. Ragged clumps of faceless people rolled in and out of entranceways. A red-and-yellow bell blinked at Gabriel in a futile attempt to ring, its sway a comical series of electronically choreographed neon. "The Hell Hotel," the sign above it read, the *B* apparently damned to *H* by mechanical malfunction. The invitation was all too clear.

In the little lobby, beside a wall streaked with dried blood, he waited for a mob of young non-Indian men in baseball caps to rumble by in boisterous tomfoolery, insinuated himself into their mass, and slipped into the tavern, he hoped, unnoticed.

The place was a veritable explosion of madness, drinkers two and three deep clustered around entire fleets of tables pouring beer and liquor down their throats as though the world would end at midnight. Amidst a knot of zombie-like figures whom he couldn't identify as human, the dazed teenager slid into a chair, pretending that this was just routine behaviour. From the carpet at his feet, another splotch of desiccated blood stared at him.

"Where's your mama, boy?" squawked a toothless hag with a shock of fuzz-ball hair. "You oughtta be in bed with your teddy, not carryin' on with us tired old Saulteaux." She laughed a terrific cackle.

"Shut up and give him a beer," burped a younger brown woman. "He's sooo cute. Hey, you know that? You're cute."

"Whachyou doin' later on, sweetie?" asked a third.

"Leave him alone," a scar-faced man commanded. "He's way too young for you."

"Give him a fuckin' beer! He's one of us. He's tribe, man."

And so the razzing went. Gabriel followed orders and drank, one beer followed by another and another until the world took on the hue of sunset, filled with warmth, then with a giddy, frothy silliness. People came, people went. Gabriel laughed when he was told to laugh, spoke when he was told to speak, remained silent when silence was asked of him. And before he knew it, he was sitting beside a man with sparkling eyes and black-tufted hair, with a "What's your name?" and a "So what brings you here?" His replies were thrown carelessly into the clangour of laughter, the weeping of country music. Finally, he leaned back in his chair, pierced the man's eyes with his, and bathed in the surge of power that shot through him. Time oozed into a haze of pleasurable pulsation, and Gabriel found himself stumbling down a dark passageway, Wayne? Dwayne? — what was his name again? — somewhere in front of him.

At the far end of the alley, he thought he saw — to his dying day, he could not be sure — a mass of bodies, men, he thought, young men with baseball caps standing in a tight circle around . . . around what? He could hear male grunting from within the ring, female whimpering, moaning, the northern Manitoba Cree unmistakable in the rising and falling of her English. Gabriel brushed past the panting, throbbing huddle to follow his new mystery friend.

Gabriel thought he caught the flash of a woman's leg, bare, jeans a crumple at the ankle, a naked posterior – male – humping. And then Gabriel and his plaid-coated friend were around a corner, and a second, and in another black passageway.

And here, the mouth of the caribou hunter's son was taken by this city-tasting mouth, its tongue moist, alive upon, around, inside his own, the teeth, the breath all beer and cigarettes. His jacket was opened, his T-shirt pulled up, his zipper pulled down, his maleness flailed. The cold November air was like a spike rammed through the hand – his feet floated above the earth – and he saw mauve and pink and purple of fireweed and he tasted, on the buds that lined his tongue, the essence of warm honey.

Two days later, the brothers Okimasis would see, on a back page of the Winnipeg *Tribune*, a photograph of Madeline Jeanette Lavoix, erstwhile daughter of Mistik Lake, her naked body found in a North Main alleyway behind a certain hotel of questionable repute, a red-handled screwdriver lying gently, like a rose, deep within the folds of her blood-soaked sex. Jeremiah would recall, with a simmering rage, one Evelyn Rose McCrae. Gabriel would say nothing.

Tock, tick-tock . . . went the old brown metronome. The fingers of Jeremiah's right hand obeyed each tick and tock – C . . . D . . . E . . . Time and again, Lola van Beethoven had promised him that such devoted attention to the development of finger technique would give his fingers the magic touch of Serkin, Gilels, and, yes, Vladimir Ashkenazy, whose name he loved to roll around his tongue. So, G . . . F . . . E . . .

Halfway into his daily marathon, Jeremiah decided he had earned his break of ginger ale on ice, with an Oreo or two for good behaviour. The crowd of bleeding saints in Mrs. Bugachski's living room stared out at him, from terracotta statuettes, from pictures, coasters, placemats, even stitched into her doilies, carved into her furniture. The white satin angels on the Christmas tree seemed to be singing to him. If only they could fly, he would send them north with knapsacks filled with presents. It was twelve years, after all, since he and Gabriel had spent a Christmas with their parents. At least five hundred dollars to fly the eight hundred miles home? One thousand dollars? For two teenaged boys? Jesus on the wall above the piano winked, and an idea rang like a gong. So thrilled was Jeremiah that he crossed himself and bowed before the Lord.

His gift may not reach Eemanapiteepitat for Christmas Eve but he could try, at least, for New Year's Eve.

SEVENTEEN

$\mathcal{A}$ gunshot pierced the starlit night, three faint echoes following. Eemanapiteepitatites who heard the blast — and who couldn't hear such noisemaking, unless they were as deaf as retired midwife Little Seagull Ovary had become of recent years? — cowered in their houses.

"Kaboom yourself," said Mariesis Okimasis as she pulled aside a corner of the floral-patterned cotton curtain and peered out at the snowbound nightscape. "I hope they kill each other, the fools. That way, we won't have to put up with these godforsaken New Year's Eves." Seeing nothing of tragic consequence as she had hoped, she dropped the curtain and was about to march across the kitchen when she decided on one more peek.

"Then why, pray tell, are you looking out that window?" inquired Abraham, with the mock exasperation that he loved to use whenever a reserve party got overheated and she took to playing the spy so she could report child murders, wife beatings, and fire bombings to the Royal Canadian Mounted Police, who almost never arrived. "They see you looking out that window and for sure they'll shoot that nosy beak right off your face, hoo-hoo-hoo-hoo-hoo."

He stood beside their scrawny Christmas tree with its strands of popcorn, cranberries, and crinkly paper angels, stubby pencil pointed to the calendar tacked to the wall above the humble brown chesterfield. Every square of December 1969 but one was filled with an uncertain X. With contented finality, the hunter crossed out the last square, just as another shot rang out and Mariesis came zooming across the room with horror slashed across her face.

"*Nimantoom!*" she hissed. "They're coming for us, quick, hide in the bedroom, turn the lights out, pretend we're not at home!"

"We are gonna sit right here on this old brown chester-field," retorted Abraham, charging through his wife's protestations like a moose in mating season, "just like we planned. And we are gonna listen to the tape that Jeremiah sent us one more time because we like his music and because that's as close as we are ever gonna get to spending New Year's Eve with those two boys so long as we live and breathe." With a prince-like flourish, he pressed a button on the tape recorder – borrowed from the priest for the purpose – sitting on the coffee table and plunked himself on the couch. The "Auld Lang Syne" that came wafting out of the machine was distant, tinny, like a child crying in the darkness for its mother.

But, at least, Jeremiah Okimasis was playing the piano for his parents.

Kaboom went another gunshot, this one just outside their door. Mariesis screamed. Four quick pounds on wooden steps and the kitchen door banged open, its hinges wailing with the pain. And who should be standing there but Santa Claus, a week late but finally arrived.

"Quick," rasped Santa Claus, "give me my gun!"

"Kookoos Cook! It's still four hours to midnight!" In the ensuing argument between the hunter and this Kookoos Cook Santa Claus driven mad by whisky, drowning in the absorbent cotton and cheap red felt of a costume torn to shreds by the twenty-seven New Year's Eve parties then raging across this ebullient reserve, Jeremiah's "Auld Lang Syne" played on with the placidity of an old church hymn. And in that most mystical way peculiar only to those who dream in Cree, the paper angels on the Christmas tree began to sing: "Should old acquaintance be forgot . . ."

"Meanwhile, back in Eemanapiteepitat," sighed Jeremiah wanly, "Kookoos Cook is loading up his rifle for the big midnight shoot-out." He and Gabriel were ambling, aimless and disconsolate, down a dim and mostly empty Portage Avenue festooned with spruce boughs and coloured lights and large red plastic ribbons. Through bulky speakers over its door, a store they passed piped out a ragged orchestration of "Auld Lang Syne." It was so cold the brothers half-expected tall office buildings to crack.

"Father Bouchard put a stop to such savage behaviour last year, I'm sorry to inform you," said Gabriel, in a hollow-voiced effort to lift their spirits.

"How would you know?"

"Dad told me. Ever since they opened up that little airport, ever since —"

"Civilization?"

"Has come within one daily flight of Eemanapiteepitat, the booze has been flowing in like blood from slaughtered caribou, as Dad puts it. So now, he says, they don't shoot guns into the air to mark the new year, they shoot each other."

The rootless pair turned north on Main. Gabriel's half-formed plot was to lure Jeremiah into the Hell Hotel – no, not the Hell Hotel, there were, after all, twenty-five other bars. Wherever they ended up, they would get plastered, as city people did to mark the greatest evening of the year.

The great hall reared its regal brow a distance to their right. To feast on it, however, Jeremiah's eyes had to pass the lights of Indian skid row, a vision that stayed with him, even when he slept.

"Mom's keeping Uncle Kookoos's Winchester thirty-thirty locked up in her closet every New Year's Eve until he behaves himself," Gabriel's narrative hobbled on. "'No way Kookoos Cook is murdering the vile and slovenly Jane Kaka on my front step,' she says." He hopped over a ridge of hard-packed snow.

Like a galleon on a nighttime sea, a figure surfaced from the silver-lined half-light. Visible only in silhouette at first, she commanded the summit of the concrete staircase that swept up to the entrance of the theatre. Resplendent in a black velvet, fur-lined cape that fell to her feet in folds, a constellation of diamonds twinkling, she scanned the street impatiently, waiting for a husband, a friend, a lover?

"So." Gabriel took a deep breath. "Wanna go for a drink?" praying that the offer sounded as throwaway as a simple "how-dee-do."

But Jeremiah was rooted to the pavement, staring across the street, at the entrance of the Leland Hotel. A woman so young she could have been a child leaned against a wall, lost, lonely, a halo of blood-red neon hovering above her head. Wearing a summery della robbia blue windbreaker, her legs exposed between a miniskirt and brown suede boots, the pale blue rose in her hair appeared to vibrate from her shivers. She was pregnant, five months, maybe six. She staggered, just as a hulking junk heap of a car pulled up, springs groaning from the weight of young white men out looking for a thrill. Could that be Rob Bailey, the football star from his history class, in the driver's seat?

"Hey, chickie." Rob Bailey's reedy voice insinuated itself into the gauze-like wash of light. "You look like you could use some cuddling." Evelyn Rose McCrae and Madeline Jeanette Lavoix appeared, keeping vigil by their teenaged sister with the sad synthetic rose. The impulse to race across the street overwhelmed Jeremiah, the need to scream: "Go! Go back inside the bar! Go home, go anywhere, but don't stay here!"

"Jeremiah!" Gabriel's voice. "Jeremiah, what are you doing?" Gabriel took a step towards him just as the woman in the cape of midnight velvet burst, like a gust of wind, down the staircase.

Perfumed air billowing before her, hazel eyes glimmering, she stopped directly in front of Gabriel. Admiration — for his beauty? his bearing? — flickered across the woman's fiery glare. Then, from her cape, a slender hand dropped a small pink envelope into Gabriel's gloved hand.

"What the hell was that all about?" Jeremiah was beside him. Gabriel almost tore the envelope in half. Inside were two white strips of paper, of the kind gift boxes are made. "Hold them up," Jeremiah's voice more bark than suggestion. In the insufficient light, they read: "New Year's Eve Gala. The Royal Winnipeg Ballet. December 31, 1969, 10:00 P.M."

Before they remembered to breathe again, the brothers Okimasis were drifting through the large glass portals of the Jubilee Concert Hall, their hearts a jumble of disbelief.

"Just a minute please, sirs." A stern male voice hooked them from behind. "I'm afraid you need tickets to get in here."

"Indeed you do." Tauntingly, Gabriel waved them in the doorman's face.

A gorgeous blush fanned out across the peach-smooth cheeks. Gabriel had half a notion to kiss his cherry-red lips.

EIGHTEEN

*I*n the second-floor foyer, Jeremiah gazed at the grand piano, a nine-foot Bösendorfer gleaming by the light of a chandelier so enormous it looked like a spaceship. A waxen, priest-like gentleman sat stiff-backed at its keyboard, his skeletal, liver-spotted fingers trembling over the keys as though stricken with Parkinson's disease. No matter, thought Jeremiah, Chopin's "Harp Etude" still sounded like springwater gurgling in moonlight.

Behind him, Gabriel stood gaping at the tables groaning with bounty. Shrimp he had never tasted. These he might begin with. As satin whispered, as champagne glasses clinked, as laughter and chatter swirled – everyone there pretending he didn't exist – he reached into the nearest platter. For the next half hour, he would not take a moment's pause, from charred buffalo croustade and venison terrine, from smoked trout with beetroot and cornbread, from rabbit spring rolls with spiced pears, from grilled marinated quail.

"Northern Manitoba?" a fragment of conversation finally trapped the brothers' ears. "Ripe for the plucking," the voice a finely modulated southern Manitoba drawl.

"The last frontier!" trumpeted a neighbour. "Uninhabited." The brothers stole a flabbergasted peek. "Or might as well be."

"Kieran-Watson's already put its money on diamonds," a third offered. "It's been, what, three years now they've been prospecting up north of Mistik Lake?" So that's what they had been in search of, those flatulent, hirsute men the Okimasis family had run into that summer on Nameegoos Lake.

"Diamonds?" the first gentleman chuckled. "Try uranium, try natural gas . . ."

The tuxedoed businessmen's northern Manitoba was miraculously transformed: mines spewing diamonds at the northern end of Nameegoos Lake, oil wells on the shores of Kasimir Lake, uranium gushing from Mistik Lake – the nickel, gold, and copper deposits of Smallwood Lake, Thompson, and Flin Flon were piffle by comparison – pipelines, skyscraper jungles, freeways, the Churchill River a leviathan providing light and heat to half of North America. The boys' dreams were on fire: they saw Cree Indians so wealthy they could commute to Las Vegas for blackjack every weekend, to Rio de Janeiro for Carnival, to Disneyland on a moment's notice to teach Kookoos Cook's favourite jig, "*Kimoosoom Chimasoo*," to Mickey Mouse – Chopin's arpeggios had become mere ambience, Gabriel's ravenous chomping slowed to a meditative chew — the Okimasis family living in a thirty-seven-room palazzo, Abraham owning a fleet of yachts, Mariesis drowning in mink and pearls, Jeremiah proud owner of a nine-foot Bösendorfer, Gabriel, in a Cadillac, cruising up to Eemanapiteepitat Concert Hall to feast on all the caviar his heart desired (he actually hated the stuff but it seemed fashionable). The twenty-first century had dawned — glorious, golden — on their home and Native land.

Suddenly, the boys noticed they each had a champagne flute in hand and that the foyer was almost empty. Snapped from their reverie, they toasted their hometown's heavenly future: "Happy Year! Happy Year! As Kookoos Cook would say." And they bumped and tripped their way into the cavernous hall.

If it wasn't for the hair in front of them, piled so high and sprayed to such brutal hardness that it could have passed for a volcanic rock formation, the brothers Okimasis would have had an unbroken view of the stage. But at least they were there, ensconced like princes in red plush seats only seven rows from the front.

When Gabriel caught sight of a host-like pate popping up just below the stage's edge, he assumed a janitor or a maintenance man was tending to last-minute business. But the janitor was wearing a tuxedo, and when he bowed to the audience, he elicited a flurry of genteel claps accompanied by lowing. Thinking to minimize their conspicuousness, Jeremiah clapped soundlessly and murmured twice. Gabriel, hearing the rumble in his brother's throat, likewise mooed politely. When the little bald man raised a chopstick above his head, Gabriel was sure he was about to perform a magic trick, but no white rabbit was pulled from a hat. Instead, a respectful hush descended.

When the chopstick came down, a bassoon whined, serpentine, penetrating. Then a shimmer of strings bled in, to cling, like dew, to the reed's exquisite legato. It dawned on Jeremiah that a live orchestra was hiding beneath the stage, and he leaned over to apprise Gabriel of this novel circumstance. He was about to explain the precise instrumentation of these opening bars to Ludislav Buchynski's *Prism, Mirror, Lens* when the chunky matron in front of him swung about the litter of otters on her shoulders — the animals' cute little faces smiled at the boys, as though in recognition — clamped her steel-trap glare on Jeremiah and hissed. The red velvet curtain parted.

At first, the stage was dark. When the coo of an alto flute entwined itself around the bassoon's sustained high A-flat, a shimmer of watery light revealed a clump of dancers standing, heads bowed, arms hanging lifeless. When, like distant thunder, the timpani and contrabasses rumbled, the grey-sheathed clump began to undulate. Pair by pair, arms wafted up, bodies moved apart, and the dance began.

The blue haze shifted, stars began to pock the sky; the northern lights had found their way into the hall. Under them, through them, with them, fifteen dancers fanned out and regrouped, fanned out and regrouped, their feet strangers to gravity, their patterns as unpredictable as air.

Jeremiah quickly found the spectacle repetitive, the dancers too conscious of their beauty, too anxious that it be admired. He found the play of lights on a star-filled sky much more to his liking. But, finally, it was the music that captured him. He closed his eyes, the better to take pleasure in its beauty. What came to him, however, surfacing like a dream from the great dome of his blindness, was the streaks of neon above the entrance to the Leland Hotel, the "o" crowning the Indian girl, large with child. Falling snow turned her transparent, ethereal, the foetus in her belly full-formed and glowing. Disengaging from the womb, the child tumbled seemingly forever, to a bed of broken beer bottles and screwdrivers filed sharp as nails. The shards loomed closer. And closer. And it was Jeremiah's own groin that suddenly rammed into them, again and again.

Shaken, repelled, he opened his eyes, willed the vision away. Then he turned to peek at Gabriel, prepared to see him squirming restlessly or nodding off. The boy, however, was wide awake.

Beat by beat, step by step, the dance had seduced and then embraced Gabriel. The dancers burst from their spinning circle, swivelled and shimmied, their upraised arms describing ornate figures, the company one throbbing mass.

In one breathtaking glissando, a solo oboe soared above the orchestra and wailed a series of wavering semitones, like the keening of old Cree women at a wake. As trumpets punctured air with arhythmic, discordant shrieks, the timpani and basses raised a thunderous vibration.

The arms were a sea of moving antlers. And Gabriel Okimasis, three years old, was perched on a moss-covered rock, the warm breath of a thousand beasts rushing, pummelling, the zigzaging of their horns a cloud of spirit matter, nudging him, licking him as with a lover's tongue. And whispering: "Come with us, Gabriel Okimasis, come with us . . ."

"So," Jeremiah said, "what did you think?"

Slumped into his seat, his eyes glazed, Gabriel stared at the curtained stage.

NINETEEN

$\mathcal{P}$retty as Miss Muffett on her tuffet, Marie Antoinette, queen of France, sat on a stool, pink crinoline with white frilled hem spilling around her like a foam bath. Her shoulders draped in ermine, her poker face all but hidden by a powdered wig and a crown that resembled a clipper at full sail. Behind her, the fabled guillotine; beside it, one terrified presenter.

"And this woman, born with . . ." Jeremiah's tongue could have been anaesthetized for all its gummy thickness, "born with . . . ahem, born with her mouth wrapped around the biggest silver spoon the Western world has ever known," he had practised his English-Canadian accent for this occasion until his tongue had hurt, "was about to prove this theory." Never before had he had to address a room filled with white people. He could hear them shifting in their seats, embarrassed, no doubt, by his backwoods ungainliness.

"So while France starved, the queen ate cake. Now if I . . . now if I were . . ." He cursed the flamboyant, sadistic Herr Schwarzkopf for his insistence on what he termed teatro verismo class presentations. "Ahem, now if I were to eat cake while you were eating straw and the boiled s-s-s-soles of your shoes and couldn't even pay your rent rent rent, what would you want to do? To me?"

Finally, and mercifully, Herr Schwarzkopf redirected his chilling German glare at the grade-twelve history class.

"Vell?"

"Cut your head off," the jock Rob Bailey responded with an undisguised lack of interest.

"Right." Jeremiah plunked the queen of France under the blade of the midget guillotine and viciously pulled the string. The razor blade, weighted with magnets and radio batteries, slid down and struck with a muffled thud. The stringy neck of the hapless royal doll flew open. A jet of blood sprayed out, two specks landing on Jeremiah's forehead. The laughter was explosive. And sustained.

"Theory proven: Never take silver spoons for granted." Finally, Jeremiah's presentation was the laugh-provoking spectacle he had planned with such meticulous care. There was applause. Rob Bailey's stuttered taunt "War war warpaint!" failed to register. Instead, the caribou hunter's son, his confidence in glorious bloom, threw off one last flourish. "And she wasn't the only one." His ts and ds had improved these past two weeks, and he was determined that this become public knowledge, "for there were hundreds whose heads fell to the guillotine in what was surely . . ." He wiped his forehead, he felt the goo, his voice began to quaver, "What was surely the most violent and bloody peer . . ." his hand came down, he saw the ketchup, and thought Marie Antoinette a most fortunate woman, "bloody period in the his . . . tory. Of the world." His first theatrical production had been a disaster.

"I disagree," a low, rich voice cut through the din. The laughter stopped. Heads swivelled.

"Yes, Amanda? And vat is it you disagree vis in Mr. Okimasis's interestink presentation?"

Amanda Clear Sky, dusky Indian maiden of eighteen years, disengaged herself from her desk and stood for all to see.

"There were many bloody periods in human history," her tone unflinching, with a sheen of anger, "many of them occurring right here in North America."

Once he had summoned the nerve to meet her stare, Jeremiah's eyes stung. "Such as?"

"Such as the Cherokee Trail of Tears." Her English was impeccable, not a speck of accent. "Such as Wounded Knee, smallpox blankets, any number of atrocities done to the Indian people. Was the colonization of North America not every bit as bloody as the French Revolution?"

"Yes, but Miss Clear Sky," the doddering teacher crawled to Jeremiah's rescue, "zat is Nors American history. Zis is European history vee are studyink . . ."

"Ugh. The Princess Pocahontas has spoken." Two rows from the front, Rob Bailey was holding court, the same person, Jeremiah wanted desperately to believe, who he had seen in the car that pulled up to the Leland Hotel on New Year's Eve. The bell shrieked.

Jeremiah was crouching at his locker rummaging pointlessly, his mind a jumble of rage and embarrassment, when Amanda Clear Sky came striding airily out the door of Herr Schwarzkopf's history room.

"So what you're saying —" Amanda winced as the warm spray from his words hit her face. "What you're saying is that Indians aren't supposed to know about the rest of the world, right?"

"No," Amanda replied, not stopping, her buckskin purse swinging wildly from a hand.

"That they should limit their knowledge of history to their own kind?" Jeremiah continued.

Amanda stopped so suddenly that Jeremiah had to save himself from crashing into her. Her eyes hovered inches below his, her breath bubble gum, pink, cherry.

"You just shouldn't forget that we have a history, too, that's all." She marched off. "I was doing you a favour. Trust me."

"Doing me favour, come on. You were just trying to make a fool of —"

"Look." Amanda whirled around. "What use is there pretending to be what you are not? You and me and your little brother, we're the only three Indians in a school filled with two thousand white middle-class kids. We can't let them walk all over us."

"What do you mean, we can't — ?"

"Don't you get it? *They* were making a fool of you, not me. You looked so . . ." Her voice suddenly grew soft. "So . . ."

"So what?"

"In need of help." She turned and walked away.

Was he to run and thank the woman for assistance kindly rendered or should he conceive some bloodless vengeance? He started rummaging again, but couldn't remember what he was looking for. He heard footsteps.

"See you later," Gabriel rushed by.

"Gabriel! Gabriel, wait!"

Gabriel raised a cheap vinyl gym bag. "YMCA."

"I need to talk to you." I need to talk to someone was more the point. And who else was there for him to talk to? Mrs. Bugachski's piano?

Gabriel turned, his smile nervous, vaguely fearful. "Bodybuilding," he chirped, flexed an arm, and disappeared.

TWENTY

"And second position and two and plié . . ." Miss Churley's steely voice sliced through the music like a razor blade. From the rear of the studio, Gabriel followed her stern-faced commands; he gripped the barre, thrust his pelvis out, and bent his knees, amazed that such a simple move could be so downright painful. Still, he was glad that he had finally dared advance from mere observer to actual participant.

The chipmunks in front of him were so damned cute that he yearned to scurry through their ranks and pinch each plump little cheek. But the mothers were sitting by the door, watching their daughters with nodding heads and brimming eyes. Instead, he held his right palm up as though feeling for rain, and he stretched his neck to the point where he wondered when his head would touch the ceiling.

"And third position and two and three . . ."

Pink as cotton candy in their leotards and slippers, the buns on their heads like inverted acorns, the baby ballerinas stretched out to infinity, the mirrored walls multiplying them into the hundreds. Thank God there were only twenty-four of them, cringed Gabriel momentarily, for his masculine self-image had never been subjected to such a humbling low. Avoid his reflection in the distance as he might, the fact remained that few of these five- and six-year-old girls came up to his navel, making him look, and feel, like a Weetigo. When a mother smiled his way, he interpreted the look as one of wild amusement; the black leotards exposing his bulbous, quivering groin would make a priest yodel *"Weeks'chiloowew!"* Still, he forged on manfully, scraping his dainty-slippered right foot from third position back to first in an approximate execution of Miss Churley's unbending will.

The ghost-pale, muscle-bound young woman in jeans and white blouse began wading her way through the bobbing columns as the creaky old woman at the piano continued ad infinitum with the flabbiest waltz Gabriel had ever heard. As she progressed, Miss Churley paused to adjust a little arm here or a little leg there, here a waist, there a neck, fully confident that such touches would result in a splendid harvest of Manitoban Pavlovas. The closer she got, the higher Gabriel raised his ribcage; it felt right, somehow, to strike such a pose when danger approached.

"Too tense, Mr. Okimasis, way too tense. Relax, this is not kung fu." She nudged his right foot in and turned his palm over: "And your palm is down, not up. You can do your praying to the *Gitche manitou* when class is over." With a vise-like grip, she grabbed his hips and turned them out. "Pooh!" she gasped, as if she had just been hit by a soundless blast of gas, "tight as a bedspring." She jiggled his arms, and slapped his thighs around like a Swedish masseuse.

Gabriel took a deep breath and willed himself into a state of rubber-like pliancy. His left hand poised on the barre, his right floated up, his neck grew, his hips no longer bedsprings. The pink little girls were now mere plumage on the wings of some fabulous subarctic creature. Still caged in Studio B of the School of the Royal Winnipeg Ballet, he was free of gravity, trying out this newfound language that spoke to him in a way nothing else had ever done.

"And back to first and three and plié . . ."

TWENTY-ONE

"Now a gavotte performed sedately; offer her your hand with conscious pride; take an attitude not too stately, still sufficiently dignified," quavered an oily, undisciplined male voice over a squabble of strings, woodwinds, and one untuned piano.

Oh, well, Jeremiah thought as he sat grappling with the tired instrument in the school gymnasium, at least I got the job. For despite the cacophony and the amateurishness of his fellow musicians, he was thrilled to be playing in a real live musical. And it may only have been the Anderson High School production of *The Gondoliers*, but to Jeremiah, it was as good as Broadway. If only Uncle Kookoos could see him now. He capped off the second verse of the gavotte with a robust little thump and plunged into the chorus.

The cadaverous Mr. Long rammed his claw-like left hand into the score before him and flung the page back with such passion that the paper almost ripped. His right hand beating four-four time as if the Vienna Philharmonic were at his feet, Mr. Long thrust his left so high that Jeremiah thought he might well snap his back brace, summoning into the unruly fray his even more unruly flute section. The hefty twins in honey-blond milkmaid braids and ruffle-sleeved Bavarian beerhall dirndls puffed their cheeks like Dizzy Gillespie and pursed their lips like wursts; the resultant sound could have passed for an air-raid siren.

In a plot that was a virtual quagmire of misinformation, there were two facts of indisputable and universal clarity: first, the pianist in the orchestra was as Indian as Sitting Bull and, second, one of the gondoliers-cum-princes, as identical as Tweedledum and Tweedledee, was white as nougat, the other brown as cocoa.

Gabriel Okimasis beamed like a torch. He was walking on air, his toes were tingling, his heart atwitter, for never had he expected to be a star in a real live show with lights and tights and wigs and music and choreography. Instinctively, he knew that he was doing something revolutionary, perhaps histori-cal, definitely head turning. For murmurs had coursed like electric charges through the audience when he had made his first appearance on stage. Jeremiah would later inform him Amanda Clear Sky had clapped her hand to her mouth, sup-pressing a minor heart attack.

It had all happened so fast that Gabriel's head was still a whorl, a snow dome turned upside-down inside his head. His dream had been to become a member of the chorus, a lowly

Venetian gondolier. He had had four months of elementary dance training. His voice, if not that of a Cree Caruso, had been found capable of holding a simple tune, in the tenor range. As this was Anderson High, not La Scala, Gabriel was a gondolier.

Then the stunning, self-obsessed Alex Brisbane had fallen victim to bronchitis, plunging Mr. Long into a tailspin of panic. For he now had to reassign the principal role of gondolier-cum-prince Giuseppe Palmieri on one week's notice. Mr. Long's emotional contortions had been prolonged and tortured. But Gabriel Okimasis had been most crafty in his manoeuvres.

Daring to anticipate such a possible development, he had not only increased his dance classes to daily sessions, not only taken on weekly singing lessons, not only committed to memory the roles of both Marco and Giuseppe Palmieri, he had even rustled up lessons in basic Italian from a woman on Corydon Avenue named Annabella Bombolini. And all accomplished with utmost secrecy. Even Mr. Whiting at the education office of the Department of Indian Affairs, from whom Gabriel had had to wheedle tuition fees for these lessons, had promised to tell no one but a certain anonymous superior in far-off Ottawa from whom he needed approval for such unusual expenditures. The final step had been to convince Mr. Long, in the privacy of his classroom, at twilight, that he, Gabriel Okimasis, youngest son of a caribou hunter from the distant north, was capable of being as Italian as Giuseppe Palmieri. For this crucial encounter, Gabriel, who knew he could be as prince-like as a maharaja, had displayed his looks to best advantage. Mr. Long had relented.

Word had leaked out that the casting was, for want of sensitive nomenclature, nontraditional, which had proved great box office. For here it was, opening night, and not an unsold ticket remained for any of the five performances. Ticket buyers had found the Indian pianist curious, even thought-provoking, but an Indian-Italian gondolier, a Cree-Spanish prince, whichever the case may turn out to be, they had never imagined.

Gabriel preened his feathers and shimmered. For, at this moment, he was the king of Barataria, the king of Spain, the king of Manitoba, the champion of the world.

Gliding up to the lip of the stage, Gabriel bowed, bobbed his head to the side, and winked at his brother. Jeremiah caught the wink and, by way of a love-bedazzled smile, threw it back. The withered Duchess of Plaza Toro yanked Gabriel's arm and they twirled upstage, back to the front steps of the cardboard Baratarian palazzo that leaned as dangerously as the fabled Tower of Pisa.

The orchestra landed with a screech on the final chord of the dance, the duchess and her gondolier-cum-prince swished up to a semi-dignified finish, and the Duke of Plaza Toro, clapping delicately, squawked, "Bravo!"

TWENTY-TWO

"So where did you pick up them fancy steps?" Hoping idle banter might quell the turmoil of his post-performance adrenaline, Jeremiah tossed out a question that seemed innocent enough.

Gabriel, however, wasn't ready to share his little secret.

He deflected the query by making a ghost-like face in the mirror. Then he burst out laughing, and began scraping his face, the cold cream and make-up clinging to the tissue paper like jam and peanut butter.

"There," he said, "the mask is off." He looked past the tremulous corneas into the depths of his pupils and there perceived, already, the other Gabriel eyeing him, beckoning, enticing.

Jeremiah stood behind his brother, tugging at the knot of the second necktie he had ever worn. One mirrored face appeared above the other.

"So." Jeremiah decided that teasing this Manitoban gondolier-cum-prince might take some of his edge off. "You're not gonna tell me?"

"Tell you what?"

"Where you learned to dance like that?"

"Here . . . here and there." With concentrated fury, Gabriel worked a puff of cotton around the lobe of his ear. "Mr. Long was helpful."

Jeremiah sank a comb thoughtfully into his hair. Why should a simple question cause such a flutter in Gabriel's answer? What was that flicker he just saw skittering across his eyes?

"Coming to the party, Gabriel?" Barry Sexton, the blue-eyed, blond Baratarian Grand Inquisitor, was the host of the opening-night festivities.

"*Neee, nimantoom!*" Gabriel snuck the Cree out like a sin. "We're actually being asked to one of their homes. Or did I hear wrong?"

"*Tapwee,*" confided Jeremiah.

"What was that, Gabriel?" Duncan Riley scrunched his freckled nose from a neighbouring mirror.

"Nothing," Gabriel snapped back into English. "I was just . . . talking to myself."

"He said he was coming," Jeremiah offered as graceless ruse. "And so am I."

"All right!" crowed Barry Sexton, the remainder of his exclamation swept away by the tidal wave of chatter. In the mirror, the brothers' mouths smiled but their eyes welled up with an inexpressible loneliness.

Gabriel brushed it off by shimmying into his shirt and starting on his socks.

"*Maw neetha niweetootan*," he said, his face hidden over his knees.

"You're not going?" So taken aback was Jeremiah that answering in Cree was the last thing on his mind. His English rang out like a white boy's.

"No."

"Do you know how many times we've been invited anywhere?" The clatter in the room conveniently covered their clipped exchange. Or so they hoped.

"He's not coming?" Gabriel heard someone behind him exclaim with mock surprise, then, "Aw, ain't that too bad."

"Why aren't you coming?"

"Going —" Gabriel could hide his irritation no longer. "Doing. Something else." There. That sounded less abrasive. He must not do anything that might jeopardize his mission.

"You're missing out on a good time, Gabriel," Barry Sexton cried out.

Gabriel slipped on his coat, strode down the hall. Like a drug his body needed if it was to live another hour, the night pulled at him.

"So you're not gonna tell me where you're going." Jeremiah was pursuing him.

Gabriel continued walking, zipping his coat, his face expressionless. "I'm going out to meet a friend."

"What friend? Why don't you bring him to the party?" Jeremiah almost had to run to keep pace. Gabriel rammed his tuque on his head. "I really resent you making a fool of me like you just did, Gabriel. In front of that big-eared fag, Duncan Riley? I mean, come on."

"I can go out and meet whoever I choose and it will be none of your goddamn business." The words took even Gabriel by surprise.

In the classroom, the cast began to pound on desks and sing Marco Palmieri's love ballad. "Take a pair of sparkling eyes, hidden ever and anon . . ."

Jeremiah grabbed Gabriel's arm and pulled him to a stop. "Why do you have to be so goddamned secretive? Gabriel, for God's sake, I'm your brother, you can tell me any —"

"Exactly. You're my brother, not my mother."

Glaring at each other was like glaring into a mirror, their eyes, their rage, identical. For siblings battling each other, wrestling with the darkness that had come scratching at their door, the sound from the room beyond suddenly resembled wordless chanting underpinned by bass drums, as in a ritual for warriors of some long-lost tribe.

"Fine," Jeremiah resigned himself, "just. Just. Go."

Suddenly, Gabriel wanted to wrap his arms around his brother. But right now, he had to leave.

"Go," Jeremiah whispered, and walked away.

When Jeremiah opened his locker door, a page of lime-green paper fluttered down, landing at his feet. A photocopied picture stared out at him — two luxuriant sprays of feathers radiated sun-like from the man's back, one above the other, a rooster's

crown of something brush-like sprouted from his head, his
wrists were bound in bracelets, his legs and feet in buckskin leggings and moccasins, all replete with floral-patterned beadwork.
Bent at the waist, the man could have been searching for some
small object in the grass, except that one hand held aloft, as if
to recognize some luminous presence towering above him, a
large bird's wing, a hawk's, perhaps an eagle's.

Jeremiah recoiled. There was something so . . . pagan about
the image, primitive – the word made his eyes sting – Satanic.

Frightened by his reaction, he concentrated on the print:
"Pow Wow, The Winnipeg Indian Friendship Centre, 371
Ballantyne Avenue, Saturday, May 16, 1970." He skimmed to
the handwriting at the bottom: "Show up. I dare you," its sig-
nature elegant, "A. Clear Sky, Ojibway."

"Nervy broad." He crumpled the paper and flung it aside
just as twenty-one pale-skinned high school boys roared out
of their makeshift dressing room and went howling down the
hallway. "Take a pair of sparkling eyes . . ."

He dropped his *Gondoliers* score into the locker, grabbed his
coat, and skipped off to join the marching throng. He even
sang, though quietly, "Hidden ever and anon, in a merciful
eclipse . . ."

PART FOUR
Molto agitato

TWENTY-THREE

"*B*aby, baby, whoa, whoa, whoa . . ." Gabriel could hear the siren screaming for him, "Oh you can do-oh-anything, oh-anything you want with me tonigh-igh-ight . . ." drums, guitars, and horns driving her rhythm-and-blues contralto. It took only seconds for Gabriel's toes, knees, and hips to surrender to the rhythm. The church and country music he had grown up with, the smattering of white-boy pop from Brother Stumbo's radio, seemed prissy by comparison now. This music meant business.

But would they let him in? He passed for eighteen, but this wasn't some two-bit blood-and-beer-soaked dive on North Main Street whose hold on life was precarious at best. This was the Rose, a downtown establishment, so Gabriel had heard, of "pedigree." Though he had also heard in the hallways and showers of Anderson High, including from Jeremiah: "Wanna blow job? Go check out them faggots at the Rose." Such yearning as had simmered just beneath the convulsive, near-hysteric hatred had only fuelled Gabriel's hunger.

"Wayne" had told him that he did look "more mature" than fifteen, had assured him that he wouldn't have a problem. Where was Wayne, anyhow? To hell with him. Gabriel summoned the wile that had become a way of life and pushed the door open.

Instantly, he felt the change that took hold of the room. Even blind men would have sensed it. Chatter stopped, laughter went unfinished; cigarettes hung in midair, beer bottles went undrunk, whisky tumblers untouched. Even the music seemed to have been cut in half, the singer now wailing, a cappella, an ornate, soulful blue cadenza.

Like a surplice of fine linen, a hundred eyes enveloped Gabriel. A thrill shot up his spine until he was confident his hair ends were on fire, crackling, emitting sparks.

As through the glow of stained-glass windows, the bronze Cree angel fluttered, the whirr of his downy wings like rustling taffeta, sending out redolence of campfire smoke, pine needles, of reindeer moss after rain. Only when he came to roost on a stool at the far end of the bar did life in the room trickle back to normal, clink by clink, laugh by laugh, word by word.

The bartender had missed the entrance and Gabriel had time to disguise himself. He scrunched his forehead, deliberately softened his gaze, as if a woebegone expression would add the requisite three years to his age.

Beyond the bottles that lined the mirrors, young and old were scattered at bar stools and tables, engaged in raucous, laugh-cluttered conversation, or sat solitary, lost in fantasy. Women too, though those few could have passed for men. Clandestine, enticing impurity that outcasts, freaks of nature, and mortal sinners seek out as refuge from tormentors. Half of Gabriel had an urge to run, to Barry Sexton's party and Jeremiah, the other half to dive in and wallow shamelessly.

"Got ID?" a mellow voice addressed him. The bartender, a slight man with a thick moustache, had materialized as if by condensation. Gabriel had no idea what to say, his nerves were a tangled knot. "No ID. No service." The man's face hung impenetrable. "Sorry," and awaited Gabriel's departure.

"Aw, let him stay." The whisky-sodden cowboy two stools away lurched to uncertain life, when, as if on cue, Wayne with the laughing eyes and the black-tufted hair sidled up to the barman.

"It's okay, Jack, he's with me." And before twelve words had crossed the bar, a full brown bottle sat foaming at Gabriel's elbow.

The conversation – with Wayne, with the glowing cowboy, with sundry others who drifted up and drifted off – meandered around Gabriel's sultry beauty, desirability. And as it roamed, so did Gabriel's focus, drawn to the small dance floor just beyond Wayne's left shoulder.

One meal from emaciation, a tall figure reeled about like a devotee in the throes of charismatic entrancement. Two features about this person struck Gabriel as most arresting, and most disturbing: he was the only other Indian in the room, and he was neither male nor female. Or perhaps both. The creature was blessed or cursed, one of God's more vicious jokes, the soul of a woman trapped in the body of a man. He willed the creature away; he-she should leave, disappear, disintegrate.

Instead, his eyes remained hostage as, inch by inch, the dancer extracted a threadbare white feather boa from a sleeve, as if for Gabriel's exclusive view. What did he have in mind? A striptease? A disappearing act? Suicide by hanging? Perhaps. For the man-woman was wrapping the wispy garment around his-her neck, but then stopped to wave and twirl its ends flamboyantly about, as though baptizing Gabriel with sprays of holy water, a sorceress, a priestess, clandestinely reviving a sacrament from some dangerous religion. Would God, in all his wisdom and power, not have good reason for peopling his Earth with such bold freakishness?

Gabriel found himself in a wood-panelled living room. Somehow, time had passed through him. A dozen other men were present, that much he remembered. Coats, shirts, jeans, underwear, socks lay scattered on the floor, over chair backs, across coffee tables. Everywhere he looked, naked limb met naked limb met naked limb, an unceasing domino effect of human flesh, smell, fluid. Whisky, beer, wine swirled, splashed like blood, smoke from marijuana rose like incense.

And the body of the caribou hunter's son was eaten,

tongues writhing serpent-like around his own, breath min-
gling with his, his orifices punctured and repunctured, as
with nails.

And through it all, somewhere in the farthest reaches of
his senses, the silver cross oozed in and out, in and out, the
naked body pressing on his lips, positioning itself for entry.
Until, upon the buds that lined his tongue, warm honey
flowed like river water over granite.

TWENTY-FOUR

$\mathcal{T}$he Winnipeg Central Library saved Jeremiah Okimasis from killing himself that spring.

For if he hadn't come across, by accident, the record-listening booths, he would never have discovered the antidote to the suicide-inducing loneliness of city Saturdays. There, that first dream-and-music-filled day, he had whiled away the hours, at times near tears, visualizing himself on stages from Leningrad to Rome. How, after all this time, could he have missed such a gold mine? From then on, Saturday would not be Saturday without the George Street edifice.

On his third visit, on a day so sombre the clouds were shaped like coffins, he was on his way to drown himself in the bittersweet melodies of Chopin's mazurkas when avoiding North Main Street became an absolute necessity. If only for the champion of the world, the caribou hunter Abraham Okimasis, would Jeremiah live beyond age eighteen. Which was how, slinking down an unfamiliar street, he came upon a sound that would have made the dead Polish composer rise from his grave in protest.

Inside a church, a pail was being banged, with maddening insistence, to accompany a terrible yowling. Dogs? In church? Were southern city animals trained to sing, even if it was some primitive, half-formed species of tune? Loping up the concrete steps two by two, he didn't even see the sign above the entrance.

What he saw took him by complete surprise. For where pews should have been — with mutts in choirboy regalia singing praise to the good God on high — bobbed a clutch of feather-tufted dancers, while watching from the sides stood Indians civilized enough for jeans and other human dress such as T-shirts.

Had he just walked into a Buffalo Bill Wild West extravaganza? A John Wayne movie? Where were the horses, the tired pioneers, the circle of dusty chuckwagons? And where was the howling and the pounding coming from? From the middle of the circle these paint-streaked warmongers were describing with a pointless shuffle? Or might this be a fair, like the Red River Ex, where one could pay a dime, shoot a medicine man dead, and win a Huckleberry Hound the size of a moose?

He scanned the sanctuary for a shooting gallery, slot machines, wheels of fortune, even merry-go-rounds and Wild Mouse rides. But no, the place was more funeral than fair. But for the refreshment stand, he would have left at once; a Mr. Big, at least, might justify ten minutes of Chopin thrown to the wind.

Gnawing at the candy bar, Jeremiah leaned against a pillar and watched the spectacle. On a wind-blown plain, back-lit by a sunset, an orchestra tremoloing away behind a grassy knoll, such dross might pass for something. But, confined by the walls of this church gone to seed, blasted by fluorescence, the outline of a giant crucifix high above the place where the altar should have been, it looked downright perverse. Who did these people think they were, attempting to revive dead customs in the middle of a city, on the cusp of the twenty-first century? Bored, he polished off his snack, threw the wrapper on the floor, and made for the exit.

"Oh my gawd, it *is* you!" the voice, at his back, resonated. He turned. And would have burst out in hysterics if his mouth hadn't been a mire of chocolate, caramel, and nuts. For there, likewise jostled by the burgeoning throng, stood Amanda Clear Sky as the Princess Pocahontas. "I don't believe it! I don't be —"

"Amanda?" Jeremiah squinted at the spectre. "Is that you? In that . . . get-up?" stopping himself just this side of the adjective "ridiculous."

"What do you mean, 'in that get-up'? This is my regalia, my dancing outfit. This is *moi.*" Poutily, she planted hands on hips. "Where's *your* get-up, Mr. Northern Manitoba, your moccasins, your plumage, your *noble* Cree heritage?" Her laugh bounced like bubbles from one wall of his heart to the other.

"Disney Indians," he scoffed, "Hollywood Indians dress like that, dance like, sing like . . ."

She rolled her eyes in melodrama fashion. "Oh, forget it. You got my invitation. You're here. And God up in the clouds is smiling on her people." And she laughed again, though uneasily.

Then he remembered the lime-green notice. He almost fell backwards, it was all so ludicrous.

"So?" With a saucy grin, the dusky Indian maid held out a slender hand, "Wanna dance?"

"Me?" Discomfort speedily truncated by a flushed-faced embarrassment. "Dance? I don't think so."

"Come on!" She grabbed his hand, her breath all cinnamon. He pulled it free.

"You just told me I'm not dressed for —"

"You don't have to be." Grabbing both his hands this time, she started dragging him. "Not for the inter-tribal, anyways," evidently the dance a deep male voice was announcing on a microphone. "Come on!" People were not only staring, for God's sake, they were pointing, laughing! "Come on, come on, come on, come on!"

"I can't dance!" Fuck off! was more like it.

"What are you *doing* to that poor boy?" a female voice interjected, not a moment too soon. When a sweat-faced Jeremiah turned to look, a tiny, brown woman, cute as a blueberry, blinked up at him.

"Oh, Granny," Amanda relented, her mock disgust not mock enough for Jeremiah's liking. "It's just Jeremiah, the guy

I've been telling you about, playing hard-to-get. You know these Cree."

"Oh, these Cree." The marble-eyed septuagenarian sighed and fanned her cracked-earth face with some dark bird's wing — a hawk's? an eagle's? "Sometimes I wish they were more like us lusty, enthusiastic, gung-ho Ojibway," she bobbed at Jeremiah. "Don't you?"

Well, no, not exactly, Jeremiah felt he should say. I don't even know if I enjoy being Cree, he knew he shouldn't say. That his embarrassment had descended to a simmering dislike dismayed him. But why shouldn't he hate this place, these cheap goings-on, this conquered race of people?

"Ann-Adele Ghostrider." The old woman regaled Jeremiah with two robust handshakes. "But I have a Cree name, too: Poosees." She batted threadbare eyelashes.

"Hmph." Jeremiah took some comfort in the fact: imagine, a woman called Cat or, better, Pussy.

"I travel too much," Poosees sighed. "For a girl my age? Way too much! Pooh! Anyways, some old Cree fart away up in South Indian Lake — Parliament Moose, can you believe that for a name? — takes a shine to me. Five years ago. Gave me that name because I have a kind of . . . cat-like personality, this Parliament Moose says to me. Now I ask you: what in the name of Jesus Christ is poosees-like about me?"

"Your whiskers," Jeremiah suggested, as a sudden burst of sunlight announced that the withered upper lip on the merry old dame was adorned by a caragana-hedge of fine white bristles.

"Why, thank you. My granddaughter here tells me you play piano better than ten white people jammed in a blender. Might this be true?" Green and pink beads sparkled from her white deer-hide tiara. "Or is she just goofin' around on me again?"

Her pupils spewing sparks, Amanda brushed past her flustered Cree captive. "I'll make you dance yet." And quicker than a sparrow, she was off through the crowd and into the dance. Jeremiah followed her progress with panic-struck eyes. What was he to say to this ancient stranger? Nothing, apparently — to his immense relief — for she took the initiative.

"You northern people," she sighed, as with nostalgia, "it's too bad you lost all them dances, you know? All them beautiful songs? Thousands of years of . . . But never mind. We have it here." She, too, was looking at the dance now. The drumming, the chanting crescendoed — pentatonic mush, Jeremiah opined.

And what the hell was this tired old bag yattering on about anyway? What dances? What songs? "*Kimoosoom Chimasoo*"? The "Waldstein Sonata"?

"Them little ol' priests," Poosees persisted, "the things they did? Pooh! No wonder us Indian folk are all the shits."

Jeremiah turned away. Then he saw her, on the dance floor: the della robbia blue windbreaker, the calf-length boots, the pale blue rose in her hair, now ten, eleven months' pregnant, her womb engorged, mountainous. In a circle of dancers coruscating with magenta, turquoise, luminescent orange, she looked like a handful of dirt. Evidently, however, this was of no concern, for she was possessed, her eyes glazed over, her feet inching along as if her body had neither heart nor soul. How could she find the strength to stand, never mind to dance? How had she — they — survived that freezing New Year's Eve?

"Devil worship," said Ann-Adele Ghostrider. "That's what they called this. The nerve!"

Yes, Jeremiah thought, the nerve. And right on the money. He mumbled some excuse and left. Chopin's mazurkas could wait no longer.

TWENTY-FIVE

$\mathcal{A}$s if artfully arranged, Jeremiah and Gabriel knelt in the tenth pew, the fresh June sunlight that fell across their faces, shoulders, arms, rendered doubly rich by the stained glass of windows. Gabriel's gaze, however, was directed at the walls between the windows, bristling with images of blood, agony, cruelty, superimposed with games of make-believe at Birch Lake Indian Residential School.

Our Lady of Lourdes must have some well-heeled parishioners if it could afford such expensive-looking sculptures. Each painstakingly carved out of some rich dark wood, the depictions were so life-like that Gabriel swore he could hear whips snapping, Christ sighing in reply.

No one in this sparse and motley congregation looked particularly devout. The women in their flowery hats may have been involved enough; some had the decency to rattle their rosaries from time to time, move their lips like fish, or hold their hands to their hearts. But the men, in suits as non-descript as muskrat fur, gave the distinct impression that they were really at the races, or in some fishing boat on Falcon Lake.

From the rear balcony, a small choir was making mincemeat of the harmonies to Abraham Okimasis's favourite hymn, "Faith of Our Fathers." Fortunately, thought Jeremiah, Holy Communion was on the way, and he wouldn't have to listen much longer. Withdrawing into his conscience for the words, "We will be true to thee till death," he prepared for the feast.

Unlike Jeremiah, who had been to this church a dozen times before, Gabriel reminisced, unimpeded, merrily. What else was a first-time customer to do? The service was boring, interminable, and, when all was said and done, unnecessary. He contemplated the carving of Jesus being spanked across the buttocks: he envied the man. Yes, Father, please, make me bleed!

Jeremiah rose and took a step towards the aisle. "Well?" he whispered.

"Well what?" Gabriel whispered back.

"Are you coming?"

"I haven't been to confession" — a ruse; Gabriel wanted nothing to do with communion, holy or otherwise — "so I can't go."

Jeremiah knelt back down. "You don't need confession. Not these days."

"I'm *not* going."

"We promised."

"Promised? Promised who?" Gabriel was suddenly so annoyed by the turning heads he could have ripped the moss-like eyebrows off the stubby small man in front of him.

"Mom. *And* Dad." If they hadn't been in church, Jeremiah would have slapped him.

"*You* promised Mom and Dad. I didn't."

"Come on, Gabriel. Just this once."

Jeremiah looked so pitiful that Gabriel relented. What did he care? It would be an act of kindness, for their mother, nothing more.

At the communion rail, the brothers squeezed between two well-nourished, black-garbed Italian widows, the space so confined they had to take turns breathing. Gold chalice in one hand, paper-thin wafer in the other, the priest turned his back on the tabernacle and started down the altar steps.

Natty in pretend red cloak and ankle-length white tunic, Jesus sat straight-backed and princely at the table's centre. Judas leaned over to offer him bread stolen from the school kitchen. The six-year-old Lord took a slice, turned to his guests — the boys of Birch Lake School, six to his left, six to his right, including Jeremiah-Judas — and told the starving crew that they would each get a piece, on one condition: that they refrain from speaking English. The table exploded with a flurry of Cree so profane and so prolonged — the scandalous ditty "*Kimoosoom Chimasoo*" the most profane and pro-longed — that the feast would have been sabotaged but for Brother Stumbo's piercing whistle announcing bedtime.

Past the scrap of cardboard on the fence — "The Okimasis Brothers present 'The Last Supper' " — stampeded the midget Cree apostles.

At the communion rail, the line of faces went on forever, every size and shape of nose well represented. Gabriel imagined their owners anticipating the great event by moistening their tongues. The very thought made his taste buds harden.

One by one, the tongues darted out as the priest, with a confidential murmur, placed the wafer on them. One by one, the tongues darted in, the straw-haired altar boy deftly catching wayward crumbs with his gold-plated paten.

Here was a sturdy specimen, mused Gabriel, square of shoulder, generous of chest, with a dimpled chin, grey-blue eyes partly obscured by glasses, no more than forty years of age. In Superman leotards, the priest would look none too shabby.

When the mumbling celebrant reached him, Jeremiah hurriedly asked God to accept Mariesis Okimasis into His Kingdom upon her death. When he realized that the prayer had sprung up in his mind fully formed, that he had had nothing to do with its conception, he was genuinely in awe. His mouth fell open, his tongue unfurled.

"The body of Christ," the priest confided, and deposited the host.

"Amen," replied Jeremiah, swallowed, and rose.

The Jesuit's crotch was arrestingly level with Gabriel's line of vision; but there was little to amuse the eye, the green silk chasuble so jealously concealed all possible event. Rebuffed,

Gabriel's gaze raked its way up the belly, chest, and neck to the face, where he knew he had induced a flashing spasm in the holy man's gaze. The Cree youth curled his full upper lip – and watched with glee as celibacy-by-law drove mortal flesh to the brink.

Flailing for his soul's deliverance, the priest thrust out a hairy, trembling hand. And by immaculate condensation or such rarefied event, a length of **raw** meat dangled from his fingers. What was a humble caribou hunter's son to do? He exposed himself. And savoured the dripping blood as it hit his tongue, those drops that didn't fall onto the angel's paten below.

"The body of Christ," said the wizard. But the instant the flesh met Gabriel's, a laugh exploded where his "Amen" should have been. The laugh was so loud – the joke so ludicrous, the sham so extreme – that every statue in the room, from St. Theresa to St. Dominic to Bernadette of Lourdes – even the Son of God himself – shifted its eyeballs to seek out the source of such a clangour.

"*Madre di Dio!*" gasped the widow to Gabriel's left, crossed herself, and clutched a rosary to the earthquake of her bosom. The priest turned pale but soldiered on; a dozen more diners were waiting, screaming with hunger.

Up the aisle Gabriel bumped and clattered, his mouth spewing blood, his bloated gut regurgitant, his esophagus engorged with entrails. At every step he took, ghost-white masks and gaping mouths lunged and shrieked: "Kill him! Kill him! Nail the savage to the cross, hang him high, hang him dead! Kill him, kill him! . . ."

TWENTY-SIX

"What's wrong with going to church?" Jeremiah pummelled Gabriel with the question, in Cree.

"Only old people go to church," Gabriel replied with cavalier insousiance, "when they know they're running out of time. Look at Uncle Kookoos." No response from Jeremiah, who was trying to marshal his thoughts. The church receded behind them. "I mean, how many kids at Anderson High practise some form of religion? How many of them believe in something?"

"You don't know that."

"The churches sit empty and the malls get bigger." Word by word, Gabriel's confidence, like his Cree, bloomed. "Some day, the world will have a mall the size of Manitoba, and then everyone will be happy. Back home people may take their religion dead serious. But we're city boys now, Jeremiah. To us, it should mean nothing."

"Speak for yourself."

"Well, then, what *does* it mean to you, this . . . Catholic thing?"

Flail as he might, Jeremiah couldn't find the words to express what he believed.

"These church-goers," Gabriel felt obliged to fill the silence, "they talk about respect, and love and peace and all that jazz, and the minute they're out of that church, they're just as mean and selfish as they were before. It's as if going to church gives them the right to act like, well . . . like assholes. You know what I mean?"

"They're not all like that," Jeremiah all but yelled back. "Take our parents. They're Catholics and they're good people."

"Yes, they are, but what about all those Catholics and Protestants in Northern Ireland? Blowing each other's brains out over the love of Jesus Christ."

"That's political," said Jeremiah. Thinking how childish Gabriel sounded, how simplistic his argument. "It has nothing to do with religion or, or, or spiritual belief."

"Yes, it does. Every war in the history of the world has had religion at its root. And what about those guys who beat the shit out of their wives while the host is still melting on their tongues? All that does is make one lose respect for organized religion."

"But what else is there?"

"There's Indian religion. North American Indian religion."

"There's no such thing," Jeremiah spluttered.

"Yes, there is," countered Gabriel. "A religion that's one hell of a lot older —"

"How do you know all this?"

"— and makes a whole lot more sense than your Catholic mumbo-jumbo. And how do I know? Because Amanda Clear Sky told me."

"Amanda Clear Sky knows fuck all. How can anything make more sense than Christianity? You're being sacrilegious, Gabriel, just to get my goat."

Twirling to trace a falcon's flight, Gabriel spied the priest, briefcase in hand, emerging from his church.

"Amanda said that Indian religion listens to the drum, to the heartbeat of Mother Earth."

"That's pagan, Gabriel, savages do that kind of thing. How can you listen to people like — ?"

"Christianity asks people to eat the flesh of Christ and drink his blood — shit, Jeremiah, eating human flesh, that's cannibalism. What could be more savage — ?"

"Jesus wasn't a man. He was the Son of God."

"Hah! Do you wonder why the world is so filled with blood and war and hate when it has, as its central symbol, an instrument of torture?"

"The crucifix is a symbol of hope, for God's sake, Amanda, I mean Gabriel! It's an instrument of love!"

"Sure. An instrument of love. If you're into whips and chains and pain. Where do you think them priests get their jollies?"

Gabriel could feel the clergyman now a mere ten yards behind them. He lowered his voice. "How do you think they get their rocks off? All that sticky white fluid? Tell me, Jeremiah. Where does it go?"

With a lingering handshake, the priest took his leave of Gabriel, nodded pleasantly at Jeremiah, and strode off smiling into the white light of noon.

"There," said Gabriel, turning towards Mrs. Bugachski's boarding house, "we've gone to church. Now we can fly north and face the music." He snuck a peek at the seven-digit number in his hand, then slipped the little white card into a back pocket. Already, he could taste warm honey dripping.

The night before TransAir flight 273 was to leave for Oopaskooyak, Thompson, and points north, Gabriel made a phone call. The rectory was busy — out-of-town guests, apologized a tight-voiced Father Vincent Connolly. In response, the ever wily Cree boldly offered him tea at his residence, actually the home of lawyer Stuart H. Everett and his wife, Diane. There, in his basement room, while the Everetts watched *Bewitched* upstairs, Gabriel Okimasis got to know the mouth-watering Father Vincent Connolly in a way that had him yodelling "*weeks'chiloowew!*" by nine that evening.

TWENTY-SEVEN

Bored as a weathervane on a windless day, Christ loomed
silvery white. Gabriel felt he could almost reach through
the airplane window and pluck the corpse, crucifix, spire,
and all. One seat ahead, Jeremiah leaned forward to assess
how far the village had grown to the north in the three
years since his last trip home. The treeless south, where
their aunt Black-eyed Susan Magipom and her terrible husband, Happy Doll, used to fight like Tasmanian devils,
appeared desert-like by comparison. In fact, not a single
log shack remained. Over the pilot's shoulder, true to
Gabriel's hallelujahs, he spied the new airstrip awaiting
their arrival.

In the seat across from Gabriel's, Kookoos Cook sprawled
snoring off seven nights of drinking Five Star whisky, smoking cigarettes, and jigging to the jukebox. The Smallwood
Lake Motel, the Legion, the liquor store, all had closed their

doors until further notice, for Kookoos Cook had drunk the little mining town dry.

Now descending over the yellow-brown ribbon road that snaked from the lake through the village to the airstrip, the boys could see a half-ton truck bumping along to meet the plane. It quite amazed Jeremiah — never had he dreamed a truck would one day grace his home reserve. Like ants to a picnic, knots of people followed on foot. How close to the treeline their hometown was. In fact, if the inhumanly tall Magimay Cutthroat wore five-inch heels, so local theory went, the surrounding forest would look like a lawn.

As the aircraft banked for its final approach, Jeremiah counted the crisp new houses that lined the road; plywood bungalows in pastel shades, as indistinguishable as peas in a pod, they could have been cakes at a bake sale for giants. There were tricycles and bicycles, as unimaginable as trucks in the old days, careering between the bungalows with four, five, twenty-one children balanced circus-like on their seats, backs, handlebars. Men perched on a roof installing a television antenna while Crazy Salamoo Oopeewaya argued with God right beside them. What was Crazy Salamoo Oopeewaya saying today? That television was the Weetigo finally arrived to devour, digest, and shit out the soul of Eemanapiteepitat?

The aircraft landed in flawless Cree. So much dust rose that, for one dark minute, according to Jane Kaka McCrae's subsequent confabulations, Eemanapiteepitat resembled Hiroshima on that dreadful day. Only through the haze, as through the Fur Queen's breath, could the brothers discern the small crowd clustering like mosquitoes around the little plywood terminal. When Gabriel pointed out the outhouse that had claimed the third of Annie Moostoos's reputed nine lives, the thrill inside their throats expanded to the size and texture of chipmunks. But for the vomit-inspiring reek of stale cigarettes and third-rate liquor from across the aisle, the moment would have been perfect. Fortunately, just then, the red Twin Otter Beechcraft shuddered to a stop.

"That's them. That's them over there!" And there, to be sure, the kingly world champion and his short, brown wife were, stepping off the terminal's flimsy little stairway and up to the wire-mesh fence, there to smile with a vengeance.

Annie Moostoos came trundling behind their parents, her solitary tooth a virtual pearl for, as the brothers would be informed within the hour, she had soaked it in Javex — "for days, weeks!" — especially for their arrival. Now approaching her eightieth year, for all anyone could remember, she was still as vibrant as "ten young caribou tied in a knot."

Eemanapiteepitat now attacked the plane en masse, for ever since the first p'mithagan had landed on Mistik Lake in 1929, the population had never been able to resist swarming like bees to machines that flew, even kites. The dark green truck rattled up, the door popped open, and Father Bouchard alighted; by which time, Gabriel had banged his uncle's pomegranate-like proboscis awake, the pilot had flung the passenger door open, and the gaggle of gawkers stood exposed as a picture.

Gabriel took a step down the ladder, Jeremiah immediately

behind. Suddenly, with a thunk, Kookoos Cook smashed into Jeremiah, who smashed into Gabriel, whose testicles smashed Father Bouchard's, who collapsed back to bosom on Annie Moostoos. The event sent all bystanders skittering off with a shriek so piercing Choggylut McDermott's new colostomy bag was said to spring a leak. And there in the sand lay a club sandwich of humans, a groaning Kookoos Cook its topmost layer.

"Kookoos Cook," Annie Moostoos squeezed out the one breath left her, "you fuckin' goddamn bleedin' caribou arsehole!" her invective followed by a bell-like poot. Had Annie's poisonous gases found heavenly release at last? As it would be revealed years later, and then only in the context of myth, the nether-region sotto voce had sprung not from the humble, one-toothed laywoman but from the learned, elevated cleric.

"Your father says you can get work at the store, *nigoosis*," said Mariesis to Jeremiah, in her exquisite Cree, "now that you're finished school."

Jeremiah shivered. How to reply? "But I'm not finished school yet"? Or, "I'm going back to play the music of Chopin like no Eemanapiteepitatite has ever played it"? How, for God's sake, did one say "concert pianist" in Cree?

Mired tremulously in his father's embrace, Gabriel sparred dexterously enough with the usual overtures — "hi, how are you, fine, how are you?" — but promptly met an impasse when the hunter asked, "Do you still pray, *nigoosis*?" his Cree impeccable. Gabriel held his breath. He plumbed the pupils of his father's eyes even as his own widened with terror.

"*Eehee*," he lied, "*eehee, Papa, keeyapitch n'tayamiyan,*" his voice incapable of masking shame or guilt. Supposing this beautiful man could see, in his son's dark eyes, Wayne's naked skin flush against his son's. Supposing this kind old hunter could see the hundred other men with whom his last-born had shared . . . what? Supposing this most Catholic of men could see his baby boy pumping and being pumped by a certain ardent young Jesuit with grey-blue eyes.

Dust radiating from his frame like a saint's penumbra, one shoulder graced by a bulging blue mailbag, Father Bouchard strode up to the family cluster and was about to speak when Jeremiah broke in.

"So, Father," he huffed in as chummy a Cree as he could muster. "I hear you're thinking of retiring." All he knew was that he needed a pretext — true, false — to deflect his mother's too-painful pleas.

"Why?" the priest hobbled on in a Cree so mangled it might have been German, Chinese, and Swahili. "You thinking of taking over my job?" He reached for Jeremiah's hand.

"*Ho-ho!*" Abraham sang out, "I'll buy the church a piano, throw your tired old *organ* smack in the lake." Their father's joke plummeted, for on matters sensual, sexual, and therefore fun, a chasm as unbridgeable as hell separates Cree from English, the brothers were sadly learning.

"About what *mon père* just said," mused Abraham, as they started down the road to the village. "About Jeremiah taking over? It's a thought, isn't it?"

"Absolutely!" thumped Mariesis, maternal pride straining

at the seams of her home-sewn smock, "Our son would look excellent in one of those long black skirts, don't you think?"

"In the wind, it would inspire nothing but the holiest of thoughts," concurred the hunter, though only in partial jest. Luggage dangling, the brothers walked ahead, their parents behind, the ebullient quartet trailed by Annie Moostoos, Jane Kaka McCrae, now doddering Little Seagull Ovary, and a chorus of yowling mongrels. Kookoos Cook would find his way home in a couple of weeks, when his twenty cases of Five Star whisky were down to zero.

A mongrel burped. Annie Moostoos kicked it. The animal keeled over and expired.

Jeremiah clung to the image of himself in a cassock, floating through the village, blessing people left and right, listening to the words of small brown boys in dark confessionals, and, in the morning, serving them the body of Christ piled high on a plate. What surprised him was that the notion, far from repelling him, shot a thrill up his spine. If the world, after all, could lionize a singing nun, could it not then, as well, a pianist priest, even an Indian one?

"How do you say . . ." English, today, tasted like metal to Jeremiah. "How do you say 'university'? In Cree?" Northern Manitoba sunlight clear as glass, dry as a bone, touched the brothers' skin, even as its edges were laced by the fragrance of reindeer moss, pine, campfire smoke.

"*Semen*-airy," grinned Gabriel, the closest he could get, in his native tongue. The word flooded his palate like a surge of honey.

TWENTY-EIGHT

"*T*ake a pair of sparkling eyes, hidden ever and anon . . ." Gabriel and Jeremiah sang as they leaned, one on each side, over the bow of their father's blue canoe. Like lightning, their reflections flashed under them — the lake a perfect mirror — as the vessel sliced dark liquid. At the stern, Abraham Okimasis pushed the motor's steering handle left, the boat veered right — waves grazed pebble-beached Awasis Point — and the fish camp leapt to view. There the dock, fish house, ice house, at a distance behind the spruce-log structures, another trio: white canvas tents poking spook-like through the tops of live spruce, of birch and poplar.

The little motor died. The canoe glided. Then a loon pierced the silence with a cry so close, so raw it made blood sing: "*Weeks'chiloowew!*"

Up to Gabriel on the dock flew the crate of gutted fish, Abraham heaving then bending over for the next. A dozen

more sat stacked in the fifteen-foot-long vessel, trout, pick-
erel, whitefish, no box less than sixty pounds. One by one,
Gabriel piled the crates behind him.

The hunter glanced at Jeremiah, who stood by idly, smoking a cigarette. "Not helping, son?"

"He doesn't do heavy work, Dad," Gabriel's disdain unhid-
den, "it's bad for his hands." The air hung thick with the wet
smell of fish, of entrails fresh and gleaming.

"Bad for his hands?" frowned Abraham, and toiled on deep
in thought. The signs had not escaped him: visit by visit,
word by word, these sons were splintering from their subarctic roots, their Cree beginnings. Yet he knew that destiny
played with lives; the most a parent could do was help steer.
He passed the seventh crate to Gabriel.

Lisztian octaves pounding like hooves inside his head,
Jeremiah stepped off the dock and up the slope, past the nest
of Achak and Peesim, their pet young eagles, and towards the
centre tent. Of what use would it be to explain that lifting
sixty pounds of fish a dozen, fifteen, fifty times a day would
make mush of his arpeggios and appoggiaturas? And should
he be thought a snob, an elitist, an insufferable egotist, too
bad. His father had had his chance at a trophy. So would he.

The needle in Mariesis's hand flashed with such rapidity,
such deadly accuracy, that a sewing machine would have
blushed to be seen beside it. A gorgeous pelt of arctic fox,
whiter than snow, hung from the rafters close by her head.
Though destined as trim for hats, gloves, moccasins, the

animal's extremities remained so defiantly intact that its tail twitched. The carpet of spruce boughs around Mariesis was strewn with scissors, thimbles, spools of thread, squares of multicoloured cloth – quilt-in-progress. So intent was she on catching the last of daylight that Jeremiah's voice came as a surprise.

"*Neee, ballee sleeper chee anima?*" he asked from the door. For how else, in this language of reindeer moss and fireweed and humour so blasphemous it terrified white people, could one express a concept as nebulous as "ballet slipper"?

"I haven't got a clue what a *ballee sleeper* is but these sure are funny moccasins you city folk wear," replied Mariesis, snipping the thread from the shoe in her hand. "Want me to make you a pair?"

Jeremiah would have declined but spied the conspicuously plastic bag beside her outstretched legs. For what should be poking out but more of this most bizarre footwear. Had Vaslav Nijinsky come hunting for moose and bear and wild caribou? Had Rudolf Nureyev defected to the frigid waterways of northern Manitoba? What the hell was going on?

"You make the fire, *nigoosis*," said Mariesis, "and I'll have supper ready faster than you can say *ballee sleeper, neee.*" With a small, cupped hand, she quashed a pig-like snort and stuffed the worn black slipper into the opaque plastic.

By the time the Okimasis clan sat down to campfire-broiled whitefish and fresh-baked bannock, midnight had almost arrived. The sole illumination a kerosene lamp, the only sound cutlery meeting metal and hot tea being sipped.

Down the slope, on a lake drenched by a great half-moon, the loon cried one last time. Immediately, its song was answered, first by wolves five miles away, then by the hunter's sled dogs sequestered on a nearby islet.

"So what's with these . . . ballet slippers?" Jeremiah's Cree voice cracked the spell.

"Speak English, *nigoosis*," said Mariesis. "It takes me back to the first time I heard it, on Father Thibodeau's radio. That old priest had to translate for us, of course, but people across the ocean were killing each other. A story so terrible, but the words sounded like music, I thought at the time. 'Great war, great war,' I used to sing and skip — I was five years old — until my father, your grandfather Muskoosis, told me to shut up, that the words meant death."

"Ach!" broke in her husband. "That's all them white folks ever do is kill each other. No wonder they packed their bags and swam over here to be with us plain ordinary old Indians, hoo-hoo-hoo-hoo." He chortled and popped into his mouth a fish jowl the size of a host.

With a wry little smile at Jeremiah, Gabriel bit into a triangle of bannock.

"So what's with these *ballet slippers?*" Jeremiah asked, in English this time. Mariesis shuddered, so pleasurable was the sound to her. "You haven't been taking ballet, have you?"

Gabriel would take his time. If Jeremiah had unearthed his secret, he would have to work for it.

"Well?"

"What else is there for me to do? After school?" Gabriel

struggled through a mouthful of the lumpy starch. "Besides hang out on North Main?" How he would love to throw his tea at his brother's face, scorch that supercilious smirk off.

"Yeah, but ballet?" What was this guy, anyway, one of them limp-wristed pansies?

"You take piano. I take dance. What's your problem?"

"So why do you have to make such a big secret of it?"

"*Mati siwitagan,*" quietly requested the hunter, for "salt" in English was beyond his ken. His eyes holding Gabriel's hostage, Jeremiah passed the small tin receptacle.

"I didn't want the boys at school to call me . . ." Gabriel flailed. "You know, a poof, a sissy, a girlie-boy. So I lied. YMCA. Bodybuilding. Just like you told me."

"I didn't tell you to lie . . ."

The boys, however, had learned not to court their father's ire when he had cracked Chichilia's skull with a canoe paddle for speaking badly of Father Bouchard.

"Why?" Gabriel rebounded. "You jealous? Of my body?"

Jeremiah's cheeks turned a brilliant red. But he had no answer.

In the silken light, above the hunter's head, the white fox winked. Somehow, its askew little grin made Gabriel think of the wicked Chachagathoo.

"One hundred years ago, when this mission was first established . . ."

Grey and sombre, the crucifix loomed through the driving rain as the two brown eagles, Achak and Peesim, curved gracefully above it. Their summer pets were now full-grown, and Gabriel and Jeremiah sat astride them, knights on steeds with wings. As the ice-edged September wind whipped their faces into sheets of white, Gabriel pulled his mother's white fox pelt up closer to his ears.

"There was a woman here who flouted the church, who did not worship the one true God, who practised witchcraft . . ." Father Bouchard's rant still shook the landscape like angry thunder. "Who made communion with Satan. Whom God punished," the priest had roared from his pulpit. "This woman was sent to prison in the south, where she died a lonely death . . ."

Gabriel and Jeremiah had sat with their father on the right side, Mariesis with the women on the left. The sermon, for once, had riveted them: who was this Satan that had his own communion? What did he look like? Who was this woman — Chachagathoo — with whom he had done business?

Through the heart of a coal-black cloud, the red Twin Otter Beechcraft plunged south.

"Away from friends, from family, from community. And away from heaven, for the soul of this woman went down to hell . . ."

Where, exactly, was this hell?

TWENTY-NINE

$\int$wooping like a hawk, a gleaming young man scooped a sylph-like girl and flung her so high that she floated, free of gravity, a grey-blue curve. In a flash he caught her and swung her back down to join five others crawling like crabs on the worn pine floor. Each time the action was repeated, Gabriel, gaping like a child at a circus, forgot to breathe.

The black-garbed man with his back to him owned these dancers, Gabriel was certain. How else could he, with a wave or a shout, manipulate their limbs, mould their torsos, control their breathing? "Yes, Eric, up, two, three . . ."

Who was this man, wondered Gabriel, this lord of Studio D with the carriage of a gymnast, the voice of honey, and the will of iron?

Later, alone in the change room — naked, tumescent — Gabriel stood before the mirror, imagining the stranger.

"And three and four and strrretch . . . ," the Slavic alto soared as, to a rousing polonaise, teenaged girls in tights blew in one clean line diagonally across Studio C. Gabriel stood shyly in a corner behind the only other male flesh in the class: two pink-skinned boys so gangly they teetered.

"Now, Gabriel, now!" cried Olga Ichmanova, and Gabriel leapt, his bulk thudding like a tank on the hardwood. Mercifully, by the fifth grand jeté, he had traversed the room. What on Earth was he doing eviscerating his crotch when he should be on Mistik Lake gutting trout with that redoubtable fisherman, Abraham Okimasis? Madame Ichmanova's revulsion clung to his back like the scales of a whitefish.

In the second round, Gabriel's one hundred and fifty pounds made the building shake. The crone at the piano botched a chord and Olga Ichmanova glared shards of glass. The thought of joining Jeremiah at a seminary glowed irresistibly.

As the third round approached, he caught sight of someone at the doorway. Chestnut-haired, dressed in black, briefcase in hand, the man stood staring. At Gabriel. Mother of Jesus, now he had an audience! He took a deep breath and leapt again.

"Those muskles must strrretch, Mr. Okimasov, they must strrretch!" trilled the matronly Olga Ichmanova, and *bang* went Gabriel, *bang, bang,* right up to the wall of mirror on the opposite side, drenched in sweat and so embarrassed he could have shit his leotards.

After hours, Gabriel stood — "And three and four and strrretch . . ." — chest and forehead pouring sweat across a thigh slung over the barre, which he suspected was a communion rail in a vengeful second coming. How could he get his groin to open further without ripping? "And one and two . . . ," he panted. Save for sporadic thumping on the ceiling – a late rehearsal in the studio above – the room was as silent as a chapel.

"May I make a suggestion?" How long had Gregory Newman, guest choreographer and teacher, been standing there examining him?

Unencumbered of coat and briefcase, smelling of some rich, masculine perfume, he stood hard by Gabriel, his face next to his, his fleshy fingers nudging at the Cree youth's spine, at his neck, his thigh, his knee, his foot, his arm, his wrist, his thigh.

"Think of your pelvis," suggested Gregory, "as a plate with an offering."

Flying into yet another grand jeté, Gabriel felt his whole groin area opening, breathing. Suddenly, he felt himself devoured.

THIRTY

"*I*t's this way." Gabriel's tone was hushed, obsequious in the lab-white corridor.

What is this, Jeremiah itched to ask him, the witching hour? Were they at the gates of a cemetery?

"God," he exlaimed instead. "How much does he pay for this place?" Down a blood-red carpet the thickness of muskeg they floated, Jeremiah afraid to breathe, sure uniformed security would swarm them from some unseen alcove.

"He doesn't pay rent," mumbled Gabriel, apologetic yet proud. "It's the dance company's." At the door numbered 2204, he pressed the button.

How many times, the question jabbed at Jeremiah, had this secretive young man been to this address?

"You made it!" Flawlessly turned out in black, accessorized with silver, Gregory Newman stood swimming in the view of a Gabriel mesmerizing in white. A froth of laughter artfully diluted by sentimental jazz trickled from the room behind him. The choreographer embraced his guest, so pleased to see him that he closed his eyes.

Gabriel stood aloof. If Jeremiah had been upset by the ballet slipper, how, God help them both, would he react to Gregory – a friend, that was all, a mentor, a professional associate who offered him possibilities?

Gradually, the host's eyes opened, only to see, over Gabriel's right shoulder, a large, dark lump. Instantly, the man let go of Gabriel.

"I . . . ," Gabriel cleared his throat, "brought someone with me." Why, in the name of Jesus, had he moved into an apartment with Jeremiah? To have his night life monitored, documented, filed for posterity, not to mention be driven mad, like Mrs. Bugachski, by the piano *Sooni-eye-gimow* had been fool enough to rent for the dump?

The choreographer made a devastating sweep of the Cree pianist's person. The pianist's scrotum shrank to raisin size.

"Ahhh, come in," his mouth cooed anyway, "party's just . . . raging away."

Like reeds at a riverbank, thirty silhouettes stood bending, swaying, the living room flawlessly conceived, its light the consistency of gauze. Framed posters, *objets d'art*, sculptures of nudes, dancers – the place was a virtual gallery; admission should be charged, thought Jeremiah. Candles, greenery, flowers, so profuse that all that was missing was a widow sniffling into a damp white handkerchief. Where was the casket, the wax-faced corpse grinning one last time?

Gabriel summoned all the bravado he could muster: he would shrug away his pique, focus on the positive. The subdued music, the elegant company, the view — all far from the cacophony of a Jane Kaka event.

Jeremiah stood propping up a wall, fingering a beerless beer glass. How, in these parts, did one request a refill? Whistle for a waiter? Bellow like a moose?

"Funny, you don't look like brothers." Gregory's voice seared through the sandalwood haze. What was that hint of accent? British? Australian? Scandinavian? He sucked at a roll-your-own cigarette whose fumes reeked bittersweet, arresting. Handing the cigarette to Jeremiah, the diffident host sailed for the kitchen. What remained for a lowly aboriginal but to indulge in the object that hung from his fingers?

Suddenly, the air around him swirled, the Persian carpet slid, swayed, shimmied. People, plants, even stone-cold objects came to life. *Oh my God!* He had just smoked marijuana! What if his brain was fried to a cinder? Too late.

With a rhythm South American, possibly Brazilian, a man wearing purple sang of children lost in space and parents who were dead. Sprouting heads like huskies and wings like crows, three bare-shouldered women sidled up to the singer and taunted Jeremiah. A daisy-chain of dishes clattered out of the kitchen, shouted "*eematat!*" and bossa novaed out the window. A mile above the city, their red lips parted and snakes slithered out singing, "Jeremiah, you are not, you are not, Jeremiah, you are not."

Not what? Not like this high priest of culture and his art gallery of nubile flesh?

"True!" Jeremiah silently, defiantly sang back. "My nostrils yawn like graves, my head is melonish, my complexion pocked, scarred, yellowish, and my hips are wide enough to bear twelve children!"

"True!" The reptiles slid into a cool-blue diminished seventh. "True, Jeremiah, *eematat, eematat!*"

Around Gabriel, mouths hung everywhere, mouths with no heads, no bodies, just arms and hands, a hammock of veins and blood that scooped his body up and rocked him and rocked him, like an infant in a cradle, the mouths singing lullabies in tongues that he had never heard. He squirmed himself free of all earthly weight and, naked, bathed in the billow created by the songs.

Jeremiah could see Gabriel, a three-year-old child, frolicking, laughing. How beautiful his baby brother was: spirit, pure, unsullied. How could any mortal hope to touch him?

In the moonlight, Gabriel's face, his neck were bathed by male breath, hot, minty. Until the silvery, naked Jesus that hung from the chain around this whiteman's neck came to rest across his own neck, hard, cold. He caught sight of Jeremiah walking by in the hallway outside.

Pulling on his coat, fending off his misery, Jeremiah stopped breathing but walked on anyway. For there, against the bedroom wall, black on white, Gregory Newman hung nailed to his brother, by the mouth.

Through the elevator walls, like the breathing of a corpse, Jeremiah heard the voice: "Is big, eh? Is big."

He clamped his eyes shut, swallowed hard, and willed his body dead. It existed no longer; from this day on, he was intellect — pure, undiluted, precise.

THIRTY-ONE

*E*ven from the hallway, Gabriel was certain that Jeremiah's scale was uncharacteristically stiff that morning, and ponderous: C-minor, so a certain Cree with intellectual airs had informed him, the key Beethoven used to express the most tragic and suicidal of his innumerable yearnings.

"Where were you?" Jeremiah neither turned nor stopped his exercise; the notes — and that insufferable metronome — dripped on like some ingenious method of torture.

"I . . . ," said Gabriel from the doorway, "stayed over."

"Where?"

"At Greg's."

The scale, and the ticking, stopped. Jeremiah swivelled. "When are you gonna get serious about your life?"

Gabriel shed duplicity, evasion, untruth with his parka on the tired old sofa.

"You don't want me to dance. You don't want me to hang

out on North Main. You don't want me to make friends. What am I supposed to do?"

"Who is this . . . Gregory Newman?"

"What are you? The FBI? Mariesis Okimasis? Father Lafleur?"

Gabriel was all of seventeen, for God's sake, barely past childhood – cradle snatcher! "Mom and Dad told me to look after you," Jeremiah lied.

"You try too hard. At everything. You and those lily-white fingers. That's what you want, isn't it? To become a whiteman."

Jeremiah's hand hit Gabriel so hard his cheek, for a moment, turned pale.

"What were you doing with . . . that guy . . . last night?"

"Nothing . . ."

"You . . . you had your tongue shoved down his throat, for God's sa –"

"So what? It's not your tongue."

Jeremiah slammed Gabriel against the wall. Knocked off the piano, the metronome crashed into a corner, landing upright: *tick-tock, tick* . . .

"How can you let someone do what that disgusting old priest did to you? How can you seek out . . . people like that?"

"And you?" Gabriel grabbed the wrist and flung it to the side with such force that Jeremiah reeled. "You'd rather diddle with a piano than diddle with yourself. You're dead, Jeremiah. At least my body is still alive."

When the roaring in his ears subsided, Jeremiah was lying on the floor, Gabriel standing over him, his face smeared bloody.

Clutching at his belly, Jeremiah whimpered, "What would Dad say?" His body went limp, his voice sepulchral, "Sick. That's what he'd call —"

Gabriel landed with the whole of his weight. He would gouge out his brother's eyes. Where was a knife, a screwdriver, a pencil? Fine, he would use his naked fingers. "And you," between pummels, he spat, "how can can you still listen to their sick propaganda? After what they did to us?"

With his last drop of rage, Jeremiah pulled Gabriel's neck to breaking point, then hissed into his ear: "Is big, eh? Is big."

"Noooooo!" Gabriel smashed his elbow into Jeremiah's face. "I. Am gonna break your arm. You will never, ever play another note on that fucking piano."

Atop the Yamaha upright, the Fur Queen smiled.

THIRTY-TWO

Gabriel watched lather travel from his chest down his belly to the forested isle from which a quivering spire protruded — most majestically, so had sworn the hordes of pilgrims. He hadn't been back to the apartment in three months.

"Gabriel," through the double barrier of door and shower torrent, Gregory was almost inaudible, "telephone!"

"So," Jeremiah's voice was still scarred by grievous injury, "you coming?"

"Would I miss it?" Gabriel's voice may have been chirpy, but a plum-sized lump had rammed into his throat. "But I'm leaving right after."

"Leaving?" This was new. "You're not coming to the reception?" If I win? Jeremiah ached to add.

"I'm moving to Toronto. Leaving tomorrow. Eight P.M." There. Had he thrown that off with sufficient nonchalance? "With Gregory." Gabriel shut his eyes, waiting for the blast.

"Gabriel! The concert's tomorrow night, not afternoon!"

"Gee, Jeremiah . . ." His cheeks flooded crimson.

"Didn't you get my note?"

What note? Had one come? If so . . . Time. Gabriel needed time.

"Gabriel," pleaded Jeremiah, "I've been working towards this for fifteen years. Mom and Dad and the rest of them, they're a thousand miles away. You're the only family I'm gonna have . . ."

"Just a sec," said Gabriel and put a hand over the mouthpiece. "Greg, it's Jerem —"

"I know." Gregory slid a Gitane between his lips.

"It's about this competition . . . I made a mistake about the time and —"

"Plane tickets read tomorrow night, 8:15. I have appointments next morning."

"Greg, please. We can at least change my ticket."

A jet of cigarette smoke enveloped, then swallowed, then obliterated Gabriel.

THIRTY-THREE

*T*ry as he might to think exclusively of the technical complexities of Sergei Rachmaninoff's "Preludes," all Jeremiah could think of was airports, planes, taxis. Even the long red carpet that led to the stage, and the double row of miniature floor lights, looked like a runway. Fine, he was a big, fat jumbo, taking off for parts unknown.

Pale white faces hovered, staring, probing, judging him. Just who the hell did this cheeky brown man imagine himself to be, walking to the spotlight with such a graceless gait, such an unmusicianly trundle? For since his fluke acceptance into the final round one week earlier, controversy had raged.

It was said, among the judges — being from England, they had to be excused their ignorance of facts aboriginal — that he was a Commanche Indian whose forebears had performed the chase scenes in the movie *Stagecoach*. Others claimed he was Apache and therefore a cousin to that drunken lout Geronimo.

Still others claimed that he came from the country's most remote and primitive hinterlands, where his father slaughtered wild animals and drank their blood in appeasement of some ill-tempered pagan deity. And all because this tuxedo-clad, flowing-haired Indian youth — Apache, Commanche, Kickapoo — was about to perform Rachmaninoff.

When Jeremiah sat down at the nine-foot Bösendorfer — the bench still hot from the ardent posteriors of such up-and-coming stars of the keyboard as John H. Smith, Mary Perkins, and that Ukrainian upstart, Inka Radnychka — the silence was so thick that a Winnipeg *Tribune* photographer took a picture of it for the next day's paper. And through it all, Jeremiah could see nothing but his brother, emerging from Mayfair Towers, laden with luggage, a taxi waiting, a gentleman in midnight black two steps behind him, as in an ecclesiastic rite.

Jeremiah raised his left hand. Their fingers extended, it came down, hitting with a bang an octave: B-flat.

At first, the process was laborious. His left wrist still ached, though Gabriel, thank the living Lord Jesus, had only sprained it. His constitution, moreover — of an athlete, a fisherman, the doctor had squeaked — had ensured that it sprang back to normal in no time flat. The ideal therapy, the doctor had merrily capped off the consultation, would be "something like playing the piano, preferably daily." After prolonged visualization of amputation, Jeremiah had been so relieved he had rushed into Our Lady of Lourdes on the way back to the university for ten quick Hail Marys.

He shifted from B-flat to its relative minor.

Gabriel, in the back seat of a sleek black taxi, a chestnut-haired, emerald-eyed Svengali. With a yank into the sun-splashed key of D, Jeremiah sent the vision reeling like a drunk into the shadows.

Decibel by decibel, he built his crescendo on the runway of Winnipeg International Airport. The pianist was so angry, he screamed, causing the trio of white-haired judges to remark, at the reception afterwards, on this contestant's positively animal passion. Never had they heard a melody line so scorching.

The Air Canada DC-10 sank its talons into the pianist's heart, its wing-lights twinkling, its wheel-spin accelerating, the rubber losing contact with the tarmac.

Jeremiah played a northern Manitoba shorn of its Gabriel Okimasis, he played the loon cry, the wolves at nightfall, the aurora borealis in Mistik Lake; he played the wind through the pines, the purple of sunsets, the zigzag flight of a thousand white arctic terns, the fields of mauve-hued fireweed rising and falling like an exposed heart.

Straddling the back of Achak, his pet brown eagle, Gabriel curved sadly over the office towers of Winnipeg, the Jubilee Concert Hall a candle-lit basilica, his brother's octaves the hooves of a thousand caribou surrounding, enveloping him, crying, "Gabriel, please, please, don't leave me!"

Jeremiah clung to the ivory until his knuckles equalled them in whiteness. These weren't keys on a piano but a length of curved, peeled spruce, the handlebar of a sled. Mist rose, silence paralysed the air. Where was he? What was that? The cracking of spring ice on Mistik Lake?

These weren't dogs pulling at his sled, these were young, naked men, winged like eagles, straining at the harness, panting out whorls of vapour. And at the lead, where Tiger-Tiger should be labouring, his little brother, cutting through swirling clouds, sailing past the moon for the planet Jupiter. The cities of the world twinkled at his feet — Toronto, New York, London, Paris: the maw of the Weetigo, Jeremiah dreamt, insatiable man-eater, flesh-devourer, following his brother in his dance.

Then Jeremiah saw it, or thought he could: the Fur Queen's cape — the northern lights — the finish line was near! And there she was, the Fur Queen herself, smiling from the great dome of space, holding out the legendary silver chalice.

Hands reached for him, clutched at his arms, his shoulders, his back. Champagne glasses, cameras, microphones were aimed at him. Men with notepads and pencils, women with pens and large red moving mouths, babbling in this language of the Englishman, hard, filled with sharp, jagged angles.

Something about "Jeremiah Okimasis, twenty years old." Something about "Jeremiah Okimasis, from the Eemanapiteepitat Indian Reserve." Something having to do with "Jeremiah Okimasis, first Indian to win this gruelling contest in its forty-seven-year history . . ."

"Your cheating heart . . . ," bled Hank Williams's wailing tenor.

Where was Gabriel? Didn't he come here on Saturday nights with his cheating heart in search of what, diversion? Inspiration? God the Father? Proud King Lucifer?

The table was a battlefield of beer glasses, surrounding a silver bowl, the Crookshank Memorial Trophy, the launching pad for many a concert artist. So drunk that only the starch of his tuxedo collar – soiled, punctured by a cigarette – held up his head, Jeremiah stared at his reflection in the trophy. Try as he might to will Gabriel into its smoke-obscured universe, the image remained infuriatingly alone. Beyond it, across the room, drunken Indians as far as the eye could see.

He had tried. Tried to change the meaning of his past, the roots of his hair, the colour of his skin, but he was one of them. What was he to do with Chopin? Open a conservatory on Eemanapiteepitat hill? Whip its residents into the Cree Philharmonic Orchestra?

Oops. A broken beer glass. Hey! What more appropriate tool with which to bid the noble instrument farewell. He lay his left hand on the table and, with his right, raised the shard. First, he would slice into the thumb.

"*Oogimow! Oogimow!*" the voice high-pitched, yet strangely euphonious. "*Tantee kageegimootee-in anima misti-mineeg'wachigan?*" Cree? In Winnipeg? Why not? He was, after all, in the Hell Hotel.

Teetering among the chairs and tables, Evelyn Rose McCrae smiled her gap-toothed smile; long-lost daughter of Mistik Lake, her womb crammed with broken beer bottles. A white fur cape fell away from her shoulders, her forehead rimmed by a Great Bear formation of seven glimmering stars.

"I won it," Jeremiah slurred, "playing the piano. See?" He showed her his left thumb, bleeding from the nick. Evelyn Rose lurched forward and laughed, now Madeline Jeanette Lavoix, erstwhile daughter of Mistik Lake, skewered in the sex by fifty-six thrusts of a red-handled Phillips screwdriver, a rose of legend.

"Can I touch it?" cried Madeline Jeanette. "Can I play with it?" Again, she laughed, and fell across Jeremiah's table.

"You can even sit on it if you want," slurred Jeremiah. "Have yourself a good long pee." Madeline Jeanette and Evelyn Rose laughed together, their voice one voice.

And, suddenly, the Madonna of North Main stood before him, the sad blue plastic rose in her hair, peeking through the star tiara. Twenty-seven months' pregnant now, her belly protruded ten feet, translucent, something inside stabbing, slashing, only the skull vaguely human.

"Hey, Luce!" she cackled to someone way across the room. "You ass-fuck devil, you! Come on, take a pictcha!" Then, with a sigh as vast as the north, she heaved the trophy to her milk-heavy breasts and grabbed Jeremiah. "You make me so proud to be a fuckin' Indian, you know that?"

PART FIVE
Adagio espressivo

THIRTY-FOUR

"You see," Jimmy Roger Buck gurgled deep, wet, and, Jeremiah imagined, slime green-yellow. "If us Indians are the thirteenth tribe of Israel," the chubby brown Saulteaux rolled the phlegm around his mouth, "then we oughta be going back to Israel." He spat. "Before the Apocalits, Jeremiah Okimasis. We got to get there before the Apocalits."

Jeremiah would have burst out laughing if his jawbone wasn't frozen near solid, his skull pulsating with a hangover that he swore had haunted him for six years. "Are you kidding?" his teeth clattered. "Them Palestinians would laugh us clean out of the country." Steam rose from the sidewalks, the streets, from buildings, enshrouding the slumbering city in a ghostly fog.

"Palace Indians!" Jimmy Roger Buck jumped on the word. "See? Told you they have Indians in Israel." Jimmy Roger Buck's humour, more potent than Chopin and Bach and Rachmaninoff combined.

"Hup!" Jimmy Roger Buck exclaimed merrily. "Looks like we got a live one." The two men flicked on their flashlights and, like burglars on the prowl, slunk down the steaming passageway.

"I wouldn't talk so fast," Jeremiah whispered back. "Remember that guy last year?"

"Deader than a door knot," concurred Jimmy Roger Buck as they approached the large lump. "Careful now." For one such lump had recently leapt at its saviour with a kick so accurate a testicle had burst, so it was said in Street Patrol circles.

As the skulking duo were about to poke the body with their toes, it exploded with a megalithic fart.

The rotund Jimmy Roger Buck broke into a back-alley jig. "It's alive, it's alive, it's alive-alive-oh!" The stench was so hideous it was a while before either could squat down for a closer look.

Her ragged skirt hiked almost to her hips, the woman lay beside a toppled garbage can whose multicoloured spew included a rat's frozen corpse. An object by her head caught Jeremiah's eye. Metal. Empty. Lysol.

"All right, up and at 'em." Jimmy Roger Buck shook the heap with a heavy-mitted hand. No response.

"Come on, girl," Jeremiah pleaded, "you're gonna freeze to death out here." The woman was ageless, her face a ground-beef patty, holes for eyes.

"Come on, Jimmy Roger Buck. Help me," and, together, the men hauled on the passed-out wretch, "heavy as a tombstone," as Jimmy Roger Buck would trumpet later to the staff at the centre. The team had to grunt for a good minute before the bulk achieved enough verticality to be dragged down the alley to the old van. "Winnipeg Indian Friendship Centre, Street Patrol," it said on the side. Jeremiah had always thought the sign should include, "See a passed-out Indian? Call us first."

One more grunt and Jimmy Roger Buck reached for the van's sliding door. The hulk lurched forward, Jeremiah jerked her back, and, with a *thunk*, she landed with her face across his chest. What was that? Something wet? Across his coat? Then he saw it: white lumps of starch, peas half-digested, mutilated hunks of what must have been roast beef, all swimming in a tomato-red goo with stripes like pus.

"Mmmm," said Jimmy Roger Buck, "jus in time for breckfas."

The woman was moaning now, and spluttering something to do with *Machimantou* — Satan — waiting for her in the Hell Hotel, that she had business with him, owed him something, had to let him fuck her till a dozen baby Satans popped from her cunt.

Jeremiah gazed wanly at the falling snow. How much longer could he endure in this . . . purgatory? Was six years of scraping drunks off the street not enough? Against the towering silhouette of the dark concert hall, he could see the grey, stoop-shouldered Cree, Sioux, Saulteaux — his people, shuffling, to where? To Israel for the Apocalits?

A bus whooshed by, ferrying the new day's early workers — short-order cooks, nurses, radio announcers, who knew, maybe even an earnest Cree student on his way to Chopin.

The van kicked to life, taking client 2,647 off into the dark February morning. His fingers stiffened to claws, gnarled from the cold, the twenty-six-year-old Cree social worker gulped from a flask.

THIRTY-FIVE

"Nothing we can do now, us old folk." The hunter's voice wound its way through the candle light. "Not one goddamn thing." Jeremiah had travelled so quickly to be here, and so suddenly, that his head was still a whirl, his body still sitting on that plane. Across the old man's craggy face, Mistik Lake shimmered, ice covered, studded with islands, a straggle of caribou crossing from the mainland.

Why wasn't Gabriel here? How can he be in goddamn Tokyo dancing for the goddamn Japanese?

"So much fighting on our reserves now, so much hate, rage." The ailing man had lost his eldest son, William William, thirty-seven, to a bullet at a Jane Kaka drink fest. "Who is going to get us out of this stinking mess, huh? Who?"

Above the elder's defiantly full head of silver hair, his last-born climbed the stars, a crescent moon strapped across his bare chest. A wild-maned, tuxedoed Jeremiah pounded at a grand piano whose rumble the patriarch would never hear. Next to the brothers' portraits sat a third: Tiger-Tiger regal at his feet, the world champion stood beaming, receiving his trophy — and his kiss.

"You're not going to die!" Jeremiah cried suddenly. "*Papa*, you're not —"

"*Ash! Kagitoo!*" Mariesis Okimasis snapped. "Of course he's not going to die!" Her fingers a jangle of rosary beads, the admonishment left her current Hail Mary unscathed.

The ninety-seven relatives who stood crushed like maggots around the diminutive matriarch agreed: they would have none of death. And none stood more firm-jawed than Kookoos Cook.

"Now I may have reached the eighty-sixth year of my life," the grizzled geezer would proselytize to all daft enough to listen, "but look at me. Feisty as a furball, tricky as a trout." With that, Kookoos Cook rushed out the room so nimbly the candles had to fight for their lives. Briefly, the Weetigo stomped across the ceiling.

"*Astum*," rasped Abraham.

Spooked by the shadow, Jeremiah moved his head closer. "*Keegway kaweetamatin.*"

But Kookoos Cook came charging back, scraping Abraham's battered old accordion across the floor like a frozen thigh of caribou.

"Jeremiah Okimasis, goddamn you young pup," wheezed Uncle Kookoos. "You play one verse of '*Kimoosoom Chimasoo*' on your father's old titty tickler and he'll be up and jigging faster than you can say 'tickle my titties.'" The sprightly elf yanked the instrument by its straps and banged it into his nephew's face.

Mariesis swore she'd stab the pestilence with her rosary crucifix. "*Ash!* Kookoos Cook! Put that *kitoochigan* away *seemak*, right away, *awus!*"

The crowd parted, and there, bag and snow-sprinkled beaver hat in hand, stood Gabriel Okimasis, twenty-seven years old, his face blue, his hair a wonderland of icicles. The wind having grounded all air travel north of the fifty-fifth parallel, he had jumped on a Smallwood Lake–to–Wuchusk Oochisk diesel truck and bribed a hunter from his bed to his Ski-Doo, to traverse, by night, seventy-five miles of subarctic lake so brutal they had almost died.

"I never thought I'd see you again," Abraham whispered, the voice so feeble, Gabriel feared his breath might extinguish it.

From the living room, women could be heard rattling off "pray for us sinners, now and at the hour of our death" in such breakneck Cree that sparks were seen shooting out of Jane Kaka's fetid mouth, thanks to Black-eyed Susan Magipom, who, not having spoken to her brother since Father Bouchard's edict twenty-three years earlier, had finally dared enter his house with the whispered theory that five thousand Hail Marys recited quick-as-a-mink was the one sure way of scaring "the fucking shit right out of death."

"I've been . . . busy," Gabriel finally replied.

"Busy? With . . . what?"

"Dancing."

"Dancing? Hmph. Are you . . . married?" Another jab of pain. "Do you . . . have . . . children?"

The words jammed up in Gabriel's throat. He was going to retch.

What choice did Jeremiah have? With his eyes and his heart, he took his brother's hand. Together, they would risk hastening the old man's death, together, the brothers Okimasis would kill their father.

"*Papa, kigiskisin na . . . ?*" Gabriel's Cree was rusty, but functional still. "Remember . . . when you sent us . . . to that school, when we were —"

The door behind him opened, the smell of pipe tobacco billowed, and in strode Father Bouchard, a worn leather satchel dangling from a hand. The still handsome priest stood darkly radiant, his crucifix wedged like a handgun in the sash of his cassock.

Knowing a dying man when he saw one, the ageing priest nodded. Once. Which was enough to send Mariesis and Annie Moostoos zooming to the dresser. Off came the candles, the photographs. The priest rummaged in his satchel and presto: a stole and a maniple in black, gold-tasselled taffeta thrown over starched white surplice, an altar bearing three blessed candles, paten and chalice, a small bottle filled with holy water, and, in left hand, a black missal.

The priest paused to whisper at Mariesis, who shuffled to the bed and whispered to Gabriel. Gabriel shook his head. She tugged at his cardigan. Gabriel pulled free.

"But, my son," Mariesis exploded, "your father's soul will burn in hell if he doesn't take his last communion!"

"He's not finished talking to us," Gabriel shot back, suddenly gripped by hatred of the priest, of the power he wielded.

Father Bouchard knew precisely whom Gabriel's fury was meant for. But he knew, too, that Holy Orders were as impregnable as granite.

" 'My son.' " Abraham startled the assembly with a voice surprisingly strong. " 'The world has become too evil. With these magic weapons, make a new world,' said the mother to the hero, the Son of Ayash."

Shocked that this most Catholic of men should resort to pagan tales for the third time that his sons could recall, they moved onto the bed.

"So the Son of Ayash took the weapons and, on a magic water snake, journeyed down into the realm of the human soul, where he met evil after . . ." Slipping into the world of dreams, the hunter beheld the Son of God nailed to his gold-plated crucifix, the priest's Gallic visage hovering like a storm cloud.

"This I know." In their grief, what the brothers heard, and remember, of the priest's reading was: "That my Avenger liveth, and he, at the Last, will take his stand upon the Earth . . ."

"Evil after evil," continued the hunter, "the most fearsome among them the man who ate human flesh," the Cree descant whirring, light as foam, over the English dirge. The priest plumbed the chalice, emerged with the host to place it on the hunter's tongue. The tongue darted out, grabbed the body, flicked back in. The lips fell closed, the hunter ceased to breathe.

Taking bottle in hand, Father Bouchard cast three sprays of holy water on the death mask.

The Fur Queen raised her lips from the world champion's cheek, exhaling a jet of pure white vapour.

THIRTY-SIX

One week later, mist on Mistik Lake thinned to reveal a man on a Ski-Doo hauling a sledful of firewood. Off Chipoocheech Point, he came upon a body lying face down in the snow. If Uncle Wilpaletch hadn't found him, Jeremiah Okimasis would have frozen to a corpse by nightfall, is what they say.

It had all begun innocently enough at Kookoos Cook's kitchen table, after the funeral and Gabriel rushing off to reconnect with the Gregory Newman Dance Company in San Francisco. Laughing, drink-crazed Cree were tearing through a case of Five Star whisky, Jeremiah keeping up shot for shot while ripping off a Kitty Wells record and ramming in its place Johnny Cash. It had been night then. But Jeremiah recalled waking with a pounding head, splayed on the floor, fully clothed and filthy, and it was day.

He recalled the fresh case of whisky Uncle Kookoos had

banged down at his side, and his aunt Black-eyed Susan Magipom waltzing with the stove, howling along with Loretta Lynn in her off-coloratura soprano, and it was night once more and, suddenly, Happy Doll Magipom had Black-eyed Susan by the hair, banging her head with a piece of firewood and blackening her eyes and the blood was spurting and the screams were piercing and Big Dick McCrae and Bad Robber Gazandlaree were trying to restrain Happy Doll Magipom but couldn't and, suddenly, it was daylight again.

Jeremiah recalled escaping – Filament Bumperville had charged in with a rifle and shot the cuckoo clock to smithereens – with a bottle and his goose-down parka and finding himself inside a snowfall, a forest of crystals, the hush cathedral-like, as if the world had died.

Where had it come from, this fog? He found himself peering into an endless tunnel, a flame appearing, disappearing, reappearing, teasing him, taunting him. He raised the bottle. His lips had no feeling. The walls of his heart had crumbled. The flame was fading. He would lie down, right there in the knee-deep snow, and sleep forever. Where was he? The edge of the world?

"God! Someone! Help me!" Whose voice was that? It couldn't be his. It sounded too far away.

"Ha-ha-ha-ha-ha-ha-ahhhhh," a giggle insinuated itself into the whorl of mist, throaty, arcing, like notes from a xylophone, as if it gave its owner immense pleasure to hear herself laugh. For it was most definitely a feminine voice.

Who the hell was that? Was he raving like Crazy Salamoo Oopeewaya, arguing with God?

The honeyed giggle swooped again. "Sometimes you humans just make me laugh."

Jeremiah squinted. He had lost his glasses.

"Hello, Jeremiah," someone cooed with a voluptuous, full-fleshed languor. Like a curtain, the mist parted. And there, leaning against a grand piano made of ice, stood a torch-singing fox with fur so white it hurt the eyes. "I take it you are *the* Mr. Jeremiah Okimasis?" She was far too spectacular: missile-like tits, ice-blond meringue hair.

Jeremiah rubbed his eyes. Had he died and stumbled into some freakish afterlife? "Who are you?"

"Ohhhh," the arctic fox flicked at her kewpie-doll lips with a cute pink tongue, puffed on her cigarette-holder, and purred, "Just a showgirl takin' a break she thought would never get here." She breathed out a small jet of smoke. "Name's Maggie. Maggie Sees. It used to be Fred but it bored the hell outta me so I changed." With an arm sheathed in white chiffon, she flipped her bushy tail, like a boa, over a slender shoulder. Her eyeshadow was so thick she could barely lift the lids. "These audiences are too much for me. If you really wanna know, my little honeypot, they're a buncha fuckin' pigs."

"Do you know how far north we are?"

"Do I know how far north we are?" mimicked the wily little beast in feigned umbrage. "Ha! Where d'ya think I was born? Miami? Where d'ya think my mother was born? Not to

mention my father, my grandmother, my great-grandmother
— honeypot, I have ancestors in these parts that go back to
when the moon was a zit-faced teenager." She spat. "What's
the matter? You never seen a girl before?"

"I'm sorry but I've just never seen a . . . a fox that could
talk, that's all."

"Honeypot, the way you been suckin' back that whisky
these past three days, you're bound to see a few things you
never seen before. C'mon, gimme some o' that shit." Jeremiah
obliged. The fox tipped the bottle and, delicate as china,
took a little sip. "Can't smear my lipstick," she tittered, "I'm
due back on stage in minutes and wouldn't you know it, I left
my Raspberry Dream back in Vegas, fuuuuck." She pulled a
tissue from her cleavage and dabbed daintily at the corners
of her lips.

"May I ask . . . ?"

"Does your bum hum when you cum?"

Jeremiah tried again. "Why are you putting on . . . a show
. . . five thousand miles north of Caesars Palace?"

The fox flicked the butt from her holder, pulled a fresh
doobie from her cleavage, and, *poof!* She was smoking once
again. "Because they need me here, honeypot. Name a place,
they need me."

"I don't get it."

"Why do you think I put on these faaabulous shows?"

"To entertain?"

"And why do I entertain?"

"Well . . ."

"Because without entertainment, honeypot, without distraction, without dreams, life's a drag. No?"

"Well . . ."

"Without celebration, without magic to massage your tired, trampled-on old soul, it's all pretty pointless, innit?"

"What's pointless?"

"Life, honeypot, life." She sashayed to the piano bench, perched cross-legged in her strapless sheath of white chiffon and Cinderella-petite glass slippers. "Do *you* think there's a point?"

"Let's see now." Jeremiah had to think so hard that his lips disappeared and his forehead turned to corduroy. "You are born. You grow up, you go to school, you work – you work like hell – you get married, sometimes, you raise a family, sometimes, you grow old. And then you die."

"Exactly. This is what Miss Maggie thinks. We dance, we fight, we cry, make love, we laugh and work and play, we die. Then we wake up, in the dressing room, with make-up all over the goddamn place, sweating so you smell like dog's crotch. I mean, get over it, Alice. You ain't got much time before that grand finale. So you get your little Cree ass out there. Just don't come here wastin' my time going, 'Oh, boo-hoo-hoo-hoo, poor me, oh, boo.' "

"And who are you to tell me what I should or should not – ?"

"Honeypot, if I were you, I'd watch my tongue. Cuz you're talkin' to Miss Maggie Sees. Miss Maggie-Weesageechak-Nanabush-Coyote-Raven-Glooscap-oh-you-should-hear-the-things-they-call-me-honeypot-Sees, weaver of dreams, sparker of magic, showgirl from hell. And this is what turns her crank." Her breath redolent of soil after rain, she hissed into Jeremiah's ear: "Show me the bastard who come up with this notion that who's running the goddamn show is some grumpy, embittered, sexually frustrated old fart with a long white beard hiding like a gutless coward behind some puffed-up cloud and I'll slice his goddamn balls off." She winked, then flung the cigarette over her shoulder. "Go grab yourself a seat, honeypot. It's show-time. Comp's on me." As though she had North, South, and Central America shoved up the crack of her furry little ass, Miss Maggie vamped back to the crook of the piano, which began to play on its own, and as the Cree chanteuse parted lips for her opening note, the fog swept back in.

And all Jeremiah was left with was the sound of the north wind, slow, persistent, moaning, the most beautiful song he had ever heard.

THIRTY-SEVEN

*B*linded by the darkness, the caribou hunter Abraham Okimasis lay locked inside his coffin. Though he found the satin lining strangely soothing, he could move nothing, not his wrists, not his neck, not his toes. And all he heard was wind, like the singing of a woman, the most beautiful song he had ever heard, teasing him, taunting him, daring him to venture out and find her.

Then it sounded like breathing, laboured, pained. Was that him? Or was the hunter standing inside some being's lungs? The cavern was vast, hollow but for stalagmites of moist, veined tissue, and stalactites that trickled condensed humidity.

The drip became a thump – a giant pacing aross the cavern's roof? – and the hunter was standing inside the creature's heart.

Finally, light appeared, first as a pinprick, and faint. In moments, however, it expanded to a glow, a flame, which splintered into two, three, four, until seven tall candles ringed the head of Abraham Okimasis.

From the coffin that, for some reason, hung upright in midair, the hunter raised an arm. Funny, he could move it now. And, funny, the hand had passed, unscathed, right through the satin, the pine lid, the six feet of soil, the snow, disappearing into the fog.

But where was he? In hell? The living room of the plywood bungalow he had shared with his Mariesis for near on two decades? On the barrens a hundred miles north of Mistik Lake, where no tree grew and the caribou roamed ten million strong?

The mist thinning out, his vision seeped back. He thought he could discern a thousand white masks hanging from the sky. Or were they faces? Yes, the faces of the living, it dawned on him, kneeling at his grave, the priest leading them in prayer as billowing snow waltzed, elegant, silent, around their feet. And that wind was his own lungs swelling, compressing, swelling. And somewhere in that crowd of faces his sons were weeping, from fear, fear that he was leaving them forever.

"*Ayash oogoosisa*," the hunter rasped at them, "the greatest Cree hero knew no fear, he . . ." And the wind took the words.

A note rang out, high-pitched, sustained. And from his father's corpse, slowly, Gabriel Okimasis raised his naked torso. Strings crashed, electric, twanging, catapulting the dancer on a trajectory beyond the grave, the village, the earth.

In the theatre's last row, among the thousand white faces,

Gregory Newman sat slumped, coldly assessing his creation, built on a story-line by Gabriel. His frame had thickened, his hair greyed by experience, but his heart would not be engaged. Instead, its owner kept thinking about this luminous man on stage who had learned to climb air as a spider climbs webs. Thirteen years he had lived, and worked, with Gabriel, yet he had failed to plumb something essential. What did Gabriel keep stashed so jealously, and so deeply, in those secretive corners, behind those eyes whose dark little flashes he would plead were nothing but headaches, fatigue?

He had told him stories, of course, of boarding schools, of priests playing complex games with brown little boys. But why did he disappear from time to time, for hours? Where did he go? Did it really have something to do with the limit-less freedom of the north, of endless roaming, of solitude in the midst of crowds?

His left hand gripping handlebar of chariot, his right lash-ing air with whip, Gabriel shouted *"mush!"* and, one by one, eight grey huskies reared up from the mist, each a dancer sculpted in sinew and muscle, straining at the harness.

Behind Gregory Newman, a wedge of harsh light materi-alized; a door had opened. The man stood, shoulders stooped, suitcase in hand, a tired, a travelling man. The door fell shut and the silhouette was gone.

Have you ever wondered where the universe ends? asked a voice at the centre of Gabriel's dreamworld, where the final star lives? The caribou hunter Abraham Okimasis would soon find out, and, tonight, so would his last-born.

"*Cha!*" Gabriel shouted. The chariot swerved right and now he could see it: the final star.

There, he would find God the Father, sitting on his throne of aromatic leather, sucking at a big fat cigar, and he, Cree dancer, would ask him a few key questions.

In the dressing room, Gabriel sat before the mirror looking at his wan, exhausted reflection as he manoeuvred the dryer adroitly through his shoulder-length hair, the table strewn with make-up, brushes, his father's Fur Queen portrait their dignified sentinel.

Like a ghost, Jeremiah floated into the mirror, into the reflection of this flawless baby brother who had journeyed past the sun.

His throat teetering on a sob, Jeremiah begged him: "*Weechee-in.* Help me."

THIRTY-EIGHT

*H*elp him? Gabriel, who had never been asked to help anyone? How, exactly, did one go about such a task?

Gabriel lay beside the snoring Gregory, smoking his daily
cigarette, staring blankly at the moon-mottled ceiling.
Impatient with himself, for thinking had never been his forte,
he stumbled through the possible scenarios.

A trip to Vienna, the city of music, about which Jeremiah
had dreamt since Birch Lake School? Out of the question.
On a dancer's salary? Besides, would such a trip get Jeremiah
back to music? Unlikely.

Find him a job? As what? Cook, lawyer, Indian chief?
Dancer? He drank too much, ate and smoked too much, never
twitched a muscle; in fact, he looked not unlike a sewer rat.

Pull him from the sewer, that was the answer. The country.
A camping trip, to thaw their cold war of thirteen years.
Jeremiah could flush out his lungs with fresh, clean air — not

to mention chop wood, pitch a tent, hike lustily through forests, perhaps even stalk a black bear in the likely absence of wild caribou. The only question was: where?

Mistik Lake would be ideal, of course, but too far, too remote. No time. But May had a three-day weekend, did it not?

At first, it was a blimp, though rather long and skinny.

"Sort of like a hot dog," said Gabriel, "without the bun."

"A dachshund with its legs chopped off," suggested Jeremiah.

The grey-blue object hovered above a squiggly horizon. Only as the ship advanced did it become apparent the blimp was an island floating on Lake Huron, a dinner plate strewn with parsley. Thrilled to be on water after so many years, the brothers Okimasis leaned on the railing. How gigantic islands here were, like little countries; by comparison, those on Mistik Lake were mere tufts of pubic hair.

"I have to warn you, though," Gabriel switched to English, thereby losing half his lustre.

"Of what?" From the start of the two-hour crossing, dark-skinned people with round, pudgy faces had glanced at them. Faces from here, from there, from everywhere, on their way to . . . what? A grand chief's funeral? An apocalyptic bingo?

"We're walking into the bosom of Ojibway country."

"And what, pray tell, is wrong with Ojibway bosom?" Native as a moose-hide, a chubby-chested woman jiggled by, scowled at Jeremiah, and marched into the restaurant.

Gabriel hissed that he could hear the war drums already, a

claim Jeremiah dismissed as mentally unstable, which accusation Gabriel countered in eloquent Cree: the beat was "steady, foreboding, and magisterially rhythmic, though thoroughly unsyncopated and therefore as simple as the mind of Crazy Salamoo Oopeewaya."

"Yeah, right," scoffed Jeremiah, though his face beamed, for each vowel had been jam, the consonants great gobs of peanut butter. He could have drowned their speaker with love slathered on love; but, like a cow, the ferry mooed, and a megaphoned voice barked: "Back to your cars!"

"*Kaaaa*," Gabriel sighed in an approximation of the vile Jane Kaka, and, tittering like chipmunks, the brothers headed for the stairwell.

Jeremiah steered their canary-yellow Rent-a-Wreck Beetle off a gravel roadway treacherous with pot-holes to a parking lot so full of cars waiting to embark that latecomers had to pray like bishops. For once off the sturdy ramp of the docked *Chi-Cheemaun*, locked into the cavalcade and ignorant of island geography, they had ended up, as by providence, in their present situation.

Welcome to:
The Wasaychigan Hill Pow Wow
Manitoulin Island, Ontario
May 21 – 23, 1983

Gabriel was beside himself. Having been to three, maybe four, such events inspired him with visions, one of which was to plaster himself with feathers and take to the stage in a glitter-crusted Las Vegas–cum–pow wow dance revue. Jeremiah merely scratched his balls, for, after ten years of southern Manitoba pow wows – scraping drunks off the street and taking them there by the van load – they still made him feel like a German tourist.

Already, the dancing field beyond enticed them with colours so excessive they wondered when the seven dwarfs would pop from a mole hole, Porky Pig come strolling down the rock-pocked hill. But, no denying it, the drum beat audible as war. Dust hung thick, and heat so high Gabriel wished he could go skinless.

"Look at these cars!" Jeremiah exclaimed, as they rattled past the Impalas, Pontiacs, Buicks, the Chryslers, Mazdas, the Cherokee Chiefs, "These southern, eastern Indians sure are . . . twentieth-century."

"You expect a parking lot lined with huskies? Of dogsleds crammed with beaver?"

"When I first moved east," Gabriel could see that Jeremiah's spiritual crisis would be quelled only with a dash of virtuosic Cree, "I couldn't believe it either: Mohawk duchesses minked and pearled, Onondaga divas in five-inch heels, Micmac mannequins straight out of *Vogue*. One night, a vision came upon me such as no Cree Indian has ever been visited with. There, on my bedroom ceiling: Mariesis Okimasis trussed up as a well-tanned Zsa Zsa!"

Jeremiah guffawed. "Zsa Zsa Gabor would murder small children for cheekbones like Mom's." Whereupon they found a parking space so tight that, in impeccable Cree, the little yellow Bug squealed.

Elbowing their way through great knots of sweaty, heaving Indians, they eventually reached the dancing field, just in time to see a dozen bronze youths throb by. Their backs sprouted feather-rimmed suns — black on yellow, red on black, pink, blue, purple, orange — two per fancy dancer, one above the other. A gust of wind ruffled the suns, a shimmering domino effect that fell against the wall of Gabriel's heart, sparking the image of the spiked, roiling spine of the mythic lake serpent, the Son of Ayash riding it across to the island of the flesh devourers.

"Say," ventured Jeremiah, "that couldn't be Ann-Adele Ghostrider over there, could it?" He craned his neck.

"Who?" asked Gabriel.

"That little old lady. The one who almost fell flat on her ass. That's Ann-Adele Ghostrider, I'm sure of it. Remember Amanda Clear Sky?" Try as he might, however, he saw no Amanda. And, by then, her granny, Poosees, had vanished.

"Come on." Gabriel grabbed Jeremiah. "Let's go dance."

"Nah. You go ahead. I'll wait here." Against all reason, Jeremiah was still frightened of this dance, this song, this drum, "the heartbeat of our Mother, the Earth," as he had heard it said on more than one occasion. Like the door to a room off-limits to children, it still made his blood run cold.

Gabriel had to admit, if only to himself, that never had his body moved with such gracelessness; a fish on land would have fared better.

There were no rules to this Round Dance that he could recognize. Feet wore moccasins, that much he could see, hide of deer, moose, buffalo, caribou, from slippers to lace-ups to knee-high mukluks. How were his feet to move in motorcycle boots that weighed half a ton? How long since they had known smoked hide of young caribou?

Midget step by midget step, he found himself circumnavigating the centre of a gargantuan, fantastical wheel, the centre an arbour of poles buoying cut tree branches, birch, willow, poplar, how were city boys like him to distinguish?

Thus shaded, five bass drums lay flat on blankets, each in a huddle of seated male players. Only one drum was at work, however, six men pounding beaded, padded sticks, chanting in a quavering falsetto. Through the day, Gabriel assumed, each drum grouping would have its say.

Suddenly, the brothers understood a word repeated by the singers, apparently the same word in Ojibway as in Cree. An old man passing Jeremiah raised an eagle plume, a woman did likewise.

The crowd shaded eyes to look up at a peerless sky. Half a mile above the field, *migisoo* — the eagle — flew lazy circles. For the song, apparently, had summoned *migisoo* — the messenger of God, according to those praying — and she had heard.

In a fit of panic — where was it coming from? — Jeremiah closed his eyes and determined he would ask, as soon as possible: where is the nearest bar?

But Gabriel saw a people talking to the sky, the sky replying. And he knew he had to learn this dance. Someday soon, he may need it.

From the heart of a fire, an old woman blinked. Each time she spoke, her mouth spouted smoke. To the brothers Okimasis, the face kept melting and regenerating, melting and regenerating, the eyes and mouths of a thousand women.

"That winter," the thousand-faced creature intoned, "the caribou failed to arrive. People in the north grew ill from malnutrition. Or starved. Then came news of men from the south," the old woman's voice soothing yet disturbing, "men with the ability to talk to God directly, people said."

The drums had stopped, but eight hours of their nonstop presence had implanted their blood-like pulse in the marrow, and the brothers Okimasis spent that evening — and the night, the week that followed — drifting in a dream-like euphoria. *Poowow*, to dream, *poowamoowin*, the act of dreaming.

"Hope rose on Mistik Lake — these men might save them. But Chachagathoo, the shaman, warned that *K'si mantou*, the Great Spirit, would not abandon them." The brothers cast each other fearful glances: that name, the name that as children they had been forbidden to speak, the name with *machipoowamoowin*, bad dream power. So that's who the woman had been, a shaman. Except what in the name of Jesus was a shaman? And why was it suddenly so cold?

"But the hunger became so severe," Ann-Adele Ghostrider's mouth exuded flame now, "first one died. Then another. And more. Until one day, a man became possessed by Weetigo, the spirit who feasts on human flesh. At this time, the first priest arrived on Mistik Lake."

Like a grass snake, as Ann-Adele spoke, a sound insinuated itself into the hush. Where was it coming from? The forest? Across the channel? The bowels of the earth? And what was it? More drumming? Or someone pounding at some great steel door, demanding it be opened?

Gabriel was perplexed, but Jeremiah knew. Suddenly, he was dying of thirst.

"The crazed man was brought to the priest, who proclaimed his soul to be possessed by Satan. But the shaman said no. When she started curing the man, when she started exorcising the Weetigo, the priest stopped her. The man died. And the priest accused the shaman of witchcraft. He had her sent to jail in Winnipeg. There, in despair, she hung herself."

Like breath, a gust of wind resuscitated the dying fire. The flames hissed. What was that it had just said?

Now the wailing was coming from the fire. Her long hair flowing, her body draped in a diaphanous white robe, an ancient woman surfaced from the coals and ascended to the sky, screaming with the agony of being roasted alive. And the brothers heard the coals moaning with the voices of women: "*Peeyatuk. Noos'sim, peeyatuk . . .*"

"Witch," Jeremiah whispered. He had to get out of here, right this minute. "Witch," he repeated, louder this time. "She was a witch. Chachagathoo was a witch." His mind, his heart were on fire.

"*No!*" Ann-Adele Ghostrider startled them with the passion, and the pain, inside her voice. "No, no, no! Chachagathoo was the last shaman in that part of the world, the last medicine woman, the last woman priest!"

"But our parents told us that she was an evil woman," Gabriel argued. "We weren't ever to speak her name."

"Your parents' generation? In the north? Lied to and lied to and lied to!"

"I think . . . I think I've had enough . . . for one night." And the darkness swallowed Jeremiah.

Gabriel shrugged, wanting to explain to their host that this was simply Jeremiah's way. What he saw, however, was her sadness, the exhaustion. And the flames inside her pupils, the burning shaman ascending to the stars.

Then it struck him: if *machipoowamoowin*, bad dream power, was obviously powerful enough to snuff out a human life, then would not *mithoopoowamoowin*, good dream power, be as strong?

THIRTY-NINE

Snuggled like a teddy in his sleeping bag, Gabriel looked up. Askew as it was, the roof was a roof, thank God, for he and Jeremiah had almost destroyed the tent trying to erect it. Their excuse, to amused bystanders, had been that the synthetic material that came pre-packaged with shish-kebab skewers for pegs took them by surprise. "In the old days," they had explained with beet-red faces, "tents were canvas and much more cooperative," and you carved your own pegs from stalks of willow. When their fire – for heating their one can of beans – had ended up a poignant little smoke curl, their audience had rewarded their Indian skills with an invitation to supper, thank the living Lord Jesus, for otherwise, they would have had to drive all the way to Espanola for chicken chop suey.

But where was Jeremiah? For if Wasaychigan Hill, being an Indian reserve, was anything like Eemanapiteepitat, would it not be as volatile, as unpredictable, as insane? What if he got shot point-blank in the forehead like their brother, William William?

Gabriel ripped open the zipper of the sleeping bag and patted in the dark for his jeans. How could good Cree campers forget a tool as traditional as a flashlight?

Wasaychigan Hill had not seen a man named Jeremiah Okimasis, Gabriel was informed at several doors, at several points on the main dirt road, "but check the forty-niner," a semi-nude, Rubenesque femme fatale named Gazelle suggested. "Lapatak St. Pierre's old corn field. All you gotta do is follow that pounding rhythm. In fact, I'll take you there myself, big boy." She raked his genitalia with glazed-over eyes.

Gabriel pleaded crabs, waited for cloud cover, and followed the pounding rhythm, away from moonlight and the hussy, through a forest so thick he wondered when a bear would tap him on the shoulder to borrow ten dollars.

Finally, a field, at its centre a fire so large it could have roasted covens of witches. Against it, silhouettes — of dogs? wolves? — baying at the moon, or crying for blood. The sound now like the gates of a prison clanging and clanging.

Four hundred young men and women stood around an aged Buick, those within reach hand-thumping at its hood, its roof, its trunk.

Gabriel circled the demonized assembly. *Poowow*, to dream. So this was a forty-niner, where drink, drugs, and song swept senses to a plane where dreams loomed clear, visceral. For not one among these hundreds was here, in Lapatak St. Pierre's old corn field, on Manitoulin Island, on the planet.

His brother stood sucking back a beer. The glow from the fire made the side of his face almost reptilian. He tossed the empty bottle and took four uncertain steps to the cases on the ground, torn open, half-finished, ravaged.

"Haven't you had enough?"

Jeremiah looked up. So, his *virginal* baby brother had hunted him down, as expected. Still, he could not think what to say. Could he even talk?

"Well?"

From the sky, black fell like an axe, Jeremiah's spirit fish guts crawling with maggots.

"Say," an oily male voice oozed in, "aren't you Gabriel Okimasis, the famous Indian *ballet* dancer?" A short distance off, four ripe young men grappled with delirium, their glassy eyes fixed on Gabriel. What was a Cree Nijinsky to say? Yes, I am? How very nice to meet you all? Which one of you would like to join me in an unlubricated, nipple-shredding, scrotum-banging pas de deux?

"So," a lanky punk drawled, on an intake of marijuana smoke, "where's your panty-hose, Flossy?"

Gabriel looked to Jeremiah: *weechee-in.*

But though the pall had lifted from Jeremiah's eyes, the dryness in his throat had thickened, the perfect alibi. For how else would he face the truth: that he was embarrassed to be caught in cahoots with a pervert, a man who fucked other men? On an Indian reserve, a Catholic reserve? He reached into the box, grabbed two bottles, and walked into the night.

"Yeah. I seen him in them magazines," a third young man sneered.

"I seen him on TV."

Gabriel looked into their eyes, and was taken completely by surprise. For where he had anticipated hatred, what he saw, instead, was terror. Of what? The fact that the flesh of the mother had formed their flesh, female blood ran thick inside their veins? Terror that the emotion of a woman, the spirit of a woman, lived inside them?

"Told you it was him, prancin' around out there."

Bottle in hand, the biggest, meanest, the most terrified and stupid, took a step forward. Whereupon Gabriel turned, and walked sadly back to the campsite.

"Hey, faggot! Where the fuck you think you're goin'?"

"Hey, shaman! Where the fuck you think you're goin'?" the ragged old drunk had shrieked as she fell on him. Jeremiah had dislodged himself, though his throat, he swore, bore the imprint of her fangs, even as her cheesy breath rankled at his nostril hairs, and her cackle, like a trapped fly, buzzed against the drum of his left ear.

His perch atop the picnic table seemed precarious at best, Jeremiah unaware that his feet were splayed, like rubber, on a bench somewhere below. What time was it? How had he gotten here? Who had given him this mickey of rye? Where was a cigarette? An oscillating ball of fire was all that he could see, in the distance, though his ears vaguely discerned the howling of wolves beyond the drumming of his heart.

Suddenly, astride the feathery back of Peesim, his pet brown eagle, he could see all of North America thirty miles below.

There they were, the caribou, feeding at the northern extremity of the barrens this summer, the tundra a ripple of wind-blown fireweed, the icebergs tall as basilicas.

And then Peesim was gone and Jeremiah was falling, hurtling through the great womb of space, aiming straight for a cotton-candy bank of snow, when his head grazed something. Like an aluminum plate, the moon twirled down, down, ending its plummet with a clatter against the leg of a picnic table. Holding his ringing head, Jeremiah rolled in the grass and groaned.

"Get out!" Hot, rank breath blasted at his face. "Get out! Oh, evil spirit, get out!"

She was back! To feast on his flesh, devour his soul, her crown, her white fur coat, her eyes of fire. And she was clutching at his throat, squeezing it shut. Chachagathoo, rising from her grave.

"Get away from me." Like a two-year-old, Jeremiah sobbed. "Get away, get away, *awus, awus, awus!*" One hand hit the lid of a trash can toppled over next to his head.

"Leave this body at once!" No. It was the monster gnawing at his innards, devouring him live, that Chachagathoo had come to get, not him. Except, she wasn't grimacing now. "Get up! Eeeeeeeeeeeeeee-ha-ha-ha!"

Laughing? What on earth could she find comical? The pustules on her face were melting, dripping down her cheeks, her neck. And, like an eggshell, her wrinkled face was cracking, another face looming from the egg's interior.

"I command you to get up!" the new face pealed, the laugh much higher this time, and younger. *"Get up!"*

Only make-up? Thank God, it's only . . . "Amanda?" Again, the woman shook him by the shoulders. "Amanda Clear Sky?"

"Does your bum hum when you cum?" Her breath all cinnamon, she laughed. Where had he heard those words before? "Granny told me you . . ." She couldn't stop laughing. "You should have seen yourself fall off that picnic table, the garbage can lid went eeeeeeeeeeee-ha-ha-ha!"

FORTY

*I*n a kitchen with room for twenty, ninety happy people stomped and jiggled with such fury that the floor was likely to collapse into the basement, so warned the crusty old veteran who had survived such catastrophes in wartime Naples. Fortunately, "the Wasaychigan Hill Philharmonic Orkestraw" was small: a banjo, a fiddle, and "my dead wife's tired old washboard."

"No, no, no," the button-eyed codger shouted at Jeremiah so his elfin voice could be heard, "not Melodius! Alodius! Alodius Clear Sky! It sounds like an ointment, but it's better than being named Bob White, eh?" Jigging so fast that her face was a blur, a stick-thin woman named Annie Cook bumped Alodius who bumped Jeremiah who bumped a jelly-bellied man with a rolling pin. Jeremiah was apologizing profusely, to a baker named Zachary as he learned, when Amanda came sailing through the horde with steaming mugs of coffee held high.

"Dad," she gushed as she handed one to Alodius, "Jeremiah is the first Indian concert pianist in the history of the world." Jeremiah just had time for one quick blush and the second mug when Alodius grabbed him. Like Moses in the book, the white-haired widower parted the sea of raging human flesh.

"Sit," he barked.

Barely held together by Scotch tape and wire, the old, brown piano grinned bad yellow teeth at no one in particular. Jeremiah wedged himself between the bench and the instrument, and sat.

"Play," barked Amanda's father. In this house of drink-mad Ojibways, what choice did a lost Cree soul have? Extending an index finger, he tweaked middle C; the three strings of the note snarled back with a virtual tone cluster. Jeremiah winced. He considered clawing his way into some twelve-tone Schoenberg but, instead, sat paralysed.

"Come on," Amanda pleaded.

"But I haven't touched a piano in ten years."

"Ten years! Come on, play some –"

"Play the goddamn thing or I'll throw you out of my house!" roared Alodius, and banged the piano top with such gusto the sound board boomed.

Distraught, Jeremiah waded into Chopin's Sonata in B-minor, its opening downward four-note arpeggio followed by thick chords ascending and descending simultaneously. The result was criminal. He skipped to the second theme, a passage more lyrical and kinder to the touch. Their bombast ambushed by a strain so untuned, the Orkestraw plunged into a simmering silence that stopped the dancers cold.

If one ignored the squeaking — a pedal so sick it should have been shot — Chopin's music was now the only sound. One by one, the rag-taggle bunch, with apple-red cheeks and beer-filled eyes, crept up to the piano and peered like gnomes past the shoulder of a pianist who wanted to be dead. Pair by pair, eyes turned slit-like, brows scrunched, thick lips puckered like assholes.

"That there is whiteman music," charged a middle-aged man with a nose like a baseball.

"Play some honky-tonk," Amanda tried.

"I can't." Jeremiah squirmed.

"Alodius!" trilled a woman in the crowed, "play some real music."

"Yay, Alodius!" bellowed the assembly. "Play 'Half a Nageela!' "

Jeremiah and Amanda slithered onto a sofa crammed with fifteen Indians jiggling like a great vat of custard. Old Alodius rammed into a "Havah Negilah" so vicious that men's balls jangled, women's nipples tittered, and Jesus fell off his wall perch, bounced off the piano, and landed on the floor with a Galilean do-si-do. The dance floor seethed with Clarabelle Cow St. Pierre, Bugs Bunny Starblanket, Minnie Mouse Manitowabi, Big Bum Pegahmagahbow, Petunia Pig Patchnose, all mixed into one riotous, bubbling stew. Like an old wet bitch, the whole house shook.

Then, smooth as an otter, Alodius slid into a sentimental

country waltz. His impromptu band followed, and the crowd mellowed, men and women pairing off intimately, romantically, hornily. The kewpie-doll Philomena M. Moosetail wove her chubby-buttocked, pie-eyed way from the stove to a window with a soup pot clutched to her belly.

"Ever thought you were born on the wrong planet?" Jeremiah asked Amanda, relieved the volume of the music finally permitted conversation. "Into the wrong . . . era? The wrong . . . ," he laughed pathetically, "race?" Amanda slid a hand over his as Philomena draped the dirty white curtain across her overpadded shoulders and, with a grunt, wrapped an arm around a prince-like man.

"Hey, Luce," ululated the Lady Philomena, "C'mon, Lucy, take a pictcha!" With a full-bodied kiss, the Ojibway monarch bestowed the silver bowl on her chosen victor.

"I just couldn't figure it out. I mean, what the fuck are Indians doing playing —" the camera flashed, Jeremiah resurfaced, "Chopin?"

Amanda was about to speak — to answer his question? Tell him she was tired? Tell him that she loved him? Even she didn't know — when the piano fell back into its dreamy three-four time.

"Oh, get off your high horse," she spluttered instead. "Who the hell do you think you are, the Saviour of the Indians?"

Outside the window, a sparrow whistled the day's first song.

"Come on." Amanda grunted her way out of the jumble of limbs. "There's . . . oof! . . . something I wanna show you."

She scooped a black box off the coffee table. Chocolates? Apparently not, if you could go by its label: *Tender Is My Heart: Episode 12.*

"I can't, Jake," said the housewife, whose dissimilarity to Amanda was not quite convincing. "I can't live with you no more." But Amanda was right; the Cree was not northern Manitoba. Liberally mixed with its sister-language, Ojibway, it was a challenge for Jeremiah. The stress on her face read like a road map.

"I already tole you, Dorothy, baby," replied her husband, a barrel-chested Indian with a belly like a bean bag, wearily unbuttoning his red flannel shirt-jacket, "it's over between me and Martha Cheepoogoot. Finished. *Kaput.*" He threw the shirt at a chair, and stood, fuming, in his sweat-stained T-shirt.

"Do you know how many times I've heard you say that?" she asked him bitterly, brushed back a tear, slipped her purse strap over one exhausted shoulder, and took a step to the door.

Jeremiah and Amanda lay naked but for a tangled sheet, watching television in a room so white they might have been in a hospital but for the furniture and prints — island fauna gambolling about a northern Arcadia — in this motel ten miles from Wasaychigan Hill. "Dorothy, please? Don't leave me."

Jeremiah couldn't quite believe it: Indian showbiz! And Amanda Clear Sky, an actress, a star!

"Yeah," she had yawned, "famous from Muskrat Dam to

Bearskin Lake." The dregs of their breakfast lay scattered on dressers, end-tables, the floor of varnished maple. As the television couple quarrelled on and on, Amanda straddled Jeremiah.

"You are born an artist." She wiggled her tongue in his ear. "It's a responsibility, a duty; you can't run away from it."

Jeremiah shuddered; a worm was inside him. Or a . . . No, no, Champion-Jeremiah, we won't think about that. Not now. Not ever. That door is closed.

Still, he was sure he had just heard skittering. Of what — mice? Bones? And what had he caught a whiff of? What was that mustiness? Mothballs in some long-forgotten holy sacristy? Incense?

"I love . . . ," he giggled instead, for, at that moment, his groin had turned to ice, "I love . . . that part, that part where you go . . . ," he mimicked, badly, " 'I can't, Jake. I can't live with you no more.' " He toppled Amanda and convulsed in the pillow. Amanda was beginning to suspect epilepsy when, sounding like a witch, her television character screamed: "Eeeeeeeeeeeeeeeeha-ha-ha-ha-ha-ha-ha!"

"Take that, bitch." His wife's hair wound around a fist, Jake banged her face against the fridge. "Now get the fuck out of my house." He threw her at the door, in his hand a bleeding clump of hair.

Amanda bit Jeremiah's ear. Half in pain, half in joy, Jeremiah wailed: yes, Father, make me bleed, please, please make me bleed.

"Okay then, bitch," Amanda parodied her soap opera husband, "get the fuck out of this room and get back to your piano." To suffocate the word, and her laugh, Jeremiah slid his tongue into her mouth. But now she was taking his penis into her body.

"If the *Gitche Manitou* ever came down to Earth," he read the card above the bed as, with Amanda's assistance, he thrust and thrust, "He would stay at the Manitowaning Lodge, Manitoulin Island, Ontario." Good for him. Or was it *her?* On television, a door slammed shut.

"Damn." Jake punched a hole through a wall.

"Next week," the telecaster's FM voice slid in. "Can Dorothy Asapap make it on her own? Can Jacob Asapap raise the children on his own? Find out in the next episode of *Tender Is My Heart.* Moosonee-TV, northern Ontario's window on Cree-Ojibway country."

Panting, Amanda reached around Jeremiah's waist and silenced the television with the remote.

"There," she gasped, and wrestled her way from under his weight.

Jeremiah moaned. And fell to the side.

He couldn't get erect. His sex was dead. The very thought made him sick, as with a cancer. Somehow, misogynistic violence – watching it, thinking it – was relief.

"Put it on rewind." He took a cigarette and lay back on the pillow. "Play it again."

PART SIX
Presto con fuoco

FORTY-ONE

"So, you coming home?" though Gabriel tried his best at sounding cold, even angry — thank God telephones transmitted sound, not sight — his performance was not quite convincing. For, naked as the day, he lay luxuriating in black satin sheets, his lower limbs entangled in some unseen task. His pleasure in the posture, in fact, was making conversation increasingly difficult. From some source equally invisible, Sarah Vaughan's honeyed alto crooned of sirens and madness.

Three hundred miles north of the rose-hued bedroom, Jeremiah stood huddled in a telephone booth, fending off a hangover so acute it was victory just to be propped upright. "I'm north of the island somewhere, outskirts of . . . Sudbury, I think."

"By land and water," Gabriel stated with machine-like

precision despite virtually surging with joy, "it'll take you nine hours." At his waist, his fingers sank into a head of golden curls. "By land alone, it'll only take five."

"Forget the ferry. I barely have enough for gas."

"Then I'll see you tonight." And see, Gabriel thrilled at the prospect, what revenge I dream up for your treachery.

Trying to keep his breakfast down, Jeremiah gulped his way back to the car. Furious with him for his recent bout of cowardice, of fraternal irresponsibility, the little yellow Beetle had not said a word to him all morning, not in Cree, not in English.

Gabriel set the telephone down, flexed his thighs, and, distractedly, gazed at the opposite wall. Zebra-striped by noonlight through horizontal blinds, the photographs of Gregory Newman in his salad days — as prince, as hero, as danseur noble — looked glamorous enough, if somewhat vintage. But they were boisterously upstaged. For there atop the oak armoire, applauded by the masses, fêted by a queen, beamed the champion of the world. Gabriel closed his eyes and let the wave sweep him off.

From the folds of black satin, like a loon from a lake, the golden head reared, lips overflowing.

In a chamber of mirrors — another church made redundant by the death of faith — Gabriel sat with legs splayed across the hardwood floor, stretching his tendons, massaging his feet, garbed in the habit of his calling: slippers, tights, legwarmers, sweat-stained T-shirt. In crumpled shirt and jeans, Jeremiah sat slumped at a creaky grand piano, the keyboard as silent as a tomb.

"Go on." Gabriel had to work at his prodigal brother. "Play something." Through his hangover, Jeremiah unenthusiastically picked out a five-finger run – up, down. But hey! The damned thing was in tune.

"Yeah, right," he feigned disgust. "The fingers are gone." In a silence this large, with only Gabriel watching, sitting like this felt eerily natural. "Gone, gone, gone. Forget it." Like a house one sees for the first time since childhood, the keyboard invited, enticed, but belonged to others now.

"Bullshit," Gabriel fired back. "You haven't touched a fish crate in fifteen years."

"What is this? Penance?"

"Yes. For running like a rat from those spineless fag-bashers? Yes. Play!"

Jeremiah began, for, indeed, was not the dear brown boy owed amends?

First came his left hand, pounding on its own a steel-hard, unforgiving four-four time, each beat seamlessly connected by triplet sixteenth notes, an accidental toccata. From where? "Ha!" Before he knew it, his other hand had joined, its discords like random gunshots: *bang, bang!*

No less surprised, and tickled bubblegum pink, Gabriel leapt to his feet and started rocking to the pulse – *peeyuk, neesoo, peeyuk* . . . Some spectacular celebration was about to begin, he could feel it in his bones. *"Weeks'chiloowew!"* he yodelled, and catapulted his dancer's frame at space.

As if sculpted from marble, five male dancers came twirling downstage, stomped up to the audience, and twirled back upstage, gull plumes in cellophane flashing from their waists like kilts made of lake spray. At one end of the line, Gabriel Okimasis executed a turn so nimble witnesses swore later that he had outwitted gravity, then snapped into a robot-like march to a circle of blue-white light.

In the crowded semi-darkness, Gregory Newman watched, impressively tanned — an interlude in Mexico, according to the press — but the light in his eyes had lost its spark; a permanent glower had seduced their emerald green.

Teacher of the young, connoisseur of beauty, celebrated artist, he would fool himself no longer. The boy-man on stage was beautiful, in his prime, poetry in motion, a choreographer with promise. But behind the show of innocence and northern piety, what a piece of dirt, a slut, a whore, a slab of meat fucked through every orifice, from Tokyo to Toronto, from Rome to Buenos Aires.

Behind him, a door flew open and closed just as quickly. Amidst a flurry of rustling cloth, hissed apology, feverish breathing, Amanda Clear Sky wedged her way to the only empty seat that she could make out in the darkness.

"Is this the piece by Gabriel Okimasis?" she ventured of her scowling neighbour.

As politely as he could, Gregory shushed her.

"Well, is it?"

"Yes, but you're sitting on my coat."

Partly concealed by a scrim behind the dancers, Jeremiah laboured at a black grand piano. As seamless as thread, his triplet sixteenth notes connected the four-four time of an unrelenting, drum-like bass. How had a casual improvisation grown, in ten months, into a showpiece stomped to by professional dancers, a sonata in four contrasting movements scored, phrased, liberally fermataed? It was quite beyond his grasp. All he knew was that he had to play or his relationship with Gabriel was history, and he'd be back in the alleyways of Winnipeg. And should the collar of his rented black tuxedo choke off his windpipe, so be it; hands on the keyboard, dressed for the casket, he would die a Cree hero's death.

Like a thunderclap, silence struck. Jeremiah leapt from his bench, and with a beaded drumstick pounded at the bass strings of the instrument. The quintet of circling dancers launched into a pentatonic chant, "*Ateek, ateek, astum, astum, yoah, ho-ho!*" And, suddenly, the piano was a pow wow drum propelling a Cree Round Dance with the clangour and dissonance of the twentieth century.

Gabriel knew that his magic had worked, for the audience was speaking to some space inside themselves, some void that needed filling, some depthless sky; and this sky was responding. Through the brothers, as one, and through a chamber as vast as the north, an old man's voice passed. "My son," it sighed, "with these magic weapons, make a new world . . ."

Amidst the storm of clapping, hooting, and shouting, Gabriel stood on stage with his dancers, glowing like the sun, proudly introducing his brother to the world. And at his bidding, the wild-haired pianist, utterly confounded, bowed once, twice. And the house went dark.

FORTY-TWO

"*Ayash oogoosisa, oogoosisa, oogoosisa.*" The sun-filled chamber danced to Jeremiah's Cree.

"*Ayash oogoosisa, oogoosisa . . . ,*" echoed four children's voices, somewhat raggedly.

"Think of it as music," suggested their instructor. "Let it swing. One more time: *Ayash oogoosisa, oogoosisa . . .*"

A dozen Indian children squatted in a circle at the centre of the room, impressively orderly for six- to ten-year-olds. Four of them repeated, better this time.

On the wall, a home-made logo identified the gathering as "The Muskoosis Club of Ontario," a round-faced bear in denim coveralls grinning toothily from the capital *O*. Such was Jeremiah's day job – providing urban Indian children, most from broken homes, with REC: recreation, education, culture.

Jeremiah launched into the next phrase. "Group B.

Peechinook'soo, three, four, *peechinook'soo*, three, four . . . ," clapping as he walked.

Dutiful as soldiers, four Muskoosisuk smiled, clapped, and talked, "*Peechinook'soo* . . . ," as Jeremiah's focus kept returning to one little boy. Because he looked so like Gabriel Okimasis at the age of six? Not exactly, but . . .

"And Group C. Now this one's gotta be sort of moany and spooky, kinda like this," and Jeremiah moaned, "*Peeyatuk, peeyatuk* . . ."

"*Peeyatuk* . . . ," moaned the last four children, then exploded into titters because the goofy little whine reminded of them of ghosts they had known.

"Now, we put it all together." Swinging by his desk, the excited Cree-language revivalist fished a gourd from a drawer. "Groups A, B, C. Ready?" He raised the object — an improvised Brazilian maraca — and shook it with a vengeance, the rattle that resulted bossa nova crossed artfully with samba.

"*Ayash oogoosisa, oogoosisa, oogoosisa* . . ." went the first four children, "*Peechinook'soo* three, four, *peechinook'soo* . . ." went the second, while the last quartet moaned, "*Peeyatuk.*" Like a priest sprinkling holy water, Jeremiah rattled the maraca, counted out the beat — "One, two, one, two." Cree rap with a Latin stamp? The patent was theirs.

"So what you're saying, people, is this," Jeremiah brought the music to a close. "Group A, 'The Son of Ayash,' over and over. Group B, 'is approaching, three, four,' over and over. Group C," and he moaned like a ghost, " 'Be careful, be careful.' Our hero, the Son of Ayash, has to be careful, for he is entering the dark place of the human soul where he will meet evil creatures like," he shook the maraca one last time, "the Weetigo. Questions?" But the undersized Natives were restless. "Jenny! Cynthia!" Jeremiah was sounding unpleasantly like a school marm, "Puh-leeze!"

"But Willie has a question, question, question," a pretty little echo circulated. "But he's too shy, shy, shy, shy." Willie Joe Kayash, whose home was a shelter for battered women and whose father was nonexistent. Willie Joe Kayash, the lad who reminded Jeremiah of Gabriel as a child.

It took some ancient Okimasis diplomacy but, eventually, Willie Joe spoke. "What . . . what . . . ," his mouth a little red cherry, ripe for the plucking. "What's . . . what's a . . . a Weetigo?" How fresh children smelled. You could take them in your hands, put them in your mouth, swallow them whole.

"A Weetigo is a monster who eats little boys," said Jeremiah, "like you." And he dismissed the assembly.

When the room was empty, Willie Joe skipped back in and jumped on Jeremiah, the rope-like arms wrapped around his waist, the hot face buried in his groin.

"A Weetigo ate me," the child mumbled into the faded blue denim. And then bit. Up Jeremiah's spine shot a needle longer than an arm. In a panic, he disengaged himself and squatted, his eyes inches from the six-year-old's. He had a raging hard-on.

"What do you mean, Willie Joe?"

Willie Joe said nothing, but, like a clandestine lover, kissed Jeremiah, square across the lips, then went skipping out: "Ayash oogoosisa, oogoosisa . . ."

Into a vortex screaming with monsters Jeremiah stumbled, clawed hands reaching for his testicles, wet tongues burrowing past his lips, his orifices pried, torn, shredded. One minute, no more, and he made it to the director's office.

"The Friendship Centre has begun the process, yes," the Mohawk gentleman behind the desk explained, "whereby the perpetrator — stepfather to the child — is being charged, yes, and, hopefully, yes, he will be jailed, yes."

For Jeremiah, jail was nowhere near enough.

FORTY-THREE

*L*ike a bear with a honeypot, Jeremiah sat hunched at a type-writer, glaring at the page in its steel-trap jaw. If it wasn't for the hum and the stop-start tap of the ageing IBM Selectric, the Muskoosis Clubroom would have been stone silent.

He snarled and tore the sheet of paper out. So disgusted was he for taking up Amanda's challenge — "Write me a role and I'll move to Toronto" — that leaping out the window looked attractive when he remembered that the Native Friendship Centre was only four floors high, and he was on the third.

Yes, he had written a spot of music — freak accident though that may have been — interspersed with words he dared to claim were poetry, if in Cree. And, yes, the work had been successful, on a very modest scale. But did that make him a dramatist? And in English, that humourless tongue?

"*Atimootagay!*" he banged out each letter and, in glum despair, scowled at the slush-bound street below.

And suddenly, Mistik Lake lapped rhythmically, July was at its peak, and arctic terns were clucking from their holding patterns high overhead — "*click*, Jeremiah, *click, click*" — telling the Cree ex-pianist of their holiday this January past in far Antarctica, where penguins threw formal-dress receptions that were the envy of the world.

And Jeremiah was nine, Gabriel six, the brothers sitting at the stern of their father's blue canoe. Squeezed into the seat — planks nailed hastily together — they rowed the narrow, pointed vessel in reverse as, from the prow, their father cast his silver net into the cold, dark waves.

"So, *Ayash oogoosisa*," said Abraham Okimasis as he wove sun diamonds with water and webs of nylon, "*eehee, Ayash oogoosisa* had to go out into the world at a very young age . . ."

A suitcase in one hand, his father's portrait in the other, Gabriel stood at the threshold of an empty living room. Lit like a rooming house, its plaster barely hung. And the smell of mothballs, mould, even stale urine, though subtle, still penetrated. Cardboard boxes spilling over with his life sat scattered at his feet.

Pensively, he set the suitcase down. He could still hear Gregory: "If you didn't do so much running around, you wouldn't get sick so often."

Cracked down the middle, a mirror sliced his image in two; he had one eye, in the centre of his forehead. He pawed at a cobweb, cleared the dust away, and peered into the glass.

The sheen of youth was fading. He was attractive, not

exquisite, not the way he once had been. What's this? The blemish on his neck still there? After two weeks?

Gabriel had had the flu twice this year, so this might be the third, but was anyone immune at this time of the year?

Still, Gregory's voice bled through: "Where did you go after the preview last night? Come on, Gabriel. Production meetings don't go to 3:00 A.M. Where do you go after the show – in New York, Amsterdam, Vancouver? How many people come by the house whenever I'm out for even half an hour? Do you think I have no nose? That I can't smell bedsheets, sweat?"

From one side of his "Holy Trinity" – the photos of his brother, his best friend, his surrogate son – Jeremiah glanced at the clock in the rusted old stove of his rooming house. Four A.M. He yawned, stretched, and vowed that he would work until the sun came up.

"Mother (to Son):" afraid the old typewriter would crumble and die if he struck it too hard, he picked at the letters gingerly, "Here, the weapons you will need: a spear, an axe, a fox's pelt."

FORTY-FOUR

"Got this feelin', burnin' inside me; got this feelin'," the wild-haired tenor snarled into the microphone. Then, chillingly, his voice swooped sky high, "And I don't know oh what to do, oh what to do."

Behind him, three black-shirted men stroked impassively at drums, bass, and keyboard while their soloist's half-closed eyes hung fixed . . . on what? Or who? wondered Gabriel. Sitting at a small round table, sipping at a beer, waiting anxiously for Jeremiah, he decided the singer could do with a more expressive body, looser at the hips, not so jerky. But this Robin Beatty, as the posters proclaimed his name to be, was looking at him, Gabriel was certain. Did that little shudder at the base of his spine not tell him so? His microphone so hot Gabriel half-expected it to melt, Robin swooped from a growl to a wail, "Every time I look into your eye-eye-eyes . . ."

Jeremiah popped his head through the black velvet curtain over the club's back wall and assessed the territory.

"Don't go away," barked the singer. "We'll be right back."

"What's this?" asked Gabriel, looking at the tattered manila envelope Jeremiah had plunked beside his beer.

"Open it," said Jeremiah, trying to contain his excitement.

Out came a sheaf of paper the thickness of a score.

"'Ulysses Thunderchild'?" Gabriel read. "'A play by Jerem . . .'"

"Well? You gonna have a peek?"

Gabriel turned a page.

" 'Remember, my son, the human soul is filled with danger, that you will meet evil men . . .' " His voice faded but his reading went on. Time passed.

"You . . . ," Jeremiah squirmed like a five-year-old, "don't think it's . . . any good?"

Robin Beatty ambled by. "Hi," the lanky jazz singer threw the greeting at Gabriel like a frisbee and Gabriel threw it back. His eyes followed Robin to the stage.

"Son of Ayash." Jeremiah tapped the script. "Closest thing the Cree have to their own Ulysses. Except I've given it this . . . modern twist, shall we say."

"Such as?" Gabriel asked, barely concentrating.

"Well," said Jeremiah cavalierly, "if James Joyce can do 'one day in the life of an Irishman in Dublin, 1903,' why can't I do 'one day in the life of a Cree man in Toronto, 1984'?"

Suspecting madness, Gabriel stared at Jeremiah, swallowed.

"You're right. Someone's gotta do it." His gaze slid back to Robin, beyond Jeremiah. "But why the modern twist?"

"Because I want my *Muskoosisuk* to get it. Could we relate to Dick and Jane and that damned dog Spot when we were kids? No. Ever wonder why the school dropout rate for Native people – ?"

"Okay, okay, I wasn't asking for a dissertation."

"And I want you . . . to direct it." There.

"Direct it?" spluttered Gabriel. "I'm a choreographer, not a . . ."

"An out-of-work choreographer."

"Are you kidding?" Jeremiah chattered at a train-weary Amanda. "No theatre in town would touch it." Leaving Union Station a hulking silhouette, the taxi rammed through the evening rush respectful of neither life, death, nor the law. " 'Your script?' this one guy said. 'No conflict. It's not a play.' " Still, he suspected that his liberal sprinklings of Cree might have thrown off its readers.

"Fools," sniffed Amanda. "They'll be sorry."

"Especially since I've snagged the best damned actress in the soaps."

"Second-best. Joan Collins, she's the first best."

"Remember, my son," Amanda advised in a voice not her own, "the way into the underworld of the human spirit is filled with danger, that you will meet evil men." She stood on the altar of yet another dead church mouthing lines with the passion of a doorknob.

"You say you are not the Son of Ayash?" a barrel-chested Cree man asked of Gabriel.

"Fuck," cursed the Weetigo, aka Bobby Peegatee of Pask'sigeepathi, Saskatchewan, when the top page of his script ripped in half.

"No," Gabriel squinted at his script, "I am not the Son of Ayash."

"No matter, *noos'sim*. You must be hungry after such a long, hard journey."

"Take this magic spear, this axe, this fox's pelt," said the mother, Amanda, with slightly stooped shoulders, "for you will have to defend yourself. I'm sorry." Amanda's voice splintered from the mother's. "I can't go on."

"What's the problem?" asked Gabriel.

"These lines, they're so . . . they're unplayable." She shimmied off the altar. "I can't do a thing with them."

"Why not?" asked Jeremiah, squirming from the sweat in the crevasse of his buttocks. "Why are they . . . unplayable?"

"They're wooden. There's no human inside this character."

"But there is," Jeremiah whined.

"Jeremiah, you're trying to write a realistic play from a story that's just not realistic."

"And what, pray tell, is this story all about?"

"Magic."

Magic? What did she want, a bunny pulled from a hat, a woman sawed in half, water turned into wine?

Finally, all diplomacy, sympathy, and tenderness, Gabriel spoke up. "I think what she means, Jeremiah, is that it's all up here –" he tapped his forehead, "when it should be down here –" he pointed to his groin. What the hell. "It's all head, Jeremiah, all head and no gut. Watch."

Before Jeremiah could pull himself back together, the actors were shouting, wailing, and snarling as, like ping pong balls, they hurled themselves across the sun-splashed space, so in the grip of improvisation they had eyes like demons.

"Yes!" Gabriel flailed his arms like an orchestral conductor fencing with an agitato. "Fill that space. Feel it with the tips of your fingers, your forehead, the soles of your feet, your toes, your groin."

Jeremiah banged at the piano – dissonance like shards of steel – though he had no idea why. "What are you doing?" he yelled at his brother.

"Play!" Gabriel screamed back. "Just play!"

"Stick to that goddamn piano" – Amanda lunged at him with teeth bared, spit flying – "where you belong!"

Who the hell did the bitch think she was? Jeremiah clawed at the keyboard, tidal waves of red smashing at his eyeballs. "*Aiaiaiaiaiaiaiaiayash oogoosisa, oogoosisa . . .*" Shooting to the ceiling, the wail dove, resurfacing as samba-metered hisses. And one by one, the company fell in with the chant, a dance, a Cree rite of sacrifice, swirling like blood around the altar and bouncing off the bass of the piano like, yes, magic.

FORTY-FIVE

*J*eremiah's "Barcarolle Ulysses Thunderchild" gently rocked as the blood rose slowly in the Plexiglas syringe. Through his earphones, Gabriel listened and envisioned, as Jeremiah had suggested, their father's blue canoe adrift, the fisherman a Cree-Venetian gondolier. Except that Mistik Lake was filled not with water but with fresh human blood. The poker-faced technician removed the needle and pressed a bandage over Gabriel's bared forearm.

Gabriel stepped from the examining room into the reception area where three young men in jeans and Reeboks flipped through magazines. A steely alto rang, "Number 9722," to which summons one of them rose.

By the exit, Gabriel stopped at a rack of pamphlets on various diseases, but these he ignored, for what attracted him was the cover photo on the tabloid next to them. As he clattered down the stairs, he tore through the pages.

"When Robin Beatty was born," the feature article led, "in North Vancouver, he claims the first words he spoke were 'da-da-da,' which is why scat-singing comes so naturally." So smitten with the text was Gabriel that, once on the sidewalk, he tripped over a poodle and fell against its master, a man squished like pâté into motorcycle leather. Finding his assailant not uncomely, the leather man's knees flagged, his eyes went glassy, his thick throat purred like an engine.

Behind the clinic, the leather man and Gabriel sequestered themselves. There, employing all the trickery he had acquired in Paris, Copenhagen, Sydney, Tokyo, Gabriel laboured at the great knot of tissue, all while the pretty white poodle watched philosophically. And not until twenty after ten did he come marching out the alleyway, his jeans pocket crackling with a new fifty-dollar bill — not the lighting budget for "Ulysses Thunderchild," but enough for a costume. Besides, late for rehearsal, he had no time for tortured moralizing, not even for a single *mea culpa*.

"Taxi!"

Nude but for a towel, Gabriel padded down the barely lit corridor, a cryptic little grin here, there a nod, here a glance fraught with meaning. The air was rife with the odour of naked male flesh.

"Oops. Sorry." The young man standing on Gabriel's foot had the smell of fresh summer lemons.

"That's okay," said Gabriel, retying the white terrycloth

around his waist. Why, so suddenly, was his heart doing somersaults and tumbles? "Aren't you Robin Beatty, the famous Canadian rock star?"

The semi-naked singer tossed off a meaty, wet chortle. Slightly crooked teeth, thought Gabriel, a human with flaws, the pattern of his thoughts having always gone askew whenever he was stoned, overtired, or both.

"Tell me," Gabriel blurted, "how do you do the publicity for your band?"

Three hours later, Gabriel had not made a penny, not for the lighting budget, not for actors' salaries. Instead, he and Robin Beatty had tripped out of the Garden Baths, skipped across the boulevard, and gone singing, sliding, and dancing through a park aglitter with moonlight and ice.

In the basement of the Church of St. Paul the Apostle, Gabriel peered into the light of a portable make-up mirror, muttering his lines and, almost viciously, slathering on his make-up. When he arrived at that now familiar blemish on the right side of his neck, he brushed it over with the honey-beige base until the purplish red could pass for a hickey.

Word had trickled out from rehearsal that Flora Jane Bustagut, first-time actress, was a natural, a genius no less. The praise had gone directly to the head of the pretty, petty Ms. Bustagut, who then took great pleasure in torturing Gabriel, in front of cast and crew — "Ha-ha, can't act, ha-ha, can't act" — followed by the announcement that she intended to become the biggest star the Indian nations had ever known. The rage still clawed at Gabriel: this nasty little cockroach prancing around thinking she is already Marilyn Monroe. Why the fuck didn't she just move back to her fish camp in Eeweecheegisit, Quebec?

American Beauty rose in hand, Robin Beatty floated into Gabriel's mirror. The neophyte actor shot his reflection a nervous smile, then went back to his ministrations.

"Just came to wish you last-minute good luck."

"Thanks." Gabriel worked his eyebrow pencil furiously. He couldn't look at Robin. Not at the moment.

"You look . . ." Robin paused: Gabriel Okimasis made up like . . . like a Cree Dionysus. "Beautiful." Gabriel bent over to lace on a moccasin. "Better leave you to your opening night." Robin reached for Gabriel's chin and forced it gently up. Ardently, Gabriel prayed to God in His Kingdom that Robin could not read eyes like he did his music. "What's the matter, babe?"

What was Gabriel to answer? The show, I'm scared shitless of the show, I'm a dancer and a choreographer, not a director, much less a goddamn actor? Or that, of all the days on Earth, how could I have chosen this day to go back to the clinic for the results?

Mouths move, words take flight. But Gabriel's demeanour said it all too clearly.

The two held each other so tightly their bones cracked. Puzzled as puppies, Flora Jane Bustagut, Anne Terabust, and

Bobby Peegatee looked on from a distance as Gabriel choked back a cry. His tongue grazing Robin's earlobe, he whispered, "Don't . . . please don't . . . tell Jeremiah."

" 'Respected Cree dancer-choreographer Gabriel Okimasis,' " read Amanda, " 'doing his first turn as actor and director, is surely the most beautiful man who ever walked the earth.' Blah, blah . . . wait a minute. Here. 'But the cannibal spirit shedding his costume at death, revealing a priest's cassock, confuses the viewer. The image comes from nowhere. And goes nowhere.' "

"What's she talking about?" Jeremiah growled.

"You didn't say it loud enough, Jeremiah," said Gabriel.

"Didn't say what loud enough?"

Jeremiah tried to ask again. But, finally, his memory opened the padlocked doors.

"Silent night," sang a crystalline soprano. To Champion Okimasis, it was the earth, serenading him. "Holy night . . ."

Beyond the aria, he could hear the endless stands of spruce groaning within their shrouds of snow, the air so clean it sparkled: silver, then rose, then mauve. Four-year-old Champion knelt at the front of his father's dogsled. He hung on to the canvas siding with one hand and, with the other, waved a miniature whip, chiming, "*Mush*, Tiger-Tiger, *mush, mush!*" The eight grey huskies were flying through the sky, past the sun, to the heaven of Champion's way of thinking. The trail curved unpredictably; who knew what surprises lay around the next bend, which creature might be feeding on spruce cones or pine needles, a rabbit, a weasel, five ptarmigans fluttering off in their winter coats of Holy Ghost white?

Behind him, his father brandished his moose-hide whip – "*Mush*, Tiger-Tiger!" – below, his mother, her back against the *kareewalatic*. Inside her goose-down sleeping robe, Gabriel lay suckling at her breast. Jeremiah laughed.

What's this? A face? Yes. In the forest and larger, blotting out the trotting dogs. Champion closed his eyes, hoping it would go away. But when he opened them again, the old man was still glaring. At him. Why did he look so angry, so embittered, so dreadfully unhappy?

Gradually, against the old man's mouth, an arctic fox appeared. The pretty white creature wore a sequined gown of white satin, gloves to her elbows, white wings whirring. And she was singing, not just to anybody but to him, the little Cree accordion player: "Holy infant so tender and mild." Such pouty red lips.

"Jeremiah," said God the Father from behind the singing lady fox, "Jeremiah, get out of bed." Thunder? In December? "Come with me."

The fox – *maggeesees* – was gone. Sleepily, Champion-Jeremiah slid out of bed.

By the light of a moon full to bursting, the now eight-year-old floated down an aisle lined with small white beds, cradles filled with sleeping brown children. Out a door, and up and down corridors, the long black robe swaying like a curtain, smelling of cigar smoke, incense, sacramental wine.

By the puffy amchair of pitch-black leather, Father Roland Lafleur, oblate of Mary Immaculate, unbuttoned his cassock, unzipped his trousers. So white, thought Champion-Jeremiah, so big. Black and white hair all around the base, like . . . a mushroom on a cushion of reindeer moss.

Now he remembers the holy man inside him, the lining of his rectum being torn, the pumping and pumping and pumping, cigar breath billowing somewhere above his cold shaved head.

What had he done? Whatever it was, he promised that, from now on, he would say the prayer in English only: "Our Father, who art in Heaven, hallowed be thy name. And make me bleed. Please, Father, please, make me bleed."

Back in bed, it was too dark to see what kind of chocolate bar it was. Sweet Marie? Coffee Crisp? Mr. Big?

FORTY-SIX

" 'What reason? God! Great Spirit! What reason?' "
Crouched against the wall behind his mother, Jeremiah
scrawled on the pad with such force the page tore down the
middle. Never mind. He would write out the scene again.
Besides, once the caribou hunter Migisoo was shrieking at the
wind, what would he say next?

"My sons think I threw away their money on my new TV,"
Mariesis confided to her guests, eight Elders playing poker
on the floor and puffing so much smoke that the living room
looked like hell. "Goddamn son-of-a-bitch!" she cursed. "I
get this fucking three one more time and I throw you pigs out
of my house."

"You should have taken someone to Smallwood Lake with
you," Jeremiah countered, "to help you read the labels when
you shopped." The hunter Migisoo collapsed beside the large
grey rock where his wife, Sagweesoo, lay dying of starvation.

288

"*Astum, doos, astum, doos,*" prayed Kookoos Cook, for if the deuce didn't come to him, he stood to lose his lead dog, Socks, to the vile eighty-two-year-old Jane Kaka McCrae.

Thrilled that she could visit her sister-in-law openly now that her self-righteous, pig-headed brother was six feet under, Black-eyed Susan Magipom said, "She can read."

"Not English, she can't," said Jeremiah. "All she knows in English are 'tank you' and 'fuckin' bullshit.' "

Mariesis tossed in three of her five cards. "Gimme three good ones, goddamnit," she said, wishing she could knock the solitary crusted black tooth out of the dealer's gaping mouth. "I may not be able to see my sons on my new TV," Mariesis adjusted the Al Capone fedora over her still-black braids, "but it cooks my goose in just thirty minutes, fuckin' bullshit, not the cards I wanted!"

Behind the 115-year-old Little Seagull Ovary, who had been decorated by the Governor-General for her career as midwife of the century, Mariesis's new microwave oven announced that the twenty-pound goose Choggylut McDermott and his wife, Two-Room, had shot on both sides was ready to be eaten.

"Tank you," said Mariesis to the third round of betting. She quelled her heaving bosom with a palm, for in her hand now bristled two aces and a deuce. Suddenly, she felt the Jesus on the rosary she used as a necklace. "Jeremiah," she asked, "do you still pray?"

My people are starving, Migisoo howled to the wind, because the caribou have not come. And you come here to tell me some stupid stupid bullshit about there being a reason?

"If you ever forgot God," Mariesis prayed to Christ on his cross that her foes be destroyed by monstrous hands, "if you ever forgot what those priests taught you at that school, it would kill your father. I tell you, he would just die."

"*Neee*," sneered the ninety-year-old Annie Moostoos, "isn't he dead already?" Finished dealing, she raked up her hand, deftly changed two for two, and sequestered her one tooth behind closed, though quivering, lips.

"Answer me," Mariesis twisted around to glare at her son, "do you and Gabriel still take Holy Communion?"

The only sound was the slash of Jeremiah's pen, the snap of cards, and the whetting of cash-hungry tongues, for the pot had hit two thousand dollars, a hunting rifle, and a dog named Socks, though the mutt was tied to a post behind Kookoos Cook's pink bungalow, unaware that she might have to relocate, tonight, to the most slovenly dive in Eemanapiteepitat.

"Well?" Mariesis was about to insist when, with a great gust of halitosis, Jane Kaka threw her cards on the quilt and trumpeted, "Ta-da!" For there before eight pairs of disbelieving, rheumy eyes lay a Jack and four mighty Kings.

Kookoos Cook cursed Jane Kaka with such blasphemy that Father Bouchard would have turned in his grave, except that "the hoary old bag" was still alive, as Black-eyed Susan had whispered to her nephew at the airport.

In the faded picture on the shelf across from Jeremiah, the Fur Queen kissed world champion Abraham Okimasis. And winked. On his pad, Jeremiah carved a line under the words: "Scene Four: 1860. The first missionary arrives on Mistik Lake."

FORTY-SEVEN

$\mathcal{A}$ styrofoam cup in one hand, a small, plastic vial in the other, Gabriel stood, running cold tap water and gazing at his image in the mirror, when Jeremiah entered. The red-and-yellow capsules danced across the floor.

"Need help with those?" asked Jeremiah, lowering to a squat.

"No."

To Jeremiah, it sounded like a bark. He noted that Gabriel was still soaked with sweat from the rehearsal just finished.

"I'll be fine. Go ahead, do your business."

Jeremiah gathered up a runaway capsule and, mystified, held it up to Gabriel. Gabriel took the offering, but his thoughts were in tatters.

How to explain pentamidine, let alone *Pneumocystis carinii*, that rare pneumonia one got only when something had kicked the hell out of one's natural immunities? How to explain the virus in his bloodstream, let alone how he had come by it? Please, brother dear, please don't ask.

With a mouthful of water, the younger brother downed a capsule.

From the urinal, Jeremiah watched Gabriel cover his face with the crumpled paper towels.

"What are those pills?"

A pause.

"Vitamins. My . . . cold feels like it's . . . coming back." As he looked at Jeremiah, a wave of love overcame him. "Come on. Walk you to the subway."

In the three-hundred-seat Belmont Theatre, a gale lashed the tundra with merciless might. And through its howl, a woman's moaning echoed. "For for for everything everything, Migisoo, Migisoo, the caribou hunter hunter hunter, there is a reason reason reason reason-son-son-son . . ."

Weakened to near death by the famine, Migisoo was thrown by the tempest against a large grey rock. Was the wind speaking? Or had he simply gone mad? Should he reply? Please, God, Migisoo prayed in silence, let ten thousand caribou stampede across this moss-covered meadow, like thunder in July, like they used to in the days of my youth. But no caribou came, just the wind admonishing.

"My people are starving," he finally screamed back, "because the caribou have not come. And you come here to tell me some stupid stupid bullshit about there being a reason?" Then the wind was gone, the only sound left his hysterical sobbing.

Done with waving Gabriel's length of white muslin – formerly a Milky Way tablecloth, now a northern Manitoba blizzard – two sprightly assistants ducked beneath the floor.

Down the aisle, the Weetigo oozed, black, slime-coated, formless.

"Come to me, Migisoo," the flesh devourer hissed through ten loudspeakers, "I've been waiting for you." The voice like water dripping in a cavern.

"Weetigo!" spat Migisoo. "You've already taken five children from us. Haven't you feasted on enough human flesh while we lie here with nothing but our tongues to chew on? Get away from us, get away, *awus!*"

The percussionist in the wings attacked his drum kit as Migisoo and the Weetigo leapt into their dance of hate.

Gabriel dodged the monster with nimble-footed grace, though as the dying Migisoo he stumbled here, tripped there, even fell. Until it looked dead certain that the struggle would be lost. Suddenly, the creature leapt into the hunter's mouth. And was gone.

"Another Hit for the Okimasis Brothers!" screamed the headline, a photograph of Gabriel dancing with the Weetigo gracing the review. Through his rasping, Gabriel could hear the applause, like the north wind lashing the caribou hunter.

The paper sat open on a chair by the examining table, Gabriel sucking at the nozzle of a respirator. The reason?

Pneumocystis carinii protozoa were filling up the air sacs of his lungs one by one, choking them to death. "Your T-cell count is its lowest ever," the ear-ringed doctor explained. "And this role you're performing, for . . . how much longer?" The patient signalled "ten" as the doctor adjusted the machine. "Ten more weeks. You'll have to be extra careful. Conserve your energy, no alcohol, no drugs." He popped the nozzle out. "But folks in your position have gone on to lead full lives for a dozen, fifteen years. It's all in the attitude.

"Now about this respirator. Twice a day, more if you feel that shortness of breath coming on."

On the street, Gabriel stopped for a light. A businessman ambled by, did a double-take, then stopped, apparently to revel in the view. The old charge shot up Gabriel's vertebrae, then back down to his groin.

Ten minutes later, he emerged from the alleyway behind the clinic, respirator in hand like a briefcase, a hundred bucks tucked away.

Gabriel found himself peering in his dressing-room mirror, studying his tongue, his throat, his palate. Yes indeedy, lead-like markings everywhere. Thrush. What next? Leukemia? Cancer of the rectum?

Jeremiah found himself at centre stage nervously facing an overheated audience. "Chachagathoo, the Shaman," a show so controversial that the cardinal of Toronto had snuck into the show dressed as a Rosedale matron, so Indian rumour rabidly insisted, had just been given the award of the theatre season.

Soaked in sweat, his head in a wet towel, Gabriel sat slumped into a chair. Behind him, Jeremiah paced, butting out cigarette after cigarette on the dressing-room table.

"It's not fair to Mom," he pleaded, "not in a situation as serious as this."

"How do you say AIDS in Cree, huh? Tell me, what's the word for HIV?"

"Gabriel, please? I'll pay her way down, I'll –"

"Not now, Jeremiah, please." Gabriel started crying. "My head hurts."

"Silent night," sang a woman. To Gabriel, it was the earth, serenading him. "Holy night . . ."

Beyond the aria, he could hear the spruce trees groaning from the snow, the air so clean it sparkled. In his father's dogsled, four-year-old Gabriel Okimasis knelt alone at the front, for Champion was away at school. One hand hanging on to the canvas siding, he waved a tiny whip – "*Mush*, Tiger-Tiger!" The eight grey huskies were flying through the sky, to God. The trail curved; who knew what surprises lay around the next bend, a rabbit, a weasel, five ptarmigans all Holy Ghost white?

Behind him stood his father, hand to handlebar, brandishing his moose-hide whip, below him his mother, her back against the *kareewalatic*, covered by her goose-down sleeping robe from the neck down.

What's this? A face? Yes. In the forest, and part of it, and larger, blotting out the trotting dogs. Gabriel closed his eyes. But when he opened them again, the old man was glaring at him. Why did God look so angry, so embittered, so dreadfully unhappy?

An arctic fox appeared, in sequined gown of white satin, gloves to her elbows, wings whirring. And she was singing: "Holy infant so tender and mild." Such pouty red lips.

"Gabriel," said God the Father from behind the singing lady fox, "Gabriel, get out of bed."

"No," moaned Gabriel in his sleep, "no, please, no." He started screaming. And thrashing. "Get away, get away, get away, you've already taken five children."

"Gabriel!" shouted Jeremiah. "You're dreaming."

"Haven't you feasted on enough human flesh?" Punching and punching, Gabriel all but broke Jeremiah's nose.

"Shut up!" Jeremiah sobbed. His face smeared bloody, he clawed at Gabriel's arms. "Gabriel, shut up!"

FORTY-EIGHT

"Who do you think met Dad? On . . . the other side?" Gabriel's soft voice drifted through the white-walled room. "Jesus? Or Weesageechak?" Reclined on pillows, the hunter's youngest son gazed at the portrait of the Fur Queen kissing his father, the hand that held the photo connected by tubes to plastic-bagged fluids. Jeremiah stood at the window, scowling at the evening traffic seven floors below.

"The Trickster, of course," Gabriel finally answered himself, "Weesageechak for sure. The clown who bridges humanity and God – a God who laughs, a God who's here, not for guilt, not for suffering, but for a good time. Except, this time, the Trickster representing God as a woman, a goddess in fur. Like in this picture. I've always thought that, ever since we were little kids. I mean, if Native languages have no gender, then why should we? And why, for that matter, should God?"

"Father Lafleur would send you straight to hell for saying that."

"When I die, I want Mom to be allowed her Catholic mumbo-jumbo. But I do not want priests anywhere near my bed. Do you hear me?"

"As if she would agree to such a thing," said Jeremiah bitterly.

"If she doesn't, I will not see her."

In the Air Canada jet, seventy-six-year-old Mariesis Okimasis sat hunched against a window looking at the clouds below, where the child Gabriel used to tell her God lived. In her purse, inside a snuff tin, a gift: Annie Moostoos's single tooth, knocked out, at last, by the inhumanly tall Magimay Cutthroat in a vicious poker game. "Give it to my godson," the now toothless crone had wept. "It will help him live past ninety, just like me."

In her bedroom at Wasaychigan Hill, Ann-Adele Ghostrider placed her white ermine cape in a small brown suitcase and closed its cover. Outside her window, the wind was rising and snow was blowing. Would she get there in time?

The Weetigo came at Gabriel with its tongue lolling, its claws reaching for his groin.

"Haven't you feasted on enough human flesh while we sit here with nothing but our tongues to chew on?" hissed Gabriel. But the cannibal spirit now had the face of Father

Roland Lafleur. Gabriel crept towards the holy man. "But I haven't eaten meat in weeks, my dear Sagweesoo," Gabriel whined, and flicked his tongue at the old priest's groin. "Don't move away."

The creature lunged at Gabriel, brandishing a crucifix.

"Get away from me," Gabriel thrashed. "Get away, *awus!*"

The door squeaked open. In shuffled an exhausted Mariesis Okimasis, Jeremiah and Amanda behind her. A string of emerald-green rosary beads wound in her hands, Mariesis took one look at her son and rushed to his bed. "*Nigoosis, nigoosis, nigoosis . . .*"

Mariesis's wrinkled hand placed the rosary on Gabriel's chest, the naked, silver Jesus glinting in the candle light, writhing in pain.

Jeremiah helped Gabriel extract a pill from a wax paper cup. Gabriel's face was wan, hollow, a damp white towel wound around his head.

"Morphine," said Jeremiah, in English, as Gabriel downed the tablet with a mouthful of water. "What's it like?"

"Dulls the pain," replied Gabriel, "for a while." He looked at Jeremiah. "Are you . . . scared? That I might die?"

Jeremiah blinked. What should he say? Yes? No? Sometimes? Finally, he pulled his eyes away, threw his hands up to his mouth, and cried; yes, he was scared. He was scared shitless that he was about to lose his brother.

"*Katha matoo,*" said Gabriel softly. "Please?"

"I . . . I promised Mom and Dad I'd take care of you. And I fucked it up. Fucked it up completely."

"Remember that day the caribou almost ran us over?" Gabriel smiled. "And you dragged me up that rock? Saved my life. But I'm not a child any more, Jeremiah. Haven't been for a long time. There is nothing you could have done about this. What I did, I did on my own. Don't mourn me. Be joyful."

"Jeremiah, you've got to get a priest," Mariesis urged, in Cree, over her older son's shoulder. Jeremiah said nothing. "If your brother doesn't get his last rites . . ." Mariesis was crying now.

"Mom!"

"His soul will go to hell, *tapwee!*"

"Okay, okay, okay." Jeremiah's Cree was like machine-gun fire. "We'll get him a priest! We'll get him a priest!"

FORTY-NINE

"There's No Business Like Show Business," read Gabriel's birthday card across the dressing-room mirror. Certain he had just catapulted through a time warp of five hundred years, Jeremiah butted out a cigarette, lit another. Everything was as Gabriel had left it: the eyebrow pencils, the make-up — magic weapons of a shaman, a weaver of spells. Only the portrait of their father was gone.

The door behind him opened, and Amanda's reflection glided into the mirror.

"Granny's gonna be late," she said softly. "Snowstorm. She's doing what she can."

"My brother is dying, and here I am playing dress-up in some stupid fucking sandbox."

Outside the Belmont Theatre, crowds jostled for admission to the closing night of "Chachagathoo, the Shaman."

Eight grey huskies crossed the tundra, Gabriel Okimasis driving them as fast as they could go. He could see, or thought he could, the finish line a mile ahead. What he could also see, however, was other mushers leading him, three, perhaps even four. Which meant forty others somewhere to the rear of him. But what did these forty matter? What mattered was these three or four ahead of him. What mattered was he was not leading.

And he was so tired, his dogs beyond tired, so tired they would have collapsed, right there, if he was to relent.

"Mush!" was the only word left that could feed them, dogs and master both, with the will to travel on.

Below the Fur Queen portrait, Mariesis's rosary lay entwined in Gabriel's fingers. Ann-Adele Ghostrider's old, brown hand removed the beads and replaced them with an eagle feather.

"Mush, Tiger-Tiger!" Gabriel moaned feebly.

About to throw the rosary into the trash can, she hung it, instead, on a Ken doll sporting cowboy hat and white-tasselled skirt. The medicine woman lit a braid of sweetgrass and washed the patient in its smoke. Her prayer now a low chant, she stood at the foot of the bed as Robin Beatty, weeping, held his lover's head gently in his arms.

Strength. Willpower. Endurance. Did he have enough? Did he have any? Did his dogs?

"Mush!" Gabriel cried to his lead dog, "Faster, Tiger-Tiger, mush!"

And then a darkness came upon him, creeping up behind him from the depths of the roaring in his ears. And at the distant end of this new darkness appeared the small, flickering flame. Growing larger with each ripple, the white flame began to hum, a note so pure human ears could never have been meant to hear it. Then the presence took on outline — the caribou hunter could discern a cape, fold after fold of white fur.

The smoke detector shrieked. Then an alarm down the hall started ringing. And another and another. Until the entire institution reverberated. Fire trucks pulled up, then ambulances.

"Open zat door!" What now, raved Jeremiah, the army? He poked his nose out. And came face to face with a towering blonde nurse.

"Vat is zat schmell?"

"Sweetgrass. A sacred herb," Jeremiah tried to explain, "like incense for Catholics!" He slammed the door, just as Mariesis came teetering around the corner with an ancient priest in tow. As hospital staff evacuated patient beds, the caribou hunter's wife charged up to the door and confronted Amanda.

"Open up," she barked, in Cree. "Let the priest in."

"No," Amanda barked back, in Ojibway.

"Nibeebeem macheeskooteek taytootew!" cursed Mariesis, with murder in her eyes.

"He will not go to hell," screamed Amanda, her native Ojibway allowing her to understand just enough Cree.

Monstrous in full kit, the fire chief came face to face with Amanda.

"Madam," he stated, "you'll have to move."

"No."

Jeremiah's sweating face reappeared in the crack. The fire

chief begged him. "Sir, unless the smoke detector inside that room is stopped, the whole hospital has to be evacuated."

"There's a man dying in here!" Jeremiah cried. "We're Indians! We have a right to conduct our own religious ceremonies, just like everyone else!" He slammed the door again.

"Jeremiah!" Mariesis wailed behind the great wall of fireman. "Let this priest in or I'll kill you!"

Jeremiah yanked the door, reached under the fire chief's armpit, shoved the midget priest away, pulled Mariesis inside, and slammed the door a third time.

The caribou hunter thought he saw a crown, made of white fur, hovering above the cape. And the crown sparkled and flashed with what could have been an entire constellation of stars. Then Gabriel Okimasis saw a sash, like an elongated flag, white, satin, draped across the bodice of a young woman so fair her skin looked chiselled from arctic frost, her teeth pearls of ice, lips streaks of blood, the eyes white flames in a pitch-black night.

Ann-Adele Ghostrider lit a tiny sprig of cedar — after sweetgrass, sage, and tobacco, the fourth sacred herb — and one last puff of smoke rose. Jeremiah stood with his back against the door, his mother biting his restraining hand. For God had finally come for his brother, banging on the door, demanding to be let in. The scream of fire alarms and engines became a woman's wail, then another, then another, until one hundred voices were wailing the death chant.

And as he moved ever closer, Gabriel Okimasis could decipher the words and the numerals printed across her sash, syllable by syllable, letter by letter: "The Fur Queen, 1987."

Through the smoke and candle light, the Fur Queen swept into the room. Covering the bed with her cape, she leaned to Gabriel's cheek.

The creature of unearthly beauty was floating towards him carrying something in her arms, something round and made of silver, carrying the object at waist level, like a sacred vessel, like an organ, a heart perhaps, a lung, a womb? He was the champion of the world. And then the Queen's lips descended. Down they came, fluttering, like a leaf from an autumn tree, until they came to rest if only for a moment, though he wanted it to last a thousand years, on Gabriel Okimasis's left cheek. There. She kissed him. And took him by the hand.

Rising from his body, Gabriel Okimasis and the Fur Queen floated off into the swirling mist, as the little white fox on the collar of the cape turned to Jeremiah. And winked.

GLOSSARY OF CREE TERMS

Anee-i ma-a? – what about those?

Arababoo – stew

Ash! Kagitoo! – Ash! Shut up!

Astum – come here (or) come to me (or) come

Ateek, ateek, astum, astum – caribou, caribou, come to me, come to me

Athweepi – rest (or) relax

Atimootagay – dog's cunt (common swear word)

Awasis, magawa, tugoosin – child, here he/she is, has arrived

Awiniguk oo-oo? – who (plural) are these (people)?

Awus – go away

Aymeeskweewuk anee-i – they're holy women (i.e., nuns)

Cha – dogsled term: turn right

Doos – Cree prononciation for "deuce"

Eehee – yes

Eematat – he/she's fucking her/him

Kaaaa — an elongation (as in "Ohhhh") of "ka," meaning "oh."

Kareewalatic — the backrest of a dogsled from which the handlebar protrudes for the standing driver to hang on to

Katha matoo — don't cry

Keechigeesigook — heaven

Keegway kaweetamatin — I'll tell you something

Keeyapitch n'tayamiyan — I still pray

Kigiskisin na? — do you remember?

Kitoochigan — music maker (e.g., record player, piano, guitar, or any instrument that makes music)

Kimoosoom chimasoo, koogoom tapasao, diddle-ee, etc. — Grandpa gets a hard-on, grandma runs away, diddle-ee, etc. (a non-sensical musical rhyme)

Kiweethiwin — your name

K'si mantou — the Great Spirit, i.e., God (also spelled and pronounced "Kitchi mantou" or, in bad Cree "Gitche Manitou")

Machimantou — Satan

Machipoowamoowin — bad dream power (a very powerful term)

Maggeesees — fox

Mati siwitagan — pass the salt

Mawch — no

Maw keegway — nothing

Maw neetha niweetootan — I'm not going

Migisoo — eagle

Mithoopoowamoowin — good dream power

Miximoo — bark

Mootha nantow — it's all right

Mush – dogsled term: go (or) go forward

Muskoosis(uk) – little bear(s)

Napeesis awa – it's a boy

Neee, ballee sleeper chee anima? – sheesh (or "good grief"), isn't that a ballet slipper?

Neee, nimantoom – sheesh, my God!

Neee, tapwee sa awa aymeegimow – sheesh, the nerve of this priest

Nibeebeem macheeskooteek taytootew! – my baby will go down to hell!

Nigoosis – my son

Nimama – my mother

Nimantoom – my God

Noos'sim – grandson/daughter

Oogimow – Chief

Oogoosisa – the son of

Ooneemeetoo – dancer

Ootee-si – this way

Peechinook'soo – is approaching (i.e., can be seen approaching)

Peeyuk, neesoo – one, two

Peeyatuk – be careful

P'mithagan – airplane

Poowamoowin – dreaming (i.e., the act of dreaming)

Seemak – right away

Sooni-eye-gimow – Indian agent (i.e., Department of Indian Affairs)

Taneegi iga? – why not?

Tansi! – how ya doin'!

Tantee kageegimootee-in anima misti-mineeg'wachigan? – where did you steal the big cup?

Tapwee – really (or) yes, really

U – dogsled term: turn left

Weechee-in – help me

Weeks'chiloowew! – "the wind's a-changing!" with childish pronunciation (a cry of joy, of boundless elation, as nonsensical yet as expressive of a point as "heavens to Betsy!")

General Notes on the Cree Language

1) There is no gender, so that, in a sense, we are all he/shes, as is God, one would think . . .

2) The soft *g*, as in "George," does not exist; rather, all *g*s are hard, as in "gag" or "giggle."